JAW

The pack leade [illegible] his chance, leaped at Joe's neck, and his slobbering jaws closed on the man's naked throat and windpipe. The teeth sank in and the dog, realizing his death grip on the man, hauled himself up onto the man's front, over the Doberman. Pulling with all his strength, the black mongrel ripped out Joe's throat and jugular vein. Blood spurted onto the animals, and for an instant, as he hit the ground, the mongrel stepped back. The pack, sensing the death of the man, stopped their attack, and Joe slowly sank to his knees. Then the leader threw his head back and howled a mournful cry of victory.

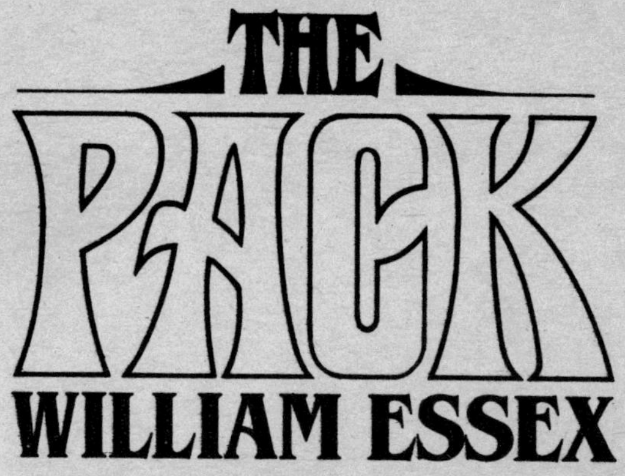

THE PACK

WILLIAM ESSEX

LEISURE BOOKS NEW YORK CITY

For Trixie, Schatzie,
Brownie, Tammy, Chiquita
and Noodles

A LEISURE BOOK

Published by

Dorchester Publishing Co., Inc.
6 East 39th Street
New York, NY 10016

Printed in the United States of America

THE
PACK

Prologue

The sun hung low in the west, ready to disappear for the night. A chill autumn breeze flitted through Jurgen's Junkyard, ruffling the drawn shade as it passed through the open office window. Karl Jurgens looked up from the ledger he was working on to peer intently at Ted Riffleman, sitting opposite him. Ted wanted to go for a beer and start the rounds of the taverns in Sioux City.

Karl knew he should finish the book work but concluded that, since the next day was Sunday and he wouldn't have the yard open, he could come down when he woke up and complete the accounting any time he chose. Slamming the book shut, he stood. "I suppose you're ready to go?"

"Christ, I have been since I walked in. How come you're so fuckin' particular about book work, for Christ's sake?"

Karl grinned broadly. "Sure can tell you're a worker and not management. Shit, if I didn't keep the books the yard would go under in a month or two."

Ted shook his head. "Fuck! I'd rather be what I am than have to sit around a fuckin' little office like this and get a headache addin' up some figures. Where do you want to go?"

Karl shrugged. "Don't make no never-mind to me. Ever since my old lady walked out on me I don't really care much about anythin' other than my business. You decide."

Ted got to his feet and ran a dirty hand over his growth of beard. "I hear they got a couple of new girls waiting on tables at Tom's Shootin' Star. What say we go down there and impress the shit out of 'em? Maybe we can get 'em to go out with us after hours and pour the ol' poontangin' into 'em."

Karl shrugged. "That's all you think about, ain't it? Fuckin' and cooze and tits. I swear, you got your brains in the head of your pecker. But what the hell! We gotta do somethin'. They gotta do somethin'. It might as well be with you 'n' me as anybody else. Right?"

"Yeah," Ted said, smiling to display a missing front tooth. "If they're gonna fuck around, it might as well be with us. Let's go."

"Hold on two minutes, my horny friend. I've got to lock the place up and turn the dogs loose."

Ted walked toward the doorway and stopped. Turning, he said, "Oh yeah! The fuckin' dogs. I forgot. You know, I always thought 'junkyard dog' was just a sayin' of sorts. Like, somebody thought that a dog would have to be mean and nasty to guard a junkyard."

"It might have been at one time, but I thought it was a pretty good idea after I got ripped off the first time."

"What'd they take?"

"What didn't they? They had to have backed a fuckin' semi up to the gate and just loaded it. Geezus! That was twenty years ago, you know?"

Ted shook his head.

Karl shut the window and turned back to Ted. "I put up the chain-link fence with the insurance money and then went to the dog pound and got a couple of the biggest, meanest-lookin' sons-a-bitches I could find there. I had 'em trained by an expert to return to their pen when a certain bell was rung in a special way. That way, nobody could fool 'em to return to their kennel. Only I could. I've kept dogs around ever since. Ain't been taken in all that time, either."

"Did you have 'em trained to attack too?"

"Goddamn right! What good would it do to have 'em trained to obey but not protect my property? You bet your sweet ass, they're trained to attack. I'd never want to be caught by 'em."

"Christ! Don't you feed 'em and water 'em and take care of 'em?"

"As little as possible. If they're hungry, they stay alert all night. A full belly and they'll lay down and sleep."

"What kind you got now?" Ted usually met Karl at the bar, or waited in the car while the dogs were set loose whenever he stopped by at quitting time.

"Couple of mongrels. A bitch and a male. The vet says they got some Newfoundland and Doberman in 'em. Maybe some Spitz or somethin', too. Wantta see 'em?"

"Sure. The cooze will wait for a couple of minutes."

"Come on," Karl said after putting the ledger book he had been working on into the small safe in the corner of the office. He followed his friend out of the building and turned to lock the door. "They're over here." He walked toward the far corner that bordered a woods, flanking the hill behind the yard.

The pen, small and confined to make certain the animals didn't get too much exercise during the day, held a dry water pan and an empty feed dish. The dogs, a large black mongrel and a black bitch with tan spots jumped to their feet when the men approached. A loud, ominous growl rumbled deep in the chests of both beasts.

"I see whatcha mean. They do look mean. How do you open their gate if you're scared of 'em?"

"Through the fence. I throw this here rope over the fence and pull. The gate swings up and they're free until I ring the bell the next morning. Then they go in and I let the gate down. Simple."

Ted shook his head. "Sure look dangerous, don't they?"

Karl picked up the rope and threw it over the fence. "Come on. The pussies are waiting for us."

Ted laughed and followed his friend toward the main gate of the junkyard. After locking the heavy metal gate Karl hurried to the corner of the fence and pulled on the rope. When the gate to the kennel lifted, the dogs dashed out, free, as far as the several acres of junkyard allowed, for the night.

Karl heard Ted's jeep motor turn over and half ran, half walked to the parked vehicle. The Cherokee roared away into the gathering dusk of a fall evening.

The dogs ran, loosening their cramped muscles and joints. They got along well despite their half-starved state. Each would hunt for and kill a rat or two before the night was out, and their hunger would be partially satisfied.

After circumventing the yard and checking the fence at different spots the dogs separated and followed their own directions, sniffing the air for tell-tale signs of prey. The male, his yellow eyes scanning the mountains of junk and old automobiles, lowered his head to the ground, sifting through the all but nonexistent smells he found there.

A rat, cowering within a wheel well of a '75 Chevy, became aware of the approaching dog. As he balanced on his hind haunches, his black nose wiggled in a vibrating way, telegraphing the scent of the large dog and assuring the rat that danger was rapidly drawing near. Leaping from the safety of the well, the rat scurried across the open space to the next stack of autos, seeking a more impervious hiding place.

The instant the rat moved into the open the male was moving. When it leaped forward the mongrel's large fangs closed on the body of the rodent and bit the spine into pieces. The rat squealed in its death throes and jerked spasmodically as the dog held it to the ground with his fore paws. Ripping open the soft belly, the black mongrel gulped down the entrails, then the body.

The bitch, hunting on the far side of the yard, heard the rat scream and doubled her efforts to find something to eat. As she neared the fence, she stopped, her nose lifted, reading the breeze blowing into the yard from the hill. A whine of hunger sounded deep within her chest and wound its way to her throat. She smelled something. An animal. Not a rat. Something like a rat, but not a rat.

On the other side of the fence a rabbit hopped into view and froze when the dog barked.

The male, hearing the female's reaction to the animal, galloped to her side. Both their tongues lolled out of their mouths as they slowly approached the chain-link fence. The male leaped into the air but fell short of reaching the top of the 10-foot fence by half that distance.

The rabbit sat, motionless, terrified into a camouflaging paralysis.

The female sniffed the bottom of the fence and

began pawing at the soft earth. Recognizing what she was doing, the black male joined her, and both dug their own channels of escape and access to the animal on the other side.

When the rabbit sensed that one of the animals was about to leap on it, it bolted away, fleeing into the night.

The female broke through first, and the male, not to be cheated of his share of the feast, redoubled his efforts rather than follow her through the hole she had dug. Within several minutes he wiggled his head and shoulders, then his body, through the opening and followed the bitch into the night, searching for the meal they both wanted and needed.

Four Years Later

Day One:

Thursday

1

Sweltering waves of heat, shimmering in the noon sun, writhed upward toward the cloudless sky. Birds, seeking the sanctuary of the shady branches, occasionally offered short renditions of their territorial songs, preferring to merely rest in the relative coolness offered by the willows growing next to the bank of the meandering stream. The creek seemed to move in slow motion, fearful that a quick-tempoed current would totally upset the heat and peace of the early July day.

Beneath the trees, lying in the shade, the pack of dogs panted, waiting patiently for the sun to go down and night to come. They would be able to roam in the darkness, hunting, killing whatever prey they might uncover. The picking had been bad of late. Even though the animals they killed were fat and healthy, it seemed that there were fewer to hunt.

On a small knoll a short distance away from the pack of panting canines the leader, a black mongrel, his yellow eyes half closed as he seemed to doze, watched over his followers. Some of the dogs were his own offspring. Most of them, however, had been picked up along the way. Since gaining his freedom the thin veneer of man's dominance had been demolished and he reveled in his wild ways. He had to fight all the males, showing his dominance, and until some other dog was able to get the best of him and he was willing to admit it with a show of subservience, he would continue to lead the pack and mate with the females.

He didn't mind the heat. It was the cold that bothered him the most. The cold and the white stuff that usually came with it. Then he found it most difficult to find food. There would be those dogs that died because of a lack of food. In turn, they offered to the pack the necessary sustenance for survival until more game could be found, killed, and devoured. There had been four times when he confronted the white stuff covering the countryside; four times since he and the tan-and-black bitch had left the place where they were allowed to run wild during the dark; four times since they had dug under the fence to chase an animal that they never did find. But the male didn't count the seasons. He counted on his ability to hunt, to kill, to defend his harem of bitches from the other males. What else mattered?

An errant breeze crossed the water, wafting toward the knoll, and the male opened his eyes wide without moving anything else. His nose quivered after a second or two, telegraphing to his brain the identity of the scent. It was the same sort of animal the pack had found to be in abundance in the countryside, the same sort of animal he and the tan-and-black bitch had chased when they earned their freedom. He stood and, after stretching, walked down from his spot above the others toward the creek, through the dozing pack. When he reached the level of the other dogs he lost the scent of the rabbit. Raising his head and half jumping with his front legs, he caught the slightest whiff of the animal on the breeze over him. Without attracting attention he crossed the stream and went up the other side of the bank.

The trail was stronger here and he followed it, making no sound as he padded through the long grass. Then the rabbit bounded away from him and he bolted after it. The animal dashed in an erratic pattern, hoping to throw the predator off his track, but the male hung tenaciously to the smell. The rabbit had waited too long to make his escape and the dog was a mere four or five feet behind him.

The dog, driven by hunger pangs, urged his gaunt body forward in a burst of speed and overran the rabbit. Rolling on the ground, the cottontail wound up beneath the dog, and when the mongrel got to his feet his jaws closed on the throat of the small rabbit. Its death squeal rang unnaturally through the quiet.

The pack, aroused by the sound of the scream, rose to follow the path their leader had taken. When they came across him he was already devouring the entrails of the rabbit. Tongues hung from their mouths. Saliva, which had been engendered by the smell of the blood, dripped to the ground. They would have to wait until their leader had his fill. The size of the prey seemed to tell the bulk of the pack that most, if not all, would not taste this kill.

When the mongrel finished he stood, stretching lazily, and stepped away from the remains of the animal. The others swarmed over it, growling, snarling, biting at each other for a bit of fur if nothing else. A half-breed collie and a smaller dog of nondescript background fought over the largest piece of skin and fur. Finally jerking it from the mouth of the collie, the other animal dashed away to devour his prize.

The black leader stood watching. The heat had lessened somewhat. Perhaps they could move out. The taste of blood and entrails had heightened his appetite and he realized how hungry he was.

The tan-and-black bitch came up to his side and he nuzzled her neck. After sniffing each other all over they moved away from the others. When the pack realized the two were leaving they followed, and the dogs treked away from the stream.

After trotting halfway through a cornfield that just managed to hide the largest dogs the mongrel stopped, searching the air with his nose. Something was ahead. Something big. He had smelled it before and had seen animals like it up close. They were much bigger than he or any other dog in the pack. Could he kill one? Could the pack kill one?

Half turning, he growled a warning, and the others dropped to the ground. He would go ahead and scout the situation. If the conditions were right, they would try. They had to. If they didn't, more would die of hunger.

Moving out alone, the black mongrel hurried through the cornfield, sheltered by the plants. He followed the smell and when he stood on the far edge of the field he surveyed the barn, house, and out buildings of a well-tended farm in the distance. A small pasture stood between him and the structures, but his attention was riveted to a pair of Hereford calves standing close to a stunted cottonwood tree, no more than 40 feet away. His yellow eyes darted from the calves to the buildings, back to the calves, around the pasture, back to the calves, to the buildings, to the calves, back over the pasture once more. He could detect no other smells. He could see nothing other than the two young animals. The Herefords were bigger than anything he had ever killed—much bigger than anything the pack had ever killed. Not that they hadn't hunted and circled cattle before. But the size and the smell of man around the animals usually drove them away.

There was always other game to hunt. But now the mongrel felt desperately hungry. Even though he could detect the faint smell of man coming from the general direction of the farm itself, he knew the pack would have to risk killing the animals before him.

Turning, he trotted back into the cornfield to summon the others.

Joe Eppson set his empty coffee cup down on the table. He had eaten lunch late and would have to hurry back to the cornfield to finish cultivating the crops across the road. The weather forecast included the possibility of rain, and he wanted his last field finished before that might happen. The weather had not been cooperative at all. First the corn had been planted late because of too much rain. Since then hardly any rain had fallen. He had most of the hard earth broken up in the cornfields and the prospect that it might rain now, in early July, seemed right to the man.

He looked around the austere kitchen. It definitely lacked a woman's touch, but he didn't care. It didn't matter to him. He had never married. He had never wanted to marry. Not after witnessing what had happened to his older brother, Leo. Ann, his sister-in-law, had proven to be a bitch—a real hellion—and Joe decided right then, after seeing her browbeat his brother, that he would never, ever marry.

Headed for the door, he stopped short. He had almost forgotten. He had to call Pete Reckels, the veterinarian from Laughton. He had to have his pigs vaccinated, and he thought it would be a good idea to have the doctor check the calves in the barn pasture. They were almost ready to wean and he wanted to milk their mother.

Striding to the wall phone, he dialed the number and waited, the buzzing ring filling his ear.

"Pete Reckels." The young veterinarian's voice rang in his ear.

"Pete? This here's Joe Eppson. Say, can you come out here and vaccinate my pigs?"

"When's it convenient for you, Joe?"

"Shoot! Any time, I suppose. How 'bout tomorrow?"

"Just a minute, Joe."

Pete's voice left the phone and, after a moment, returned. "Too bad you couldn't do it this afternoon, Joe. I'm going to be out that way."

"Couldn't anymore today, Pete. I gotta finish my plowin'. If it's goin' to rain, I gotta get done today."

"What time tomorrow?"

"You name it. I'll be done plowin' before dark."

"How about eleven?"

"Sounds good to me. I want you to check on my Hereford calves. I just want to make sure they're all right before I wean 'em."

Joe hung up and crossed the kitchen, lighting his pipe as he walked. Banging the screen door behind him, he walked to the John Deere tractor. Climbing into the cab, he turned the motor over and, after checking the gauges, put the tractor in gear. He caught a glimpse of the Herefords in the pasture. Pausing at the entrance to the farm, Joe looked both ways before easing across County Highway Y-31. Trixie, his collie bitch, followed, ready to chase any game flushed by the plowing. The tractor bounced as it entered the cornfield across the road from the farm, and Joe continued plowing where he had stopped earlier.

The mongrel left the cornfield and found the pack lying in the shade of a huge cottonwood tree not far from where he had left them. His excitement transferred to the other animals and after the tan-and-black bitch had sniffed him and he'd returned the gestures to her, the black dog turned, reentering the cornfield. Instead of heading straight back toward the pasture near the farm he circled to his right, making certain that the wind—what little wind there was —would be coming toward him and the pack.

When they were almost at the edge of the cornfield, the leader slowed and growled quietly. The others stopped, remaining silent. The calves stood close to the fence that ran at right angles to the one confronting the dogs. The mongrel studied the situation. It would have to be a quick attack, one that gave the prey no chance of recovery. The animals seemed nervous and moved in jerky steps, first toward the fence, then toward the middle of the pasture, beyond the tree.

High weeds grew along the fence near which

the calves stood. The wind moved the pack at an angle, carrying the sound of a tractor not too far away. The mongrel stepped along the fence separating him from the prey and turned the corner when he could do so with the cover of the weeds. The pack followed, a tremor of excitement flowing through each dog as though one common brain reacted to the hunt.

When the mongrel stopped it stood less than ten feet away from the animals. The Herefords looked about. Something bothered them, but neither could detect what it might be. Nervous, they half turned away from the fence, and just then the mongrel led the attack.

Before either could take three steps the young animals found themselves surrounded by the pack of dogs gone wild. The black mongrel leaped for one of the calve's throats. The other wheeled about, dashing across the pasture toward the barn, bawling for its mother. The older cow, grazing nearer the barn, had gone undetected by the mongrel. Hearing her offspring crying out, she lifted her head and saw the young Hereford charging headlong toward her. Her maternal instinct fanned to a flaming inferno, she ran to the calf.

The mongrel hung fast to the one he had attacked. He bit hard but found it difficult to penetrate the skin, even though it hung loosely where he had bitten. The calf coughed, choking as the dog's jaws closed tighter on its windpipe. In the distance the mongrel could hear the other animal bawling and a new sound, a deeper, more confident lowing, drawing nearer.

The cow galloped across the field toward the pack of dogs and her other calf. The wounded animal, the dog hanging tightly to its throat, bucked, throwing its head from left to right in a vain attempt to dislodge its attacker.

The mongrel hung on tightly and when the other dogs became aware of the approaching cow and calf they turned to attack them. The mother stopped, lowering her hornless head to protect herself and her unharmed calf. While the tan-and-black bitch attacked the second calf in the same way that the mongrel had, the other dogs launched a furious assault on the cow. Because of her size and weight the cow fared well in her efforts to protect herself. The best the dogs could do to her was nip at her legs, and she continued moving toward her twin calves.

The mongrel ground his jaws even though his feet barely touched the ground and, when they did, it was only for a split second. His teeth had finally broken through the tough skin and as the blood seeped into his mouth, his attack grew more frenzied and he locked his jaws even tighter. The calf stopped running, head hanging down, waiting, its sides heaving. The dog pulled as hard as he could, trying to tear the throat out of the young calf.

The pack continued baiting the cow while the bitch, clinging to the throat of the other calf, slowly choked it. The Herefords bawled as best they could, the young to the mother and the mother to the young she could not reach or protect.

The mongrel pulled, tugging until the calf gave one final heave with its head to dislodge him and the dog's 80 pounds. Being thrown out once more proved too much for the skin. The main arteries and veins tore loose along with the animal's windpipe. The calf went to its knees, its life's blood gushing onto the brown grass and dry earth, which quickly muddied. The animal's final breath sloshed out of the torn windpipe.

The dog stood triumphant over the carcass.

The tan-and-black bitch met with much the same sort of success, and the second animal dropped to a sitting position, its neck torn open, blood spurting in a panic-filled rhythm as its heart pumped its life away.

The cow, sensing that her offspring were both beyond her help, stood still. The dogs ignored her when the smell of death and blood and food filled the air. She turned, meandering back toward the barn, bawling out plaintive cries for her twins.

The pack, strangely quiet, milled about, ducking in, biting at the dead calves, occasionally growling and snapping at one another. The mongrel walked triumphantly toward the belly of the calf he had killed and bit at the male's penis, pulling and ripping away the skin and exposing the pink under layer of flesh. Slashing, ripping with his teeth, he tore open the belly of the animal and quickly gorged himself on the viscera. After gulping down enough of the entrails to fill his belly he moved away and watched the tan-and-black bitch open the belly of the other animal in the same way. The carcass he had just left was quickly inundated by half of the pack, while the others rushed to feast on the second dead animal.

When the cavities of the bodies lay empty those dogs who had had their fill moved a short distance away to sleep. Those who had not been so fortunate chewed on exposed meat and ribs that were easily accessible. Despite their powerful jaws, the dogs found it difficult to pull the raw meat from the bone. Still, they continued tearing at the flesh, gulping down huge pieces whenever they succeeded.

After an hour the carcasses were left behind and the pack moved away, toward the cornfield on the east edge of the pasture. Their bellies relatively full, they wanted nothing more than to sleep. The cornfield would offer shade and some degree of protection from discovery. Too, the pack could guard their kill from there.

Flies quickly discovered the dead calves, descending to have their fill of the feast and to lay their eggs. Overhead, four crows circled downward to investigate the free meal in the pasture.

On the highway a car drove past the Eppson farm, its driver not noticing anything wrong.

2

Joe Eppson eased his John Deere tractor onto County Highway Y-31 to cross over to his farm. When he entered his yard he pulled out his watch and smiled. Not quite three-thirty. He would have plenty of time to finish his evening chores in daylight. One thing he hated about farming was the fact that many times he began the day in the dark and finished it the same way. Tomorrow, after the pigs were vaccinated, he'd start haying, and he'd be working late.

After parking the tractor near the machine shed he gathered his buckets for feeding the chickens and picking up the eggs. When he had fed the hogs he'd be able to take a shower and prepare his evening meal without hurrying.

When he left the house yard Trixie, his collie, whined pitifully.

Joe stopped. "What's the matter, Trix? You all right?" Dropping into a crouch, he roughed the dog's head. It, in turn, licked Joe's face. The instant the man stood, the dog, tail between her legs, slunk to the porch and crawled underneath.

A prickle of energy ran up Joe's back, moving the hair at the nape of his neck. At best, it was a peculiar way for the dog to act. Usually the collie was active and playful until some stranger showed up on the farm. Then all hell would break loose. She'd bark and carry on, making certain that her master knew that an encroacher was present. But because the dog acted in a bizzare way didn't mean that Joe had to react in an equally strange way.

Still, for some reason he felt as if something were out of place—amiss. He eyed the farm from where he stood. Directly north of the back step of the house, he could look between the granary and barn, into the grain field. He could detect nothing there. Turning to his right, he took in the machine shed that he had been near minutes before. There was nothing wrong there. Farther to his right he saw the hog house and yard. The grunts and squeals coming to him from there told him things were normal. He turned to his right rear without moving much to check the chicken coop. The hens and roosters were busy pecking at the ground, searching for food until ground feed was brought to them. His old Chevy, parked in the open garage, appeared the same. Everything seemed absolutely normal. Then why did he feel as if someone or something was out there—watching him or taunting him by being out of place? He could see no one. Still, the sensation persisted.

Turning back to continue on his way to the granary, he stopped. The hog house and yard caught his attention. Why? He started toward it and stopped again. The pasture beyond came into focus. Where were the Hereford calves? He wanted them to be all right. They were prize animals, and he was being more diligent than usual where they were concerned. When he reached the fence of the hog yard he stepped across and hurried to the far side. The pasture lay flat. Long grass, slightly brown from the lack of rain, covered the unbroken ground with the exception of a stunted cottonwood near the far fence. He could see the entire area. The calves were nowhere to be seen.

After climbing the next fence he was in the pasture. The only place the calves could possibly be was on the other side of the cottonwood tree, lying down.

Joe cursed his luck. All he needed was a break in the fence that the Herefords had found and had gotten out of the pasture—into the cornfield on the east side. They could do themselves a lot of harm if they got in there, eating the young corn plants, stuffing themselves.

He hurried forward across the pasture.

* * *

The pack, spread along the rows of corn, lay quietly. Some of the dogs sprawled out on their sides. A buff cocker spaniel, legs sticking out from beneath its body, snored lustily. Others were content to merely rest on their full bellies, dozing off on occasion.

The black mongrel, his yellow eyes half closed and his tongue lolling from one side of his mouth, rested in the middle of the pack. Groaning, he half stood, half sat, and stretched lazily. Yawning mightily, he licked his chops and stretched again.

Then his ears shot straight up, listening intently. His nose quivered as he hastily searched the breeze coming to him from the west. Something—some animal—was coming toward him and the pack. When he realized it was a man he growled softly, ominously.

The other dogs snapped to attention but held their place when the mongrel lightly stepped across and around them to move to the edge of the cornfield.

Off in the distance, coming toward the tree and the pack's kill, a man strode along, his head turning from side to side, as if searching for something.

The mongrel growled louder and took another step. Their kill could still provide food. The pack could feast before they moved on. This man—this animal—this creature was a definite threat to the pack's well-being. In the four years since he and the bitch had left the junkyard, man had always been avoided. Now man was about to cause a problem. The black animal turned slightly, growling just loud enough for the pack to hear. The animals got to their feet and quietly moved to flank their leader.

"Here, Boss! Come, Bossy! Come! Come on, Boss, where are you?" Joe called calmly. No sense alarming the animals into running around the pasture. Something like that wouldn't do them any good. He had to remain calm even though he still felt a sense of panic rising within him. Where could they be?

He had kept the tree in line with his own route because the place he had entered the pasture and the other side of the cottonwood were in a direct line. If he could see through the trunk and low hanging branches, he wouldn't have to walk into the pasture. Any minute now the Herefords would come out from behind the tree and Joe would laugh and promise himself never to tell anyone how scared he got the day he thought his prize calves had disappeared.

When he neared the cottonwood four crows flapped their way into the air. Joe swung around to his left, circling to the far side of the tree.

Then he saw it.

The gutted carcass of one Hereford lying on its side held his attention in a powerful grip for a long minute. What had happened? How had it happened? *Who* had killed his prize Hereford?

What had killed it? Questions ran through his mind while he slowly walked forward, his heart pumping faster and faster as his blood pressure rose. Adrenaline flowed through his body, activating his muscles and mind to a peak of efficiency.

He found the remains of the second calf a short distance away. Joe couldn't help it. Tears formed, running down his grizzled, weathered cheeks. What the hell kind of animal was around that could kill two young calves and eat this much? There weren't any wild animals around that he knew about, and he had lived his entire life in the Laughton area, with the exception of the years he had spent in Korea.

People? Could people have done this? He thought back 12 or 15 years, when a series of strange animal mutilations were discovered across the United States and Canada. There had been a couple of such instances around Laughton. But he recalled that those cases always presented mysterious clues. Cow udders or external sex organs would have been removed, as if with surgical instruments, and in every such case there was never a drop of blood found.

Joe looked around the carcasses. Blood stained the bodies and the grass on which they lay. No, this couldn't be the same type of situation. It had to be something else. Something wild and hungry, to have killed the animals and eaten half of them. But each calf had to have weighed at least 200 pounds minimum. Both body cavities had been cleaned, and teeth marks bordered each opening from which chunks of meat had been ripped. What sort of wild animal could eat that much at one time?

Reflecting back to early afternoon, when he had come in for lunch, Joe replayed the sight of the pasture in his memory. Had he seen the calves then? Had they been already dead and half devoured while he sat in his kitchen, content and smug? He turned and saw the mother cow grazing close to the barn.

"Goddammit anyhow all to hell and back!" he cried out. Now he'd have to dispose of the carcasses and have the cow bred again, and get two more calves later on. Shit! It was always something. Joe crouched down to examine the dead animals more closely.

The mongrel watched the man, some fifteen yards away, walk up to the pack's kill. The hair on the dog's back stood erect and a growl rumbled deep within his wide chest. He took a tentative step toward the man when he moved even nearer the carcass. If the man sniffed at it but didn't try to claim the carcass as his own, the mongrel would do nothing.

The pack, standing on both sides of the mongrel, stood concealed within the rows of corn. Soft, quiet, plaintive whines wound through the dogs as they watched the man scuff at the earth. They grew more nervous when they heard his voice.

Then, when the man crouched down, the mongrel barked once. The short, husky sound electrified the pack and, as one, the animals leaped from their places of concealment to charge at the man. Those dogs small enough merely ran through the barbed-wire fence. Others, like the mongrel, the tan-and-black bitch, a Doberman bitch, a couple of collies, and other assorted breeds of various backgrounds, were forced to leap the fence, but the effort barely slowed them. The dogs ran without making a sound other than that of their feet padding through the dry grass.

At first Joe was unaware of their approach. The first he knew the dogs were attacking him was when the black mongrel leaped at Joe's head, knocking him to the ground. Reacting more by instinct than plan, the farmer jumped to his feet to find himself surrounded by dogs that began barking the instant he had become aware of their presence.

What the hell was going on? Where had so many dogs come from? Joe turned to run. The dogs raced after him, immediately biting at his heels and lower legs. Amid the barking and yelping of the dogs, Joe's cries of pain sounded, not unlike a mumbled prayer being offered among the curses and blasphemies of heathens. For every step he took three or four bites on each leg seemed to be his reward. A large collie caught a good piece of his calf and hung on. The excruciating pain shot through Joe's body to his brain and he cried out.

The scream of the wounded man seemed to infuriate the dogs, and they renewed their attack with a viciousness and ferocity that quickly terrified the farmer into paralysis.

The black mongrel leaped at Joe's upper body, which he protected with crossed arms covering his face, throat, and chest. Snapping jaws caught one arm and pulled it away. When the mongrel released it to jump at Joe's exposed throat Joe immediately brought the arm back up again.

"Goddammit! Get away you, sons-a-bitches! Get the fuck away from me!" Joe screamed, spinning about. His words were lost in the raucous barking and growling. At least six dogs held onto each leg, biting, tearing at his clothing. How long would his denim overalls last with this type of assault? The heavy material seemed to be protecting his legs to some degree.

The Doberman bitch, unable to find a place to attack the man, ran around and around, barking, until she saw an exposed place in front and leaped for Joe's crotch. When her teeth locked onto his penis he dropped his hands to fend her off—to protect himself as best he could.

The pack leader, seeing his chance, leaped at Joe's neck, and his slobbering jaws closed on the man's naked throat and windpipe. The teeth sank in and the dog, realizing his death grip on the man, hauled himself up onto the man's front, over the Doberman. Pulling with all his strength, the black mongrel ripped out Joe's throat and jugular vein. Blood spurted onto the animals, and for an instant, as he hit the ground, knocking the Doberman bitch from her hold, the mongrel stepped back. The pack, sensing the death of the man, stopped their attack, and Joe slowly sank to his knees.

For an agonizing moment he knelt, not quite able to comprehend what had happened. His eyes rolling back into their sockets, Joe fell forward, face down onto the grass. The dogs, standing perfectly still, stared for several minutes. The mongrel worked his tongue around his mouth, savoring the new taste. Then the leader threw his head back and howled a mournful cry of victory. Their kill was safe.

He walked forward and sniffed Joe's body. No movement. The man was dead. His quivering nose worked its way from the feet along the bloody legs to the crotch, reddened with gore, to the gaping hole in the neck. The dog's tongue flicked out once, taking more blood into his mouth. He tried it again. Then again. His taste buds awakened, intrigued by the taste of man's blood, he nipped at the torn flesh next to the wound. Mouthing it, he took more, then more.

The pack, realizing that their leader was eating, waited patiently. Still full from the feast of the calves, the mongrel tore at Joe's clothing. Ripping the shirt before one suspender of the overall gave way, he pulled, tugging at the tough material until it surrendered to the attack and the pants ripped apart. The other dogs joined in, pulling, ripping, tearing until Joe's body lay naked.

Then the carnage began anew and the pack closed over him. The Doberman bitch, not to be forced out of the prize she had originally claimed, bit a German shepherd to get him away from the dead man's genitals. When they were free of his underwear she bit down on the penis, chewing it off at the base. Bolting it down, she attacked the testicles and devoured them. The dogs, driven to a frenzy by the taste of a new animal, tore at Joe's middle, ripping open his body cavity. The dogs fought each other for a taste of the viscera.

An hour later the dogs lay in a circle around Joe's body and the carcasses of the cows. The mongrel got to his feet and stretched. A sharp bark brought the others to their feet, and the pack moved away from the field, heading in a southerly direction, away from the Eppson farm and Laughton. After going several miles the leader changed direction for no reason and headed west.

When they came to an open expanse of blacktop road they boldly crossed it and disappeared into an oat field.

3

A meadowlark proclaimed its territory from the top of a post, which held the fence separating the Cramden County Park from the neighboring oat-field. Virtually deserted, as was common during weekdays, the park lay empty except for a couple sitting on a blanket beneath a tree.

Pete Reckels tipped the can of beer to his mouth, emptying it. "I'm glad you talked me into this, Amy. It's really peaceful out here when it isn't overrun with people."

Amy Bondson smiled. "If I had known before that all it would take to get you out here during the week was to ask you on my afternoon off, I would've done it a long time ago." She picked up the paper plates and got to her feet. After dumping them, along with the rest of the refuse from their impromptu picnic, she came back to the blanket and dropped to her knees before sitting down.

"If Joe Eppson hadn't had to finish his plowin', I wouldn't have been able. He wants me to vaccinate his new pigs. I tried for this afternoon, but he said it would be better tomorrow. So tomorrow it is and today is picnic and funtime."

"You work too hard, Pete."

Pete glared at her. "Don't you start. That was Carol's song-and-dance routine. It was her harping on my working hours and habits that finally drove us apart. It's the only way I know. I'm sorry about that, but I've got to work hard or I feel as if I'm doing something wrong."

"Wherever did you get that idea?"

Pete shrugged. "I don't know. I guess from my folks. They worked pretty darn hard on their farm. I don't think they ever took any time off to go on a vacation or trip of any type. Oh, sure, they went to funerals and weddings that were away from the farm. But for the most part those trips were done in a day or two at the most. And when they got back home it seemed as if Dad and Mom worked twice as hard to catch up."

"There's nothing wrong with working hard. I just don't want to see you overdo it. You need a little time off."

Pete leaned closer to her. "As long as I don't feel as if I'm slighting my work and the time can be spent with you, I'll agree."

Amy moved closer and kissed him lightly on the mouth. He returned the kiss, embracing her in a tight hold.

"I love you, Amy. I really do. The thing I had with Carol was all wrong. Now that I look back on it it was probably the biggest mistake I ever made in my life. Our marriage was pure hell."

"Why are you bringing her up? It'll only upset you."

"I guess I'm getting ready to face her. I should have sent her the child support check, but I didn't get around to it and it's due today. I'll have to deliver it by hand because she'd be just bitchy enough to call the sheriff and have me served with a summons."

Amy patted the back of his hand and stretched.

Pete looked up. "Sky sure is beautiful, but it would be a whole lot prettier if there were some clouds in it."

Amy nodded, but said nothing.

"The weatherman's prediction will probably be like all the rest and we won't get the rain he said we would." He forced a bitter smile.

"It *is dry,* isn't it?" Amy said absently, as though it had just occurred to her.

"You're first noticing?"

"When I'm with you I seldom notice anything else. You know that."

Pete grinned sheepishly. She made him feel like a god at times, the way she talked. Hell, he was nothing more than a farm boy with a college education and a degree in veterinary medicine. He could have stayed on the farm when he graduated college, but he decided that farming wasn't for him. He had an uneasy feeling about the inflated value of the land and the tremendous investment that all of the machinery represented. When his dad said he wanted Pete to take over Pete offered his arguments and, surprisingly, the elder Reckels accepted his son's logic. All Pete had to do was promise him that he would work hard and be the best veterinarian to ever work in Cramden County.

When he opened his practice, with a sizable loan from his father, Pete catered more to the farm trade then he did the small animal and pet practice for which most veterinarians opted. In time he found there was only one other practioner who competed with him and that veterinarian, Doctor Emory Vales, was old. As a result, Pete had the farm trade almost all to himself.

His marriage to Carol Bessels had worked for a short time, but when she discovered she was pregnant their union took a bizarre turn. Carol became jealous of the animals Pete cared for, as well as of the farmers for whom he worked. She reasoned that they took him away from her at a time when she needed him. After Jenny was born nothing changed Carol's unreasonable attitude, and when their child was less than two years old they separated. That had been five years before, and Pete was watching his daughter grow up at a distance. He had his visitation rights, but the time he spent with Jenny was forced and never long enough for the two of them to really get close and know each other.

"You ready?"

Pete blinked. "What?"

"I asked if you're ready to go. It's almost four o'clock."

"I guess maybe we should. You got plans for tonight?"

Amy nodded. "Only if a certain veterinarian I know gets involved with them. Interested?"

"I might be. Remember, I have to go see Carol. I might be in a terrible mood afterward."

"So?"

"Do you want to risk seeing me at my worst?"

Amy got to her feet. "Are you hiding some deep, dark personality secrets?"

Shaking his head, Pete stood up. When she stooped to pick up the blanket he moved to the opposite side to help her fold it. When they walked toward each other, holding their respective ends of the blanket, he kissed her on the mouth. "No secrets. But if we get married, you'll know everything there is to know about me. Carol tends to bring out the worst in me right now."

"Didn't she before, when you were married?"

"Not at first. But as she changed, I changed, and it wasn't a change that I liked."

Amy took the blanket and gave it one last fold before handing it to Pete. "You take this and I'll bring the basket."

As they walked toward Pete's Bronco, they linked arms.

"Are you ever sorry you picked Laughton for a home?" Pete held back and stopped walking, forcing her in turn to stop and look up at him.

"Sorry? How could I be sorry? That was the wisest decision I ever made."

"But have you ever thought what would have happened if you had chosen Fresno over Laughton? We never would have met."

"I know that. And I'm thankful that I did choose it. After all, if the company I was working for hadn't gone bankrupt, I wouldn't be working for Al either. Nor would I likely have met you."

Pete frowned when he thought of Al Neidles, the county attorney. A wimp if there ever was one. Brilliant law mind, but a lousy front and even worse personality. How he had managed to get elected eluded Pete. But, because he had stopped in Al's office one day, he had met Amy.

Pete opened the passenger door for her. "I'll bet there are times when you wonder what would have happened it you *had* moved to Fresno."

Amy got in and turned to face him before allowing him to close the door. "Of course there have been—in the past. I've often thought that if I had gone to Fresno, and the company hadn't folded, I might be rolling in dough today. But after I met you I started adding the thought that that wouldn't have happened in Fresno either."

Pete grinned. "I know. Ain't love grand?" He

slammed the door and skipped around the front of the small vehicle to get in the driver's side. Once he had turned the motor over he drove slowly from the park toward the county highway that fronted it. Highway Y-31 would take him right into Laughton.

Laughton, the county seat of Cramden County, was a town of more than 40,000 people. Though there were no giant industrial companies within its confines, the town did have more than its share of successful manufacturing companies, most of which were home-owned. A large meat-packing company seemed to be the pulse of the local business world and, as it went, so went the community.

After they had driven several miles Pete said, "It's a shame, though, that Joe couldn't let me take care of his pigs this afternoon. Now, tomorrow I'll have to drive back out here and vaccinate."

Turning, Amy lightly punched him in the ribs. "Are you trying to tell me you'd rather have stuck a needle into a bunch of pigs then spend the afternoon with me on a picnic?"

Pete grinned foolishly. "It depends."

"It depends?" Amy stared at him.

"Come on, I'm kidding. For crying out loud. You know I'd rather spend time with you than do anything else."

"Even work?"

"Well, a guy *does* have to eat."

She laughed. "I'm glad I know you. If I thought

for a minute that you were really like that—"

"Hey, I *am* conscientious almost to a fault. I can't help it. It was the way I was raised. I've got a strong work ethic locked up inside of me, and I don't think I'll ever lose it."

They both fell silent for a long minute. Suddenly Pete slowed down.

"Hey? What's that on the road?"

Amy snapped out of her reverie. "Huh? What did you say?"

"Look! Up ahead. What are those? Dogs?"

Amy squinted, focusing on the movement on the road ahead of the Bronco. "Almost too far to say. You're the animal expert. But they do look like dogs, all right."

"All sorts of breeds," Pete said, pressing down on the accelerator.

The car leaped ahead, and in seconds they were approaching the spot where they had seen what appeared to be many dogs crossing the road. Pete slowed the car to a crawl and then braked to a stop along the verge. He sat for a minute, looking into the grain field to his left.

"What would a bunch of dogs be doing in the country?" he asked absentmindedly.

"You've got me."

"I didn't expect you to answer, hon."

"Is it unusual?"

"Unusual?"

"For dogs to be in the country? At least, as many as we seem to think we saw?"

"Well, it's not unusual for dogs to be in the

country. Hell, every farm has at least one. When I was a kid growing up on the farm it wasn't out of the ordinary for Rex, our dog, to take off at night and gang up with the neighbors' dogs. They'd roam the countryside, hunting and playing and mating."

"The last part sounds like a normal pastime," Amy said, snickering and wiggling her eyebrows.

Pete didn't notice.

When she realized she had failed to get a laugh out of Pete she said, "If it's not unusual, why are you so interested?"

"I guess it's just my training and background. See, it's pretty normal for dogs to do that—pack together—at night. But what would a pack of dogs as large as we saw be doing out in broad daylight?"

Amy puckered her brow. She still didn't understand.

Pete opened his door and got out of the cab. Amy followed him.

"You know," he said, "there were all sorts of breeds in the pack. I spotted at least two or three collies. And at least one Doberman."

"So?"

"The collies could be farm dogs. But the Doberman—well, that's another ball game."

"Why?"

"Because a Doberman isn't a farm dog. It's a hunting dog. A guard dog. That particular breed just isn't found on a farm very often."

"Oh. So?"

"So what would a dog like that be doing with a bunch of farm dogs?"

"How do you know they were farm dogs?"

"I don't. I'm just assuming that they were. If I had seen them in town. I'd probably say they were city dogs. Then the city dog catcher could do his thing."

"Look, Pete, it's getting late. I wouldn't mind standing here on the highway talking about dogs. Incidentally, where are they? They sure disappeared quickly, considering that there were so many."

"If they were chasing something or running just to be running, they could get clear out of sight over that low hill in the grain field in the length of time it took us to get here. The hill isn't that far off. Come on. I'd better get you back to town."

He helped Amy into the Bronco and followed her. He put the vehicle in gear and pulled back onto the road.

"Well," he said when they were underway once more, "I'll tell you this much. I'm not going to worry about it."

"I'm glad," she said. "I wouldn't want to be in love with a man who worried about every dog he saw running across the road."

Pete grinned, and Amy snuggled closer to him. He slipped his arm around her shoulder and they drove toward Laughton without talking.

4

The pack trotted along the rows of corn, not hurrying. The black mongrel constantly read the air passing through the corn plants that almost concealed him as he moved along. Suddenly he stopped, freezing in position, and cocked his ears. The coughing exhaust of an approaching tractor rode on the breeze coming toward the dogs. Their ears standing upright, the dogs watched the black leader. As if in slow motion, he lowered his body to the dry earth and waited.

Johnny O'Malley intently watched the rows of corn passing beneath the Farm-all tractor despite the heavy rock and roll pounding in his ears from the Walkman. The one thing he didn't need was to hit a rock that might break one of the cultivator blades skimming through the hard ground. At 17 he had learned how to be frugal in the most reasonable ways. His father, Dan, had made certain his son would not be careless around the machinery on the farm. It made more sense to be careful than to lose a finger or hand because of one moment's disregard. It made sense to be careful when cultivating, to watch for rocks that could be avoided by stopping the tractor and getting down to move them by hand if they looked as if they could break something on the cultivator. If something broke, that meant it had to be repaired, and that could cost money and time. Both commodities seemed to be in short supply on the farm of late.

Johnny stopped the tractor and pulled the radio/cassette player from the pocket of his bib overalls. After turning the cassette over he put the machine in gear again and the Farm-all moved forward. Johnny didn't see the rock nor did he hear the crack of metal as the shovel sheared off from its mooring. He did feel the tractor give a slight jerk, and when he looked down his face fell. Braking to a halt and killing the engine, he clambered off the seat and made his way around the left rear wheel.

"Shit!" he said softly after turning off Bruce Springsteen's yelling. Crouching down, he examined the damage. The blade had broken off its pedestal, popping the rivets that held it in place. It wasn't major, but it would be a delay.

When he stood up he suddenly realized how quiet it was in the cornfield. He slowly turned in a full circle, looking over the field. Nothing. No breeze rustled the broad, green leaves. He winced when he heard what sounded like a drum beating, only to realize it was his own heart pumping blood through his body. Shaking his head, he walked around the huge rear wheel to mount the seat again.

The black leader listened intently as the sound came nearer. Without warning the sound stopped. Twisting his head to one side, he peered in the direction from which the noise had been coming. A whine worked its way through his throat and he slowly stood. The others did likewise and followed him when he started walking in the direction to their right.

After walking several hundred yards he dropped to his belly again and waited. The smell of man was strong in his nose. The other animals recognized the new source of food as well, and an uneasy restlessness passed through the pack like a wave on an ocean.

The black mongrel inched his way forward toward the smell, toward the thing he could see looming above the plants. It had a peculiar stink to it, but winding through that particular stench was the savory hint of man. He watched the boy stand after having been down, close to the ground, looking at something on the thing.

When the boy turned, looking in all directions, the dogs hugged the ground even tighter then when they had been merely lying there, watching him. He reached inside the clothes he wore and did something before walking back toward the back of the thing. Just as he was about to climb up on it the mongrel leaped to his feet and charged.

Johnny knew what he had to do. He'd have to leave the field and drive home. If his dad wasn't around, he could do most of the repair work himself, since he had helped do the same sort of thing before. At least the old Farm-all had lights, and he could plan on finishing tonight. There was rain in the forecast, and the plowing had to be finished to gain the advantage lost when they were forced, because of too much rain, to plant two weeks late. By rights they should be doing the second crop haying right now, rather than be cultivating for the second time.

Johnny adjusted the volume and continued bobbing his head back and forth as Bruce Springsteen picked up his raucous song once more.

Then he was hit. Just as he placed his right foot on the axle housing something struck him in the back of the head and he sprawled forward, whacking his head on the edge of the tractor seat.

"What the hell?" he cried out loud, barely hearing his own voice over the music swelling in his ears. Grabbing at his head, he spun around and caught a glimpse of a black dog leaping at him. Startled, unprepared for any type of assault, Johnny stood there, not quite knowing what to expect. Just as the dog's teeth closed on his throat, he saw the pack running up behind the animal clinging to his body.

Johnny coughed and tried to pull the canine from him. That only hurt more. How could he get the dog to loosen his grip? He pounded on the dog's back, but that only seemed to make him tighten his grip even more. Sharp stabs of pain tore through the boy as the dogs surrounded him and bit at his legs and body.

Grabbing at the muzzle of the mongrel, Johnny reached the lower jaw and covered the dog's nose with his other hand. Pulling with all his might, he tried to pry apart the clamping jaws. Using every ounce of strength he could dredge up, Johnny slowly separated the teeth from his neck. He had no idea if the teeth had penetrated the skin, if he was bleeding, if the dog had actually inflicted so much damage that he was seriously injured. When he felt the jaws were far enough apart he threw back with all his might, and the mongrel sailed over the pack to land unceremoniously on his rump and side. Lashing out with fists and feet, Johnny called on the reserve strength of youth and fought the dogs off. He had to get up on the tractor and get away. Turning, he ignored the bites on his backside and climbed into the seat. The tractor had to start. It was old, but it had always started without hesitation. He reached out for the key and turned. The sound of life from gasoline meeting electrical spark caught and the engine purred loudly. In all his seventeen years Johnny O'Malley had never heard a nicer sound. Slamming the tractor into gear, he started down the row of corn again, throwing all caution to the wind, going as fast as he could make the machine move.

The mongrel watched the tractor pulling away and charged. Instantly, the others were behind him. When he reached the back of the Farm-all, he vaulted over the trailing claws and hit the wheel. The dog found himself being hauled to the top of the tire, and before Johnny realized he was being attacked again, the mongrel jumped from it, full onto the boy.

Doing his best to protect himself, Johnny took his hands from the steering wheel and tried to protect his throat. But the dog had already found it, and the new assault on the wounded windpipe continued.

Growling viciously, the dog pulled against the throat, bracing his legs against the boy's chest and stomach. Top-heavy and out of control, the driver found himself teetering backward and finally falling clear of the seat, but striking the claws of the cultivator behind the wheels.

Boy and dog landed in a heap and the other animals were all over Johnny in an instant.

Kicking as best he could with several dogs biting each leg, the youth desperately tried to pull himself up. He knew he was as good as dead on the ground. Standing, he might stand a modicum of success at surviving.

When he opened his eyes he looked directly into the yellow ones of the dog. The last thing he saw was the dog suddenly pulling back with something like a small piece of bloody hose hanging from its mouth. A sensation of warmth flowed over Johnny O'Malley, and he died several seconds later.

The tractor, throttle wide open, continued plowing erratically through the corn, zigzagging its way across the rows, toward a small gulley at the far end of the field.

Pete pulled up to the curb outside Amy's house. If they got to the point of talking marriage, and he felt certain that serious talks would be forthcoming, he hoped she would consider staying in the house she lived in now. He liked it. It was on the edge of town, and quiet and peaceful. Not that Laughton was a noisy town. It was just that there was little if any traffic on this street, and the nearest house was at least several hundred yards away.

"You're coming back, aren't you?" Amy asked quietly, opening the door on her side of the cab.

Pete leaned over and kissed her. "If you really want me to come back over, I will."

"How long will you be?" she asked, slipping from the front seat. She turned to face him, holding the door.

"I'd like to spend a little time with Jenny—assuming the 'bitch of Buchenwald' will permit it. It's not my regular visiting time." He shrugged.

"Well, it's almost five-thirty. Take your time. I'll

fix a late supper. Say around eight or so? That way I can walk Duchess and have her fed before you get back."

Pete smiled. "Dinner sounds great."

Amy slammed the door and stepped back from the Bronco and Pete pulled away from the curb.

Dan O'Malley looked up at the kitchen clock and then back to his wife. "I'm telling you, Emily, Johnny's got a problem of some sort. Maybe the old Farm-all broke down."

"I don't think it's too good an idea for you to go out now. If he thinks you don't trust him and have any confidence in him, he'll never want to stay on the farm and work with you."

"That may well be true, but I'm telling you he should have been home an hour ago. I know how much he had left to do today. There's no way he would be taking this long. It's already five to seven. He should've been back before six."

Emily looked at Dan. "I—" She stopped.

"Look, Em, a tractor isn't like a car. It can tip easier'n shit. You know that. He might be in trouble. Bad trouble. I'm going."

"Maybe you should at that," she said. "I never once thought that he might be hurt. Go on. I'll hold supper. Hurry up."

In a flash Dan jumped to his feet, moving toward the door. He grabbed his straw hat and plopped it on his head before slamming the screen door .

The sun was dipping toward the western

horizon, but it would still be light for another hour and a half. Dan got into the pickup truck and turned the motor over. He'd go the back way to the cornfield. It wouldn't be as smooth as taking the county backroads, but it would be quicker going through the pasture and then skirting the grain field.

After closing the pasture gate he made his way along the roadlike space between the oats and fence. The oats looked good. They'd be ready for harvesting within two weeks. Five minutes later he stopped at the fence line separating the oatfield from the corn. Dan shut the motor off and listened. He tried to hear the tractor, but the only sounds were the normal buzzing in his ears and some crows cawing above a spot a hundred yards away.

Climbing to the roof of the cab, he looked out over the cornfield. He could see no sign of the tractor. What could have happened? Maybe he'd finished and took the road back home, but that wasn't too likely since the tractor would make much better time going the way Dan had come. He got back down to the ground and crossed the fence. Once he had walked almost 60 percent of the width of the field he found the place where Johnny had turned the last time. Beyond that the ground had not been cultivated. Half running, half walking, Dan O'Malley started along the freshturned earth.

He stopped short when he found the place where the tractor had veered off through the corn and into the area where the ground hadn't been gone over yet. Something had happened. But what? He followed the path of broken and upturned plants. When he came to the gulley he found the tractor, nose first, one rear wheel in the air, balancing on the edge.

"Johnny? Johnny? Are you around here? Where are you? Come on, son, answer me."

He waited. No answer. Only the sound of the crows that were flapping in for a landing behind him someplace, cawing as they came to earth.

"Johnny?" Dan edged closer to the tractor. He had to make certain his son wasn't underneath the tractor. In the event he had been thrown clear, he might merely be unconscious and out of danger of being smashed by it.

When he saw that the grass wasn't bent of broken below the tractor he breathed easier. "Johnny?" No answer.

Stepping back, he looked at the control panel of the tractor from where he stood. The ignition key was still on and the throttle open. Maybe he fell off someplace else and the tractor went its own way and wound up here, eventually running out of gas. He turned to backtrack.

Running along the erratic path, he kept calling out for Johnny. "God Almighty!" Dan cried out as he hurried. "Where's my boy? What's happened? Show me the way to find him. Please? He's only a kid. Let him be all right!"

When Dan found the end of the path he started along the evenly cultivated rows and stopped short when he heard the crows off to his left in the cultivated part of the field. There wasn't any corn to be eaten yet. What would crows be doing in the field? Eating at some dead animal's carcass? He ran ahead.

"Shoo! Get outta here! Shoo!"

Dan stopped when the birds took to the air, one almost hitting him in the confusion of flapping wings, cawing crows, and yelling man.

Dan stopped short after the last crow had lifted off. He tried to comprehend what it was he saw lying on the ground in front of him.

"Johnny?" he whispered fearfully. God, it couldn't be his son!

The body lay on its back, arms and legs outstretched. The yawning hole of his throat held Dan's attention until he pulled it away, only to be held in an even tighter grip by the sight of the open body cavity. Shreds of flesh hung limply from the ragged edges and the rest of the body was covered with bite marks.

Dan felt himself weakening. His stomach heaved and he fell to his knees, vomitting. Retching, he spit up whatever was left in his belly before crawling forward toward what had been Johnny O'Malley. Crying, moaning, Dan wept out his initial grief. What could have done this? What sort of animal was there in the vicinity that could do this sort of damage?

Whatever it was wouldn't get away. He'd see to that. He'd call the sheriff and there'd be a posse put together to hunt down the wild animal that had done this awful thing.

Dan struggled to his feet and, taking off his shirt, covered as best he could Johnny's remains. He stumbled back to the truck and drove all too fast along the oatfield. When he reached the gate he barely threw it open wide enough for the truck to pass through. Jumping from it, he left it in the opening of the pasture gate and rushed toward the house.

"Em! Em!" he called. "Get the sheriff. Quick."

Back in the cornfield, the crows had already landed and pulled Dan's shirt from the banquet they had found. In the sky, clouds that had hung on the horizon for the last several hours and had slowly moved overhead began forming into a tighter knot.

5

Pete wished he had gone directly to Carol's place. Now that he was with Jenny, he felt relaxed, almost at ease. A sense of trepidation was stifled whenever he thought of Carol and her attitude toward him. If he let it, an argument could be born as easily as taking his next breath. Way down deep, he knew he didn't actually hate Carol. It was more of an instinct to survive that rose to the surface whenever she attacked him. It had been his past experience since the divorce that had made him drive around until almost seven o'clock before finally stopping at the side-by-side duplex and parking in front.

"Daddy, can you swing me?"

Pete snapped out of his funk and looked down

at Jenny. "Of course. Did your Mommy get you a swing?"

Jenny nodded. "Uh-huh! For my birf-day. Come on. I'll show you." She took Pete's hand in hers and led him around the side of the house.

When Carol had uncharacteristically said it was all right for him to stay awhile to visit Jenny he had opted to go outside. He had felt suffocated in the house. He smiled ruefully when he recalled what she had said when he knocked on the door.

"Well, if it isn't John D. Rockefeller. If you've got money, come on in. If you're trying to buy some additional time, I'll call my attorney and have you thrown in jail." Carol stared at him.

Without blinking or looking away from her all-encompassing gaze, Pete reached in his shirt pocket and pulled out the $200 in small bills that he had had the foresight to get earlier. If he had had to write a check, she would have questioned its worth, simply to embarrass him. This way she had nothing to yell about. "You'll find it all here," he said, handing her the small stack of bills.

Carol busied herself counting the money and she re-folded it when she had satisfied herself that it was all there "So? Thanks. You're late with it, however."

"Not really. It was due today. I thought perhaps you'd let Jenny and me have a little time together. Possible?" He hoped it didn't sound like he was begging or that he was trying to buy a little time with his own daughter.

Carol frowned. "Oh, I suppose so. But you're not taking her anywhere. You understand? This isn't your regular visiting day. You have to stay right here with her."

Pete nodded. "What about outside? We can talk and walk around the yard."

"You stay in the yard. All right?"

Pete wanted to say: *"Yes, Mommy and I'll be a good boy and not run around the neighborhood either."* But he knew his sarcasm would only infuriate his ex-wife, and perhaps she'd wind up withdrawing permission for him to be with Jenny.

Instead, he said, "No problem with that. I've got an eight o'clock appointment so I can't really stay all that long."

Carol looked at her watch. "Some father. You come here at seven and buy a little favor with me to spend some time with Jenny and then squirm out of being with her too long by coming up with some phony appointment."

Pete wanted to scream at her that he had a dinner engagement with one of the nicest people he had ever met but bit his tongue, deciding it would be foolish to let Carol know of Amy's existence. It was better to let her think that he was miserable in his loneliness.

"You know, Carol," Pete said softly, "you might think differently if you had to come up with two hundred bucks a month just to visit your child."

"Hey, don't blame me. You're the one who said you couldn't live with me. You're the one who wanted out, not me."

"Need I remind you, Carol, that you were the one who changed? Not me. After Jenny was born it was as if you were another person."

"Nuts! You're exaggerating again, just like you always did."

"You were the one who exaggerated. You were the one who always said I had something other than work keeping me away from home."

"You didn't want to help with Jenny. That's why you stayed away." Carol pouted.

Pete stepped back. Frustration flowed through him and he knew that if they persisted, the argument would go on and on.

Jenny suddenly materialized between the two of them. She looked up first at her mother, then at her father. "Are you going to fight?"

Carol turned away and Pete crouched down to be at Jenny's six-year-old height. "No, darling. Mommy and Daddy aren't going to fight. We were just having a discussion."

"Every time you come over you and Mommy have a 'scussion. How come you never come to see me?"

Pete embraced her and said, "If it's all right, Carol, I'll take her outside now."

Carol said nothing, but nodded without turning around.

Pete and Jenny had gone outside and eventually they wound up in the backyard, with the child on the swing and Pete pushing her. She told him about Mrs. Smith, her doll, and the little boy and girl who lived on the other side of the house with whom she played whenever she could.

Pete thought that was good. At least Carol wasn't keeping the girl isolated.

"What else do you do, Jenny?"

"Oh, Uncle Mark comes over almost every night."

Uncle Mark? "Who?" he asked without telegraphing his curiosity.

"Uncle Mark. Mommy's boyfriend. Have you got a boyfriend, Daddy?"

"Huh? Oh, no. No. Daddy doesn't have a boyfriend." Pete smiled to himself. But Mommy apparently had a boyfriend. That must have just come about. Carol hadn't said anything, but then, she probably wouldn't have told him anyway.

Pete looked at his watch. Almost seven thirty-five. He'd have to think about leaving by ten of eight. Amy's face formed in his mind and he relaxed. How different life would have been if he had met her first and Jenny had been their child.

He slowed the swing down after awhile and helped Jenny get out of it. "Well, darling, it's time for Daddy to go."

When he crouched down next to her she threw her arms around his neck. "Oh, Daddy, don't go. Uncle Mark will be here soon and you should meet him."

"Another time, honey. Another time. Daddy's got an important meeting to go to. You wouldn't want him to be late, would you?"

"If you were late, would you have to stay after school? Mommy said to me that when I start school this year, I can't be late or they'll keep me there."

"Oh, I don't think I'd have to stay, but it's not nice to keep people waiting. You always remember that. Okay?"

"Okay, Daddy."

He took her hand and she skipped along at his side. They went to the front door and, thinking better of simply walking right in, Pete knocked softly. In seconds Carol came to the door. Her eyes looked as if she might have been crying. Deciding not to say anything, Pete merely said, "Well, here she is—safe and sound."

"All right, Pete. Will you be here this weekend?"

Dropping down to Jenny once more, he hugged her and gave her a big kiss on the cheek. "You bet I'll be here. I wouldn't miss my date with my best girl for anything."

He stood, saying, "See you 'round, Carol."

When he reached the curb he walked around the Bronco, hesitating when he heard a siren screaming through the neighborhood several blocks away, where the highway passed through town. He couldn't help noticing the digital clock on the dashboard when he climbed in and turned the ignition key: 7:47.

He eased away from the curb when he saw the car coming down the street pull in behind him. Driving slowly, he watched a slight built man get out and walk up to Carol's door.

"Uncle Mark, probably," he muttered, and turned on the wipers when the first drops of rain splattered the windshield.

6

Sheriff Duke Little glared at the phone. Why did it have to ring now? It probably would be nothing more than a routine call, one he could dispatch to one of his deputies who might be in the vicinity—assuming it was that type of call. Maybe it was just Gayle, his wife.

After it rang a third time he picked it up and said, "Sheriff's office, Duke Little speaking."

"Duke? It's Dan O'Malley. Can you come out right now?"

Duke frowned. Maybe Dan just needed a deputy for some reason and didn't mean he wanted the sheriff himself at all. "What's up, Dan?"

"It's—it's Johnny. I found him—his body—in the cornfield where—"

"What happened?" Duke asked, interrupting the caller.

"That's just it. I don't know. I think—I think a wild animal must have gotten him. God, it's—it's awful. Can you come, Dan? For me?"

Duke swallowed. He and Dan had been best friends ever since junior high school, when they had each gotten a detention for fighting one another on the playground during the noon hour. High school, the army, Vietnam. They had done everything together except work. Now Dan needed him, and Duke would be available to help him, no matter what the inconvenience. "Hang on, Dan. I'll be there as soon as possible. How's Em? Is she all right? Should I call a doctor for her? What about the coroner? I'll notify him and have him meet me at your place. You stay in the house till I get there. All right?"

After a short pause Dan said, "All right. I don't know about the doctor for Em. She's taking it better 'n me, but then, she didn't see Johnny's body. Hold off on the doctor. At least till you get here."

"Fine, Dan. I'll see you soon."

Duke hung up, called his wife to tell her he wouldn't be home for supper. He called his chief deputy and ordered him back to the office. With no one other than the dispatcher in the courthouse, he wanted at least one officer on the premises. After telling the dispatcher to call the coroner he left his office.

The first drops of rain hit him as he got into his

patrol car. Just what he needed. The farmers needed the rain, but as a city person he didn't really care if it rained or not.

Driving as fast as he could without becoming a traffic hazard himself, Duke turned on the siren and clocked 40 miles an hour through the business district. At least at this hour there weren't many people or cars around. When he hit the outskirts he floored the accelerator and stretched his arm muscles at the same time. He needed to work out more than he did. He was in shape, despite his 41 years, but he needed to get out and walk more. Perhaps this fall he could double up on his hunting time. Maybe he and . . .

Duke swallowed hard and forced back a tear. How would Dan ever recover from the loss of his only child—his only son? Duke was Johnny's godfather. He had no idea what he would say when he confronted his friend. Words always seemed so inadequate when death was involved.

Slowing down, he turned onto County Highway A-10 and resumed his speed. The rain, which had seemed almost afraid to fall at first, developed into a steady patter on the roof of the car. His headlights, knifing through the rain, reflected the tiny daggers of water as they sliced through the early, sunless dusk.

In the distance he could see the O'Malley farm, the old, unused windmill marking the property like a skeletal finger pointing to the heavens. Duke slowed a bit. He didn't want to turn in, but he knew he had to. It was his duty—not only as sheriff but as Dan's best friend. Pushing harder on the brakes, he turned off the red flashers on the roof and killed the siren.

The farm seemed gloomy in the rain, as if mourning for the loss of Johnny.

Duke got out of the car and hurried to the kitchen door, where Dan met him.

"What happened, Dan?"

Dan shrugged. "I don't know. Something—some wild animal got him. God. It was terrible. His whole middle—" He stopped and gagged at the thoughts ricocheting through his mind.

"Easy. Don't go into detail. Where's his body?"

"In the field. I covered it as best I could with my shirt. Jesus, Duke, there were crows eating on him. Crows were eating my son." Again his stomach reacted, but nothing happened. He had long since completely emptied it.

"Hello, Duke," Em said dispassionately when she entered the kitchen. "It's terrible. Dan wouldn't take me out to him. Why wouldn't you, Dan?"

"I told you it was somethin' you wouldn't want to see. Be thankful Duke is here. He'll know what to do."

"First thing will be to get out there. Can you show me, Dan? Maybe Em should ride along.'"

Dan glared at his friend. "I don't think she should see him, Duke."

"I didn't say she should. She can wait in the car. I'm sure she wouldn't want to be alone right now. Em?"

"That's thoughtful of you, Duke. Yes; I think I better ride along. I'll stay in the car, Dan." She reached out and put her hand on her husband's arm.

Without a word Dan pulled away and strode for the kitchen door. Duke wanted to embrace them, but knew the gesture, at this moment, would be almost meaningless. He was there in his official capacity and had a job to do. Later, when the time was right, Duke, the friend, would step in to help console the O'Malleys.

Duke turned the car in the yard and, following Dan's instructions, turned right onto the highway. At the first intersection he turned right again and drove along the narrow side road. He could hear Dan's soft sobbing at his right and caught the man's movements when he wiped away tears. It disturbed Duke to see his friend so overwrought. Still, he felt he would be doing the same thing if it were his child.

"Here. Stop here, Duke," Dan said, breaking the silence in the car.

Braking to a halt, Duke turned on the flashers and got out.

"You stay in the car, Em. You hear me?" Dan said, more in an ordering voice than a compassionate one.

"I said I would." She stared straight ahead into the darkening night, which was being splashed rhythmically with the red lights.

"Follow me, Duke." Dan crawled through the barbed wire fence after going through the gutter.

When he realized that Duke wasn't behind him he stopped and looked back.

"Hold on, Dan," the sheriff said from the rear of the car. Slamming the truck lid down, he ran through the gutter and handed Dan a poncho. "Here. There's no sense in us getting soaked to the skin. We should have thought of it back at the farm."

Without a word Dan slipped the plastic rain gear over his head and turned to walk through the corn. Duke, shaking his head at his friend's upset, turned on his flashlight after donning his own slicker. One thing bothered Duke. Why had Dan left his son's body in the field?

"Over here, Duke," Dan called from the sheriff's right side.

Duke hurried through the corn and stopped when he saw Dan pointing to the ground. "There. There's my boy. What's left of him. Maybe I should have taken him to the house, but I didn't think I should disturb him. 'Sides, I didn't want Em to see him like this. She should remember him the way he was. Did I do the right thing, Duke?"

His unasked question answered, Duke nodded. "You did exactly the right thing, Dan."

Duke flashed the light around the body. The rain was soaking into the dry ground, but any prints that might have been made in the hard earth would have been destroyed by the force of the falling drops.

"What animal kills like this, Duke?" Dan stared

into the eyes of his friend. "I gotta know. I gotta kill the goddamn thing, whatever it is."

The sheriff played the light along the body of the youth. His middle had been ripped open and the entrails, stomach, liver, heart, lungs—everything was gone. Moving the beam toward the head, he stopped at the spot of the boy's neck. Torn wide open, the neck showed a large section of the windpipe gone. Duke shuddered. What a horrible way to die. He thought back to the things he had read about wild animals and the way they killed. In Africa there would be animals that would kill like this, but the bodies would be worked over more than Johnny's had been. He brought the light down to Johnny's legs. Bruises and what appeared to be bite marks covered his limbs and face.

What animals would there be on the North American continent that were classified as predators—predators large enough to kill a husky 17-year-old boy. Cats? Cougars? They were rare in the Western states and in Florida, unknown around Laughton. Bears? Bears could be vicious killers under the right circumstances. But Duke doubted if there had been a bear on its own in the Laughton area in over 100 years. Wolverines? Not hardly. He knew they were the most elusive of all animals in the wild. Wolves? Coyotes? He shook his head. Not around this part of the country. What then?

"You got any ideas, Dan?"

Dan shook his head. "I've been hunting a lot

and I know I've never seen a carcass left like this. What do you think? Wolves? Bear? Cat? What?"

"Not around here, Dan. For crying out loud, your son was ripped open by what appears to be a pretty good-sized animal. Christ, his clothing was stripped away. What's the largest predator around here? Fox? A few. Racoons? They can kill a good-sized dog, but they'd have to be rabid to attack a human. And if they were rabid, they wouldn't be able to eat."

"Shows what you can overlook if you don't watch out." Dan stared at the lawman.

"I don't catch your meaning, Dan."

"Remember a couple of years ago? A moose from Canada wandered down through Minnesota, into Iowa, and finally wound up in a game preserve or park down in Missouri. Remember that?"

Duke half grinned when he recalled having read about the animal moseying through cornfields and timbers, heading south. "Yeah, I remember. What about it? A moose didn't do this."

"Didn't say it did. But the thing you're forgetting is the fact that the moose managed to slip away whenever it wanted to. They lost sight of it in Minnesota and no one saw it until it was around Cedar Rapids or someplace nearby. Then it just as easily disappeared again and was seen south of Des Moines, entering Missouri."

"What's your point, Dan?"

"If something as big as a moose can come and

go as he pleases and walk around without being seen, why couldn't a cougar or a bear be in the vicinity and elude everybody?" Dan thrust his jaw out in a determined way, gesturing that he wanted Duke to prove him wrong.

"All right, I'll give you that. But tell me, why haven't there been any reports about dead livestock or attacks on other people?"

"I don't follow you. I just said—"

"I know what you said and I agree. An animal could get around the country without being seen if it were careful. But it had to eat before now. Here, all of a sudden, it gets hungry and attacks Johnny? I don't buy it. There would have to be reports about dead animals or attacks if your theory is correct. There haven't been any. I would've seen them if there had been."

"Then back to square one. Right?"

Duke nodded. "Did Johnny have any enemies?"

Dan shook his head vigorously. "Hell no! Johnny was well liked. Nobody, but nobody disliked him."

"That's what I thought."

"What's that mean?"

"Just what I said. I thought Johnny was pretty popular. You haven't seen any strange cars hanging around, have you?"

Dan shook his head.

"Remember ten, fifteen years ago when the cattle were being mutilated? Did you lose any then?"

Dan shook his head again. "Are you trying to say somebody did this to my boy? A person? A human being?"

Duke held his hand up. "I'm not saying anything like that at all. I just have to cover all the angles. Those mutilations were never cleared up, were they?"

"Not that I recall." Dan stepped closer to Duke. "Look, what's the next step? Em is going to get antsy and come out here. I don't think she should see Johnny like this."

"I agree. Let's go back to the car and call the coroner. He should be on his way out here, but he doesn't know where the body is. Come on." Duke slogged off through the muddying field and crawled through the fence, Dan right behind him.

After calling the coroner on the radio the sheriff turned to the woman in the back seat. "How you doing, Em?"

"Is Johnny really dead?"

Duke nodded. What did she expect? A joke of some sort? An awful sick joke that would have Johnny running up to the car, laughing about how he had fooled his parents? He knew Johnny O'Malley. The boy, if he were alive, could never hurt anyone—most especially his parents. Then, too, he had seen Johnny's body—or what was left of it. He shuddered. What type of animal killed like that?

Once the coroner arrived, Duke drove the O'Malleys back to their farm. His friends were in for a long night of mourning, and he had things to do back at the office. One thing was certain, he was going to concentrate on finding the animal responsible for Johnny O'Malley's death. At least Duke hoped it was an animal and not some perverted human being.

7

Pete downed the rest of his coffee and set the cup on the table. "That was good, Amy. I didn't realize how hungry I had become since we ate in the country."

"I'm not certain if that's a compliment or an insult."

"Why?"

"I made a quick lunch for the picnic and then I made a good meal here. Apparently you didn't like my picnic lunch."

"Not so. I just didn't eat that much. Besides, the country air really got to me."

"That's a likely story." She finished putting the last of the dishes into the washer and set the controls. She turned back to Pete. "Do you have anything planned for tonight?"

"Wow! Is that ever a loaded question. Would you like to rephrase it?"

Amy smiled, blushing at the same time. "All right. Are you planning on returning to your apartment or are you going to hang around here and be a pest?"

Pete feigned injury. "I think I'll go home."

"Maybe you should. After everything you've told me, your *ex* was almost civil you to."

"Meaning?"

"Meaning she might be developing a warm place in her heart for you again."

"That I doubt very much. I didn't tell you about 'Uncle Mark,' did I?"

Amy mouthed the words *Uncle Mark,* but said nothing aloud.

"Apparently Carol has gotten herself a boyfriend. At least Jenny refers to him as Uncle Mark. I think he pulled up behind me when I left."

"Well, if you're really torn apart by the idea of Carol being in another man's arms, I'll consider letting you stay—if you behave yourself."

Pete grinned widely. "I can always sleep on the sofa. In fact, I think I will. I'm getting used to sleeping alone. I found that I actually sleep much better when I'm in bed alone."

Amy threw a dish towel at Pete.

"Missed me," he said, laughing.

"Just try sleeping on the couch, *Mister* Pete Reckels. You'll be sorry if you do."

"Gee, I wouldn't want to be sorry about anything like that, would I?"

She smiled, stepping closer to him. "I can recommend a real nice bed upstairs. Only one catch."

"What's that?"

"There's another person who will be occupying half of it."

"Anybody I know?"

"You might."

"Anybody I'd like to know?"

"Could be. Tell you what, I'll give you three guesses."

"Amy? Amy Bondson? Miss Amy Bondson?"

"Right on all three." Amy started from the kitchen, turning the lights out, and led Pete through the dining room to the stairs in the front hallway.

They quickly undressed, and although Amy was first in bed, Pete followed in mere seconds. He turned the bedside light out and reached for her. Their lips met and they embraced. Caressing, fondling, they enjoyed each other's body, and when they had finished their demonstration of love, they fell back on the bed.

"Are you going to sleep right away?" Amy asked, only to be greeted by even breathing. "No one—no one other than Pete Reckels—falls asleep that fast." She grinned in the dark and snuggled next to him. In seconds the steady rhythm of the rain on the porch roof outside the bedroom window lulled her to sleep.

The mongrel lay curled up beneath the low

bush. Despite the shelter the rain seeped down through the heavy foliage, dripping on him. The other dogs sought shelter in much the same way, trying to avoid the rain. None succeeded. When the rain began to diminish, the black dog stood and shook himself, setting up a miniature downpour for several seconds. The other dogs slept or patiently waited for the rain to stop.

Moving off into the shadows of the trees lining the creek bank, he didn't turn back, ignoring the inquisitive whine from the tan-and-black bitch. Trotting along the bank, he came to a bridge overhead and easily surmounted the grade to the level of the road. Standing on the wet macadam, he read the breeze. Nothing. All of the animals that should have been out, foraging, had sought shelter from the elements. The mongrel turned to his right, then to his left, as if deciding in which direction to go.

Without hesitating he loped off to his left, easily trotting along the smooth surface of the highway.

Dr. Mervyn Wilson bent over the body on the table. Why the sheriff was so insistent that he examine the body and perform an autopsy before morning was beyond him. An autopsy wouldn't take long, considering the condition of the body. The thing the sheriff seemed to want more than anything was the manner in which the boy had died. What had killed him seemed to be uppermost in the lawman's mind.

Wilson shook his head. The boy, according to Sheriff Little, was only 17. A shame. A real shame. And it must have been an awful way to die. Most of the blood was gone and, when he finished his examination, he calculated that less than a pint remained in the cadaver. The aspect that held his interest the longest was the bruise marks on the legs and arms and face. They were undoubtedly teeth marks, but from what sort of animal? At first he thought they might be dog teeth, but that didn't make sense to Wilson. The number of bruises and the varying sizes seemed to tell him that many dogs would have to have been present to render the number of bite marks. The body had been torn up quite badly, and he wondered at the logic of continuing his work. Still, he had his orders from the sheriff: Find out what killed Johnny O'Malley.

The black mongrel stood on a hill overlooking Laughton. The lights, twinkling merrily below in the clean, damp air, were mere dots of brightness in a sea of gray and black to him. Still, he felt he had to investigate the lights and the town. He and the bitch had avoided most towns when they had first started running. Trotting down the face of the hill, he made his way toward the city limits.

Wilson poured himself another cup of coffee.

His report was half finished. At least Duke wouldn't be able to come down on him like a ton of bricks for not having completed the autopsy before morning. He played back the tape recording:

"The subject is white, male, seventeen years of age, approximately one hundred eight-three centimeters in height and the approximate weight would have been in the vicinity of seventy-five kilos. Visual examination shows tearing laceration of the throat. Closer examination shows the jugular severed and portions of the trachea and esophagus missing. The apparent cause of death is multiple animal attack with complete evisceration of thorasic and abdominal cavaties. The arms and legs display multiple lacerations that appear to be bite wounds of varying sizes."

Wilson turned off the machine and made a notation on his pad. After assuring himself he had not made a mistake he reactivated the tape player. A muffled sound brought back to Wilson the terse statement he had made after covering the microphone: *"God Almighty. The poor sonofabitch is ripped to shreds."*

Wilson knew he would be questioned by the sheriff if he put down the dogs were responsible for Johnny O'Malley's death, but what other alternative was there? He could hear the arguments of the lawmen.

"How many dogs?"

"Where are they now?"

"How could dogs do that?"

"Are you trying to tell me that household dogs and farm dogs did this?"

Of course he didn't know for certain that dogs had been responsible. All he could do was put down on tape, and in a written report, the conclusions he drew from examining the body. Deep down, Mervyn Wilson found it impossible to believe that dogs could have rendered the damage to Johnny O'Malley's body.

Every muscle twitched in the black mongrel's body. He read the scent of the breeze once more. It was a bitch. A bitch in heat, and no other animals were around. He moved forward cautiously, keeping his nose high in the air. Confronting the first house he came to, he realized that the bitch was around this house somewhere.

Stealthily moving forward, he passed a parked vehicle in the driveway before coming to a gate and fence. A deep-throated whine wound its way through his chest as he walked the length of the fence surrounding the yard and house.

The second time he whined an answering call rewarded him, and he could see the figure of a white dog coming from a kennel behind the house. From where he stood, at the end of the yard, he could see the house, which had no lights visible. He whined a third time and saw the dog running toward him. Another member for the pack. And she was in heat.

Suddenly the dog stopped short, held in check by the leash hanging from an overhead wire. The bitch barked once, short, plaintive, pleading.

The mongrel whined again, running back and forth along the fence. When he realized the bitch couldn't come to him he looked up at the top of the wooden barrier separating them. He leaped effortlessly, clearing the top rail, and landed in the yard with barely a sound.

The white bitch, tongue hanging from her mouth, danced a stutter step back and forth, waiting for the black dog to approach her. When they were mere inches apart, they began smelling each other, identifiying each other, an identification that would last the rest of their lives. The white bitch turned her hindside to the black, who intently smelled her scent before moving. The quivering in his own loins hammered at him and, rearing up, he mounted the bitch.

Several hours later the black mongrel trotted along the highway, back in the general direction from which he had come earlier. After leaving the road he relocated the stream and followed it until he came upon the sleeping pack. The rain had long since stopped and several dogs stood, wary at first and then eager to greet their leader.

When the formalities had been finished the mongrel curled up under a bush. Tomorrow the pack would have to hunt for new game, but tonight their bellies were still full.

Day Two

Friday

8

Duke Little snapped the wooden pencil between his hands. "Bullshit!" he muttered, picking up the telephone. "Darlene, get me the coroner's office."

There was no way this report could be right, simply no way. Duke had done enough hunting in his life to know a little about the outdoors.

"Dr. Wilson."

" 'Morning, Doc. Say, what kind of garbage are you handing me in your reports these days?"

"What? I don't understand."

"The O'Malley boy. What the hell are you saying?"

"Oh."

Duke waited for a moment after the one word

acknowledgment. Then, when he thought the coroner had had enough time to gather his thoughts, said, "Well?"

"What seems to be the problem?"

"Christ, you didn't say anything about he cause of death."

"I drew the only logical conclusions I could draw at the time."

"What the hell does that mean? Listen. Listen to this. I'm reading it from your report.

> "Teeth marks appear on the arms and legs of the victim as well as on the torso. The abrasions appear to have been caused by the canine teeth or fangs of some sort of animal. The abrasions could have been inflicted by cats such as mountain lions or lynx. Other possibilities are members of the dog family such as *Canis lupus*, or wolves; *Vulpes*, or foxes; *Canin Latrans*, or coyote; *Canis familiaris*, or the ordinary domesticated dog. One other possibility would be large rodents such as rats, beavers, and rabbits. (The last suggestion does not seem to be in keeping, however, with the nature of the abrasions. They seem to have been caused by conical, pointed teeth such as the fangs on those animals mentioned above. Rodents, on the other hand, have flat, long incisors that would not match the abrasions found on the corpse's extremeties.)

"What the hell are you saying, Doc?"

"I thought it was pretty clear. I don't know. All

I'm doing is giving you the possibilities of the alternatives, if you will." Dr. Wilson waited on the other end.

Duke frowned. The most he had hoped for was the type of animal. Here, the coroner was giving him the choice of just about every predator on the North American continent except— His eyes lit up. "What about bear?"

At first there was no response. Then, "I rather doubt that. This isn't their territory, is it? I never thought of bear. I suppose it could be. They have canine fangs."

"When you say you suppose it could be do you mean that, or are you just lumping the idea in with the other choices?"

"I guess you could say I was adding it to the list, Sheriff."

"Okay, then, I want you to add the wolverine and just about any other type of wild predator you can think of to the list. Coons, weasels, otters, name it. Put in on the list."

"Why, for heaven's sake?"

"Because it makes as much sense to list everything as it does to list a few. Got it?"

"Yeah, I got it," the doctor said dejectedly. "I'll amend my report and get a copy of it over to you as soon as possible. All right?"

"That'll be fine, Doc. I'm not trying to be a hard ass about this. It's just that Dan O'Malley is my best friend and Johnny was sort of special to me. I want whatever it was that killed him."

"I understand."

"God, that was an awful way to die."

"Tell me about it, Sheriff. I performed the autopsy as best I could. I've never seen anything like it before."

"Would you care to make an off-the-record suggestion as to what type of animal it was?"

A long pause followed the sheriff's question.

"Well?"

"If I had to make a guess, I'd say it was more than one animal, as I stated further on in my report. There was more than one. There had to be. The depth and spacing of the teeth marks or abrasions were different in a lot of the cases."

"That helps narrow it down somewhat, but how far I don't know. Wolves and coyotes run in packs. Fox don't. Nor do cats. Well, whatever it was, I'll find it. Goddammit, I'll find it or bust trying. Thanks, Doc. I'll wait for your amended report."

Duke hung up without waiting for the medical man to answer. Puckering his lips, he folded his hands. What would possess wolves or coyotes to come into a farming area to hunt and turn to eating humans?

Pete stepped onto the back step by Amy's house. He had a relatively full day ahead of him and wanted to start with Joe Eppson's herd of pigs. Stretching, he walked toward the Bronco parked in the driveway. When he reached it he opened the door and honked the horn. In seconds Amy ran from the back door, turning to lock it before coming to the car.

"Don't be so impatient, Pete. I've got all kinds of time before I have to be at the courthouse."

"I know that, but I don't. I've got a lot to do today, including taking you to work and—"

"Hey," she said, getting into the passenger's seat of the vehicle, "don't bother if you're pressed for time."

Slamming the door, Pete turned to her. "You know I'd go through fire and water for you. It's just that I've got a helluva lot to do today." He turned the motor over and started to back out of the driveway.

"Wait a minute," Amy called out. "I forgot to water Duchess or feed her."

Pete stopped the Bronco and laughed. "If it were your grandmother, I'd say she could get her own grub and water. But, since it's a dog, and Duchess *is* a patient of mine,I guess I'd better let you do it. Don't be long."

"I won't," she said, jumping from the car.

"Will I see you tonight?" Amy asked, getting out in front of the courthouse.

"I might be late. Want me to call or come over?"

"Why not just come over? I'll wait with supper until you get there."

"You've got a deal." Pete leaned across far enough to give her a peck on the lips. "Gotta go. See you tonight."

Amy stepped back, waving as Pete pulled away

from the curb.

He watched her in the rearview mirror until he came to the traffic light and turned left. The gas gauge caught his attention, and he knew he'd have to stop for fuel before leaving town for Eppson's farm. Half a block again, he pulled into Marty O'Connor's service station.

Before he had a chance to turn off the motor Marty was at Pete's window.

"Fill 'er up for you, Pete?"

"Yeah. How you doin', Marty?"

After thrusting the nozzle of the hose into the yawning gas pipe and setting the handle Marty stepped back and said, "Not bad, but I damn near lost my breakfast when I filled the sheriff's car this morning."

Pete stared at him. "What do you mean?"

"He asked me if I knew of any wild animals around Laughton. You know, I do a lot of hunting, but, Christ, what he told me next about finished me for the day."

"What was that?"

"Well, you know Dan O'Malley, right?"

Pete nodded. He knew every farmer in Cramden County.

"Seems Dan's boy, Johnny, got killed."

"What? How?"

"Wild animal of some sort. The sheriff went into a lot of detail, trying to see if I recognized the way the boy died or something, I guess."

"I don't follow you."

"Well, he told me that the boy's body was torn

up pretty bad. Throat was torn out and the belly ripped open. The guts and everything was eaten."

"Jesus," Pete gasped. "That's awful."

"I know," Marty said quietly. "At any rate, the sheriff asked me if I knew of any wild animal around here that would kill a person."

"What'd you tell him?"

Marty shrugged. "What could I tell him? Hell, the biggest pedator around these parts is probably racoon. And as far as I know they don't kill people."

"That's right, but if a racoon is cornered, it'll take on a pack of hunting hounds and walk away the winner, if the conditions are right."

"I know that, Pete. But for the most part, 'coons let people alone. Oh, they'll come into town and forage through garbage if the pickings are lean in the country. But kill a person—a boy? A healthy boy that could probably have outrun a 'coon?"

"Where'd the—the accident happen?" Pete wondered what else something like the death Marty was describing could be called. The killing? That sounded premeditated.

"I guess the kid was cultivating the corn. The tractor took off by itself and tipped over in the gully a short distance away from where Dan found him. Jesus Christ, that must have been awful for Dan—to find his only kid like that, ripped up and half eaten." Marty turned away to take the gas hose out of the Bronco. "How's the oil?"

"It should be all right," Pete said absently. "What's the sheriff going to do, or didn't he say?"

"He didn't say. I imagine he'll have to warn everybody to be on the lookout for some sort of animal that doesn't belong."

Climbing into the driver's seat after paying Marty, Pete said, "Yeah, I guess that makes sense. Nothing much else he could do, short of organizing a hunting party to go after whatever it was that killed Johnny."

"Yeah, and that would be pretty difficult, considering the rain wiped out all signs of tracks and spoor."

"See you, Marty," Pete said, turning the engine over. He pulled out of the service station's drive and onto the street. In 10 minutes or so, once he got out of Laughton, he'd be at Joe Eppson's farm.

He furrowed his forehead when he pictured in his mind the way Johnny's body must have looked when Dan found it, based on Marty's secondhand account. He shuddered. He'd have a helluva rotten day if he continued thinking about such horrible things. Reaching down, he turned on the radio.

"This is WKBB, Laughton. Here's Jason Roberts with the latest news."

Before Roberts could begin recounting the tragedies and traumas of the world Pete turned the dial, searching for music. When Willie Nelson's voice filled the Bronco he pulled his hand away and started singing along with the entertainer.

Hell, anything was better than thinking about the manner in which Johnny O'Malley had died.

9

Pete slowed down enough to turn into Joe Eppson's farm yard, and after easing along the muddy road, came to a stop close to the barn. He seldom, if ever, went near the houses of the farms he serviced. Why should he? His business was centered more in the animal pens and enclosures, and it would prove to be a waste of time and effort to stop near the house.

He half expected Joe to come out of one of the buildings to greet him, but didn't think too much of it immediately when the farmer didn't show himself.

Then Pete's hair began feeling as if it were moving of its own accord. An eerie sensation passed through him. What was causing that? He started to think that unseen eyes were watching his every move. Or perhaps that he had stopped at the wrong farm. That was ridiculous. He knew Joe. He knew Joe's farm. This was the right place.

Opening the door, Pete slipped from the driver's seat and moved around to the rear of the Bronco. He opened the back door and reached in, taking out the box of vaccine he had put in yesterday following Joe's call to him.

The creepy sensation persisted, and the veterinarian stepped back, away from the car, and, without being obvious, turned in a full circle while seeming to study the box in his hand. Instead, his eyes scanned each building, trying to see if someone, Joe undoubtedly, were actually watching him without letting his presence be known.

Then Pete saw the dog. He searched his mind for the animal's name. He tried to keep the identification of each dog in his memory. It was a good exercise in memory training and helped avoid dangerous situations, since dogs relaxed when their names were called. Trixie. That was it. Trixie, Joe Eppson's collie, slowly walked toward him, a pleading whine spiraling up through her chest and throat.

"Hey, girl," Pete said, dropping to his haunches, "what's the matter? You all right? Where's Joe? Is Joe around?"

The dog flicked her pink tongue out to give Pete a quick wash job on his face.

"Hey, that's enough!" Pete stood upright and read the instructions on the box of vaccine bottles. "Joe?" He called the man's name as loud as he could without actually straining his voice.

When he was satisfied that he had enough vaccine he stepped away from the Bronco again. "Hey, Joe? Where are you? I'm ready. Come on, I'll need your help with the pigs."

He waited. No answer of any sort, other than the sounds coming from the direction of the pig house, where the young animals were being held until he could vaccinate each one. The chickens hung close to their brooder house. Pete wondered why. It seemed as if they were waiting for something to happen or someone to come by.

Calling out the farmer's name once more, Pete decided to investigate the brooder house first. Taking big strides, he moved across the farm yard and made his way through the clucking, milling chickens that quickly closed around him, waiting for food. They fluttered out of his way and he entered the brooder house. Nest boxes lined the walls and he peeked in several to find eggs still in the nests. He wondered why Joe hadn't picked up the eggs. Then the thought struck him that there were an awful lot of eggs to be picked up for the morning. He wondered if perhaps Joe hadn't picked them up last night. No, that would be uncharacteristic of the man. He was methodical to a fault. But why hadn't he picked up the eggs?

When he came back out of the house, Pete

scanned the yard once more. The tractor sat near the machine shed. The exhaust hadn't been covered. Joe must have used the tractor that morning. Leaving the chicken yard, he closed the gate, but it didn't latch. He walked past the vehicle when he returned to the Bronco. Reaching out, he found the motor cold. It hadn't been run that morning.

Pete was beginning to feel uncomfortable. Something was wrong. But what? He ran toward the pig building and found the young pigs he was to vaccinate milling about, grunting, squealing, practically begging for food. The sows in the outside pen made as much racket as the young ones. If Pete knew anything about animal husbandry, he knew hungry animals when he saw them.

If the tractor wasn't there, he would think that the old bachelor had gone into the field and forgotten about Pete's coming this morning. But the tractor was sitting there, waiting. Besides, the fields were too wet after the rain. Then Pete caught a glimpse of Joe's '71 Chevy half in, half out of the garage. Joe had to be on the farm someplace. Maybe—

Pete broke into a run toward the barn. Maybe something had happened to Joe this morning when he went to milk. Throwing open the barn door, Pete rushed inside, waiting for a scant second for his eyes to adjust to the gloomy half light of the interior.

"Joe? Joe, are you in here?"

He waited, holding his breath for fear his breathing might cover up a moan or a groan from Joe in the event the man were injured or ill. Nothing.

One of the cattle, waiting to be milked, stuck her head into the barn through the open portion of the door leading to the cattle yard on the side of the barn, farthest from the yard. She lowed loudly, begging to be milked, to ease the pain of her swollen udder.

Something weird had happened. It appeared to Pete as if Joe hadn't done any of his evening chores from yesterday, nor had he done anything this morning.

The house. He hadn't checked the house.

Dashing from the barn, he made his way as fast as he could across the farm yard to the simple, two-story house. When he reached the kitchen door he pounded loudly. "Joe? Joe, are you in there?"

He waited for less than half a minute before trying the door. The knob turned easily and he stepped into the entryway.

"Joe?" Easing into the kitchen, he called again. "Joe? Joe, are you all right?"

The smell of stale tobacco hung in the air, and Pete noted the dirty dishes in the sink. When he examined them he found crusty food dried on each. That had to be from yesterday's meals.

"Joe?"

He peered through the doorway leading to the dining room, which he found empty. The parlor, closed off with sliding doors, yielding nothing. Another room, next to the stairs that led to the second floor, was empty. Pete opened the stairway door and called Joe's name again before starting up the steps. Each one creaked in its own peculiar voice, lending an unearthly aspect to Pete's search. The upstairs was empty. The one fully furnished bedroom gave no clue as to what might have happened to the owner.

Rushing back downstairs, Pete left the house and stopped on the back step. The Hereford cow bellowed loudly. Where were her twins? Pete had helped her deliver the prize-winning calves earlier that spring. They should have been with her and eaten long before this. He scanned the pasture east of the farm. He couldn't see the calves anyplace. Perhaps they were sick or hurt or something, and Joe was with them. But if that were the case, why didn't he answer when Pete called his name?

Pete felt obligated to check the pasture in the event the twin animals were in trouble of some sort. Climbing the fence that paralleled the corncrib, he began calling the calves.

"Come, Boss. Come, Bossy. Come."

Instead of getting some response from the calves, the mother cow lowed pitifully for her offspring. Pete looked at her. Her udder was swollen, distended. The calves hadn't sucked on her for quite awhile.

Suddenly, Pete grew aware of another animal's presence and found Trixie beside him.

"Come on, girl," he said softly. "Let's solve this mystery."

With the collie whining plaintively beside him, Pete struck out across the pasture toward the stunted cottonwood. The only place the calves could be was on the other side of that tree. He could see every other part.

Again the sensation that he was being watched washed over him. Stopping, he looked about and saw the Hereford cow and the milk cows standing near the barn, watching him, staring.

A brief shudder ran down his spine. He remembered the only time he had ever been frightened by farm animals. His father had told him to go to the windmill in the pasture and turn it off if the animal's watering tank was full, and as he crossed the open expanse of grass, he had suddenly found himself being scrutinized by his father's herd of short-horn cattle. Each one had had her eyes fixed on him. The bull, a large roan animal, had been lying down and when he stood up, he brushed one of the heifers, who jumped in turn, bumping into another, who bumped another, and the chain reaction resulted in the herd of 90 cattle stampeding straight at him. Pete had stood, rooted to the spot for a moment, watching the 200 yards that had separated him from the herd rapidly disappearing before his eyes. Spinning about, he found the nearest fence almost 100 yards away. There was no way he could bank on outdistancing the cattle in that direction. The nearest thing was the windmill, and he had made a headlong dash for it, just reaching the ladder and safety when the first cattle ran by the structure.

This was different. The Hereford cow was in the same pasture that he was in and the dairy cattle were in the pen next to the barn. They apparently foraged and grazed in the pasture north of the barn. He had nothing to worry about and continued toward the cottonwood, stopping short when a murder of crows flapped into the air. Trixie ran on ahead, disappearing around the trunk.

On the other side he found the carcasses of the two calves, flies covering the openings of the bellies. What could have killed them? The thought of Johnny O'Malley's fate crashed into and filled his mind. Was this the way the boy had wound up as well? If it were, and Johnny had been ravaged like the calves, Marty or the sheriff had not done justice to the description. Pete knew he had to report this to someone, but who? The sheriff? The sanitation department of Cramden County? The highway patrol? Who? Trixie, whining loudly from behind him, caught his attention, snapping him out of his funk.

He turned to retrace his route to the farm and his Bronco, freezing before taking a single step. Joe Eppson's body, the clothing torn from it, lay on its side. The abdominal area had been ripped open and Pete could see that the interior was hollow. The cadaver had been thoroughly gutted. Joe's throat had been torn out, and the look on his face was one of unspeakable horror. Trixie barked once and ran away toward the farm.

Pete felt sick, his stomach churning before it retched, violently contracting, until he threw up his breakfast—the breakfast that Amy had lovingly made for him. Spitting to clean his mouth of the bile and partially digested food, he ran a hand over his forehead, wiping away the strands of dark hair that had fallen across his face when he doubled over. He had to report this. What the hell had killed Joe? What kind of animal?

Breaking into a run for the farm yard, he decided to call the sheriff from Joe's house rather than run the risk of being overheard on the CB radio in the Bronco. Running as fast as he could, he quickly reached the fence and climbed it.

On the other side of the cottonwood some of the flies, relinquishing their place at the sites of the calves' bodies and Joe's remains, flew to the warm spot of vomit and settled in to feast anew. Overhead the crows still circled and, when they felt secure enough, glided in to continue their role of carrion eaters.

10

By the time the sheriff turned into the yard, with an ambulance trailing him, Pete's stomach had settled down. The sight he had seen in the pasture remained with him, but the constancy of it made it more familiar and he no longer felt ill. The sheriff stopped his car near where Pete stood. Pete noticed another man sitting in the front seat and wondered who he might be when the man got out.

"Dr. Reckels?" the sheriff said, approaching Pete and extending his hand.

"Right. You're Sheriff Little?"

"That's right. This here," he said, indicating his passenger, "is Dr. Wilson, the county coroner. I thought, based on the vivid description you gave on the telephone, it might be a good idea for him to see the body on the scene."

Pete nodded and took the medical man's proffered hand. "How are you?"

"Fine, Doctor," Dr. Wilson said.

"The body's out in the pasture. If you want to follow me—" Pete let the sentence hang and started toward the fence.

"Can the ambulance drive out there?" Wilson asked.

Pete stopped. "I would imagine it could, but it isn't all that far for the body to be carried on a stretcher."

"Whatever," the coroner said, and turned to the two ambulance attendants who had approached the three men. "Get the stretcher and follow us."

One attendant glanced at the other as if to say, "We gotta walk and carry the stiff?"

Pete crossed the fence and the sheriff followed him, with Wilson bringing up the rear, until the ambulance attendants joined them.

"How did you come to look for Eppson in the pasture, Doctor?" Duke Little asked without stopping.

Pete explained how Joe had called him the previous day, asking him to come out to vaccinate his herd of pigs the next morning.

"You got any idea as to what killed him and the calves?" Duke asked, half turning to Pete.

Pete shrugged. "It looks like a kill that a dog would make, or a wolf or other canine family member. That's only a guess, mind you. I don't know of any dog in the county big enough to take on a two-hundred-plus calf and kill it—let alone two of them—and a man. Then, too, it's almost too clean for a dog kill. There's not much of a mess around the bodies."

"Mess?" the sheriff asked.

"Yeah. The entrails are all gone and there's no guts or waste food laying around the kill site."

"Couldn't those crows have cleaned up?" he asked, pointing to the murder of crows flapping away to sit on the fence several hundred feet away.

"Of course," Pete said. "Then there's other animals—mice, rats, and what have you—that could have visited the kill site during the night."

"What makes you think the killing took place yesterday?" Duke eyed Pete in a strange way.

"Yesterday or last night. The rain soaked down the pasture pretty good and the clothing lying around was wringing wet. It had to have been out in the rain all night."

"I see," the sheriff said, rounding the cottonwood. He stopped short when he saw the body of Joe Eppson. "Jesus! It's just like Johnny."

The coroner, who had been walking behind Pete and the lawman, came up and stopped short. "You're right there, Sheriff." Wilson went up to the cadaver and dropped to one knee. "The MO is identical. Probably the same animal performed both killings. Or animals."

Pete jerked his head up. Of course. Why hadn't

he thought of it before? The dog pack he had seen yesterday crossing the highway, when he and Amy were comng in from their picnic. He replayed the memory in his mind's private theater. The dogs all seemed relatively small. There were big ones, but not as many as smaller-to average-size farm dogs. He remembered the Doberman pinscher and one or two others that would have been comparable size. A black one had crossed the road first, now that he thought about it. That particular dog had slipped from his memory until now. The thing he had first really noticed was the pack. That had been unusual.

"Animals? How many animals, Doctor?" Pete asked, looking covertly at the sheriff. "And why do you say animals?"

The coroner stood and confronted Pete and the sheriff. "In my autopsy report on the O'Malley boy I mentioned the fact that a multiple-animal attack was probably the cause of death."

"How could you tell?" Pete narrowed his eyes.

"Various bite marks on the extremities. Various size imprints. Various spacings. Various depths of fang marks."

Pete coughed. "Would you say the teeth marks were caused by dogs?"

The coroner shrugged. "Could be. They could also have been caused by wolves, fox, or any other animal with canine fangs. Oh, I know there aren't supposed to be any around here. But wolves have been reintroduced in Upper

Michigan and Wisconsin. Who's to say they haven't roamed farther than they're supposed to? After all, Wisconsin isn't that far from here?"

Pete looked at the sheriff, who nodded. "Look, Doctor, Sheriff, I saw a pack of dogs crossing 31 yesterday. I didn't think too much about it then. But since then Johnny O'Malley and Joe Eppson have been killed, as well as these two calves."

"Where on Y-31?" Duke asked, pulling a notebook from his shirt pocket.

"South of here, about four or five miles."

"Heading in which direction?"

"West." Pete swallowed before adding, "Right toward O'Malley's property. Right, Sheriff?"

Duke continued making notes and saying, "Right."

"I find it difficult to believe that dogs did this," Wilson said, moving toward the calves. He dropped to one knee at the first one and examined it. Then, turning without getting up, he looked at the other.

"Dogs can be pretty vicious if they're hungry enough. These could be feral. They're a pack animal by nature," Pete said.

Wilson stood. "Then tell me why they don't 'pack' together more? Hell, I've never heard of it happening."

"There was a case up in Minnesota about five, six years ago," Duke said. "Never did hear what happened to the animals."

"If they were local dogs," Pete said, "they

probably just went to their homes and forgot about roaming as a pack. See, dogs who live in town adopt the family with which they live as their pack. Farm dogs do pretty much the same thing—adopting all the animals on the farm as members of his or her pack. I remember, when I was a kid living on the farm, how our dog would take off at night to roam with the other dogs in the area. He always came home, though. In a way, he and the other dogs were living out their fuctions as pack animals by gathering together."

"What do you suggest, Dr. Reckels?" Duke asked.

"I seldom go by Dr. Reckels, Sheriff. Call me Doc or Pete. I'll answer to either one. You go on calling me Dr. Reckels and I might miss the question, thinking it's for somebody else."

"So, Pete, what do you suggest?"

"Me? God, I don't know. Maybe what I saw was an innocent gathering of dogs, like our farm dog used to take part in. If that's the case the pack I saw wouldn't even be together now, more than likely. If they were shot or poisoned, a lot of people would be getting pretty angry about their pets or farm dogs being killed in a needless way."

"So what are you saying?"

"I don't know. I guess everybody should stay alert and see if any wild animals are spotted. At the same time, keep farm dogs and pets tied up as much as possible."

"That's going to be pretty tough to enforce,

Pete." The sheriff turned to Wilson. "You got any ideas?"

Wilson shook his head. "That's not my area of expertise, Sheriff. All I know is that two calves were killed in the exact same manner as a man and a boy. Whatever did the killing has to be hunted down and shot or killed in some way."

"That goes without saying," the sheriff said. "I think I need more input before I say anything to the press or TV or radio about wolves or wild dogs roaming the countryside."

The coroner motioned for the two amublance men to take Joe's body. "Somebody had best call the county sanitation department to get rid of the calves' carcasses as well. The other animals will have to be fed and cared for."

"I'll see to that," the sheriff said. He stepped in front of the two men who had put Joe's body into a plastic bag and were about ready to lift the stretcher with its grisly load. "I don't want this talked about right now. You men understand?"

Both nodded.

"If," the sheriff continued, "word does get out, I'll come straight at you two and make your lives miserable. You understand?"

"Hey, what about these other two?" one of the attendants asked.

"Don't worry about them. Worry about your own tongues. Keep it quiet. Or else."

The attendants walked off, carrying the stretcher toward the farm and waiting ambulance.

When they were out of earshot the lawman turned to the coroner and veterinarian. "The same goes for you two as well. I feel I can trust you both more than I can those two." He motioned behind himself and grinned.

"What's so important about keeping this quiet?" Pete asked.

"Just be careful who you say anything to, that's all. The last thing I need is a panic about wild animals."

"I would think the more people who knew, the more alert the community and the county could be," Pete said.

The sheriff grimaced. "You might have a point there. I suppose you're right. I'll release a story, but not all the facts. Christ, if I did that nobody'd believe it anyway. The condition of the bodies are beyond belief, wouldn't you say?"

Pete nodded and the coroner agreed.

"Well, then, I'll amend that order. Don't sensationalize it. Tell it to people and tell them to keep their eyes open and to be careful. Can you catch up with the ambulance men, Doctor?"

Wilson nodded. "I think you're being realistic, Sheriff. Something like this should be public knowledge. If we kept it quiet and somebody else got killed, I think all of us would be derelict in our duties as human beings."

"I agree," the sheriff said.

"The thing I'm hoping is that somebody sees the animal or animals and can properly identify it," Pete said.

"Why's that, Pete," Wilson asked.

"That way we'll know what we're fighting, if that's the right word."

The sheriff smiled. "Fighting is as good a word as any I can think of. We'll have to track down the animal or animals and kill them. They've tasted human blood and humans themselves twice now. Will that be an issue down the road, Doctor?"

"I don't know," Wilson said, turning to Pete.

Pete shook his head. "I'm not positive. Wild animals, such as lions in Africa and tigers in India, have turned to a diet of human flesh when they get old or can't hunt successfully or just when their own source of food becomes scarce. I'm not the least bit sure if feral dogs would do the same."

"Why do you say that, Pete?" the sheriff asked.

Pete shrugged. "I don't know. I guess because it just doesn't seem possible for any wild predator or band of predators to be running loose around Laughton without being seen. Dogs could break up and go to their homes and nobody would ever suspect."

The seriousness of Pete's words slowly sunk into the minds of the sheriff, the coroner, and Pete himself.

11

Pete's stomach still tried doing a number on him as he drove toward Laughton. The sheriff's car ahead of him was staying at the 55-mile-an-hour speed limit and Pete didn't mind. He hoped the air gushing into the Bronco would make him feel better by the time he reached the city. The condition of Joe's body, the flies crawling over the cavity feasting and laying eggs inside, rippled through his memory. God! How awful. The calves had been in the same condition, but they were animals. He had seen animals in varying stages of death and decay. But man—man the ultimate animal—was above that sort of earthy demise.

The longer it took to get to Laughton, the

better he thought he would feel. When the sheriff slowed to 45 and then 35 to stay within the speed limit as he approached the city limits Pete was beginning to feel normal, as normal as he could under the circumstances. He caught a glimpse of a clock at a service station he drove by. Eleven-forty. He could swing by the court house and pick up Amy. He grinned wryly. But not for lunch. He wasn't the least bit hungry. If she wanted to get something to eat, that would be fine with him. But, for himself, he would abstain from food for the time being.

Finding a parking spot in front of the courthouse, he jumped out of the driver's seat and plugged a nickel in the parking meter, then walked toward the entrance. He found Amy, head down over a typewritten page, scrutinizing her latest work for errors. When he closed the door she looked up.

"Hi. I thought you had a full day."

"I did," he said, dropping into a chair in the waiting area. "You'll never believe the morning I had."

"Did the piggies give you a bad time?" She smiled broadly, but stopped when she saw her humor was falling on deaf ears. "What's wrong, Pete? What happened?"

He looked up. At least the sheriff had relented where telling people about Joe's death was concerned. He doubted he could keep something like that to himself. The idea that his imagination took over while driving into town, almost making him sick, still mentally upset him. He thought he was in better control of his senses than that.

"Joe Eppson's dead."

"What?"

He told her of the mysterious atmosphere of the farm when he first arrived and how he had found the body in the pasture. After telling her of the sheriff's arrival along with the coroner he stopped.

"What happened to him? Heart attack?"

"I wish."

Amy looked at him, aghast. "What? I don't understand."

"Have you heard about Johnny O'Malley?"

"Who?"

He filled her in on the gory details of the teenager's death. When he finished Amy looked ill.

"What has that got to do with Joe's—" She stopped. "You mean that Joe Eppson died in the same way?"

Pete nodded. "God, it was awful, Amy."

"What was awful?" a nasal voice asked from the doorway behind Amy's desk.

Pete looked up to find Al Niedles, the county attorney, coming into the outer office. Without thinking, Pete said, "Joe Eppson's death."

"Who's he?"

Pete retold the story of calling on the farmer and how his death matched almost exactly that of the O'Malley boy.

"Probably wolves," Al said confidently.

"I doubt it very much," Pete said quietly.

"Well, I don't. Lord. What else would kill a human being? Certainly it has to be wolves. Nothing else." Al pulled himself up to his full height of five-seven and stared at Pete, defying him to contradict.

"There aren't any wolves around here, Mr. Niedels," he said patiently.

"I don't believe it. Wolves are bloodthirsty monsters."

Pete did all he could to keep from laughing out loud. Apparently, the attorney had been frightened of the big, bad wolf in *Little Red Riding Hood* at one time. But what good would it do to argue with him?

"Are they, Pete?" Amy asked, breaking into the tension that suddenly filled the room.

He shook his head. "Not really. They've had a lot of bad publicity over the years, but recent studies show they're quite family oriented and kill only weak and sick animals for the most part, when they hunt."

"What do you mean by 'for the most part?' " Niedles said.

"I don't really want to discuss it, Mr. Niedles. I've had a bad day, finding Joe's body and all. I'm just not up to talking about anything that's remotely related. All I will say is, if you've got a dog, keep it tied up."

"What?" Niedles asked, his eyes widening.

"I don't understand, Pete," Amy said.

"Well, the evidence seems to indicate that a

pack of dogs might have done it. We're not sure."

"We're? Who's *we're*?" Niedles asked, sounding as if he were cross-examining someone in a court of law.

"The sheriff. The coroner. Me."

Niedles straightened up. "Hmph!"

"Really. The way the two people were killed and parts of their bodies eaten matched those of two calves almost identically. Dogs kill their prey in the same way."

"You saw them do it, right?" Niedles asked coldly.

"No. Of course not. But the evidence is there."

"Then I say it could have been wolves or bears or any other wild animals. Certainly not my little Poopsie."

"Who?" Pete and Amy chorused.

"My little cock-a-poo. She's so cute. She'd never do anything like you're describing."

"Given half a chance, your little cock-a-poo would kill in exactly the same way." Pete looked at Amy. How could she work for this pompous ass? He wanted to get the hell out of there, and the sooner the better.

"Well, you may know animals and how to care for them, but you certainly don't know my Poopsie. She's perfect."

Ignoring the man's plaudits for his own animal, Pete stood. "Can you go to lunch now or should I wait outside for you?"

Amy glanced at her boss, who turned without saying anything and went back into his office. "I guess so. It's two minutes to noon. Do you want to eat?"

Holding the door open for her, Pete said quietly, "Not on your life. How about you?"

"I was getting hungry until you walked in. Right now I don't have an appetite for anything—unless it would be talking with you. What you should do is advertise the fact that you can turn people away from eating by telling them a story."

They walked down the hall toward the exit that would lead them to the Bronco.

"I hope you don't think this is a story."

She shook her head. "Not for an instant. I think I know you pretty well. You were really upset and shaken when you came into the office. No, I believe it. Every word. Regardless of what my boss might think."

When they got to the Bronco Pete held the door for her. "Now be serious. Do you really think he can think?"

"Only on cue and in a courtroom. He's got a good conviction record, but socially the man is a total mess."

"How the hell did someone like him get elected in the first place?"

Amy shrugged as Pete pulled the car away from the curb. "Duchess is all right, isn't she?"

Pete nodded. "Of course she is. She's tied up."

"I know that. I wouldn't untie her right now for anything."

"Why?"

"Well, if dogs are running wild and killing

things—people—then won't people suspect most dogs that are running loose?"

"Probably. Even Al Niedle's bloodthirsty cock-a-poo."

They both laughed, welcoming the release it gave them.

12

Trixie watched the truck pull out of the yard with the carcasses and the calves. When the sound of the motor died away she winced. Where was her master? Why hadn't he been around to feed her? Was it because of his lying out in the field? She remembered the multi-smells she had detected in the air when she had followed him home from the field the day before. Many dogs. Dogs she didn't recognize by scent. Her sense of smell, 40,000 times greater than that of a human, was more reliable than her eyesight. She had never before smelled any of the animals she had detected in the air that day.

Trixie had crawled under the porch, looking for a hiding place, to get away from the smells of the strange animals. She had heard, after awhile, the cry of a dog howling. Trembling at the foreboding sound, she had crawled back even farther under the porch, waiting, frightened. After a long time, once the sun had gone down and night had fallen, she had come out, but her master was not around. She had followed his smell to the pasture and found the bodies of the calves and then that of her master. Lying down, she had slept next to her master's unmoving body, waiting for him to awaken. Still, she knew he was not unlike other animals she had killed at one time or another.

The next morning, shortly after she had returned to the farm, the man who called her by name had gone around all the buildings, calling her master's name. When he went to the pasture she had gone with him and come back to the house after he went inside for something. Then two more vehicles had come and taken her master away. Everybody had forgotten about her and she had stayed under the porch until the truck came. The men in it ignored her and took the dead calves away.

Now she was alone again. And she was hungry. She had managed to slake her thirst at the different animals' watering troughs, but their food didn't appeal to her. She needed something to eat and soon. Her ears pricked up when she head the sound of a car approaching. Off in the distance she could see something moving, and moving fast. Would the car stop at the farm? A crying whine threaded its way from her throat when the car sped past. Lying down on the back step, she rested her head on her front paws and whined again.

The black mongrel padded through the cornfield, leading the pack toward the site of their big kill. They were hungry, and the few small rodents they had managed to kill had not satisfied many of them—even those who had downed most of the bodies. The two animals and the man they had killed the day before would offer sustenance to them and then they would be able to hunt for more game.

When he came to the edge of the field he stopped. The others gathered around him, and he raised his nose in the air to sort out the breeze. The smells of meat and blood still rode the ether, but they seemed weak.

Leaping across the barbed-wire fence, he led the pack into the pasture toward the cottonwood. When he reached it he sniffed out the spots where the dead animals and Joe had lain. Everything was gone. He growled, then the ominous sound turned into a hungry albeit puzzled whine.

Raising his head, he sniffed the breeze coming from the west. A dog. A bitch. Not in heat, but a bitch. There was a female nearby. Trotting off toward the buildings, he led the pack to the farm.

Trixie, sleeping on the step, didn't hear or smell the pack as it came toward her from the east. Her eyes flew open the instant the mongrel growled, and she jumped to her feet.

Intruders. Invaders. She had to protect the farm even though her master wasn't there. A growl rumbled deep in her chest, but it was quickly drowned out by the answering growl from the black mongrel, who outweighed her by 20 or 30 pounds. The tan-and-black bitch snarled and stood behind the mongrel.

He advanced toward Trixie, the hackles on his back standing up, his yellow eyes unblinkingly fixed on her.

Trixie backed away. She was brave. She would have fought any dog who had the audacity to trespass. But there were too many dogs confronting her, although only one seemed to be threatening.

When the mongrel stood close to her he stuck his head forward, his nose working rapidly. She did the same thing, and their noses were mere millimeters apart. He growled again, and she answered in her own threatening way.

Deep within the recesses of her ancestoral memory, the thought of clan, of pack, of family soared through the eons of time. Her master had been her pack. The animals on the farm had been her pack. But her master was gone. He'd never come back. The animals were still on the farm, but the ones that grunted a lot had almost attacked her when she went into their pen for a drink of water.

The animals confronting her now were of her own kind. A pack. A family. The black one confronting her was the leader—the strongest one. The memory continued to grow and become clearer. She suddenly knew what she had to do, and lay down in front of the mongrel. Rolling onto her back, she offered her exposed belly to him and he sniffed her from head to tail. Lingering at her genitals, he growled once and stepped back.

Trixie clambered to her feet and the mongrel turned toward the chicken house. The others followed him and, when they stood at the gate to the yard, the leader pawed at the closed but unlatched gate. The pressure of the blow bounced the gate open. The chickens fluttered about, shrieking in terror at the presence of so many whining and panting animals.

The leader stepped through the open gate and the others followed him. Trixie hung back. She knew better than to go into the chicken yard. The dogs attacked the helpless chickens, tearing their bodies open, gobbling down the entrails. Blood, feathers, and uneaten offal spewed about the enclosure.

Smelling the blood, Trixie's appetite screamed at her, and she tentatively entered the yard, sniffing at a dead chicken pressed up against the fence. Licking a bit of blood, she quickly lost any fear of retaliation and began satisfying her hunger.

When the sound of the last chicken squawked and fell away the dogs licked and bit and chewed the fowl into an unrecognizable mass of bloody feathers and white-pink meat. The only sound was that of slurping and an occasional growl when one dog came too near another.

The chickens had partially satisfied the hunger of the pack, but they still needed food. The mongrel trotted toward the pig pen and smelled the musty odor of the sows in the yard. They squealed and grunted their annoyance at the dogs. The leader, displaying a degree of intelligence, backed away from the fence. The sows weighed more than the calves they had killed. The calves had been young and virtually unprotected, other than by their mother. These animals were adult. They were big, and the mongrel recalled having attacked one once and had found the skin too tough to bite through. These animals would do nothing for the pack. Turning, he trotted toward the road. The others followed.

Trixie stood in the middle of the yard, watching them leave. She turned to the house. Nothing there. Quiet. Her master was gone. Moving her head in the other direction, she took the farm in, in a glance. She was alone. Her pack—her family—had been changed considerably when the body of her master was taken away. These farm animals had been part of her pack when her master was alive. But he was gone. Her responsibility was gone. She barked once—a short, staccato bark.

The mongrel stopped and turned back to face the farm and the collie. He whined, then barked.

Trixie gave another short bark and ran to catch up. She had become a member of a pack once more.

The dogs ran through the tall weeds and grass in the gutter paralleling Highway Y-31 in a northerly direction, heading unwittingly toward Laughton. After the better part of an hour, during which they flushed out several gophers and a couple of pheasants that got away, the pack came to a strange area for them. The road they had been more or less following intersected with another. It meant the pack would have to expose itself by crossing this open expanse.

The black mongrel stopped and the tan-and-black bitch came up to his side. Trixie came up on the opposite side. She couldn't understand why they had stopped. She had crossed roads many times. But her leader was hesitant. Her inquisitive whine went unanswered.

The mongrel turned to her, growling. She fell silent. Suddenly his ears perked up and he turned, looking in the direction from which they had come. The sound of a car approaching filled his ears. He lay down on his belly, the others following suit, and they waited.

Chuck Adderly watched the road, mesmerized. It was late Friday afternoon and he was finished for the weekend. He still had two hours to drive before he got home to Dubuque, and it would be a little after six by the time he reached it. But he knew Ellie would have an ice-cold martini waiting for him.

He caught sight of the sign warning of an intersection and he automatically pulled his foot from the accelerator. He believed in driving the 55-mile-an-hour speed limit although on Friday afternoon, when he was headed home, he was more than tempted to goose it a little and get home more quickly. But he knew his luck. He'd be the one caught. So he drove 55 and took the extra time to get home.

At least it wasn't as oppressively hot as it had been the last few days. The rain the night before had cooled things off considerably, and he welcomed the opportunity to drive with the windows open. It meant better gas mileage if he didn't have to have the air conditioner on, and the smell of the fresh country air proved to be invigorating.

Braking to a stop at the state highway, he turned on his signal flasher to turn right and pulled out a cigarette.

The black mongrel watched the car as it came to a stop. Raising his head, without standing, he inhaled the air coming to him from the automobile. He recognized all of the scents. The grating, bitter smell that he had come across before, the last time in the cornfield when he pulled the man off that strange vehicle, came to him and he sneezed, clearing his nostrils to better smell past the odors coming from the car. The smoky smell of tobacco of the man in the pasture with the two dead animals came to him. Offensive, but not as bad as the smell from the automobile. And man. He smelled the man in the car. Could he get to him?

The high-pitched whine coming from behind him brought the head of the mongrel around, and he saw some movement racing toward the pack on the highway, blocking their path.

He turned back to the man in the car, who had to wait for the truck to pass. The window nearest the man was open. He could make a quick charge and jump. With luck, he'd get the man by the throat and that would be that.

Catapulting from his position, the mongrel was on his feet, charging toward the driver's side of the car. Totally unaware, the man didn't see him until the dog had already leaped through the air.

Unable to close the window, the man instinctively raised his left arm to fend off the attack and screamed when the jaws closed on his triceps. His foot slipped off the brake, hitting the accelerator. The car shot forward, right into the path of the gas truck that was almost to the intersection.

The mongrel hung on, but the sudden motion of the car tore him loose from his hold and he dropped to the ground, rolling over and over, holding a piece of muscle in his mouth. Getting to his feet, he dashed for the gutter just as the car and tanker collided. The cab of the semi rolled over the smaller car, smashing the roof onto the passenger section, squashing the driver inside. The Escort's tank burst, soaking the interior. The tractor careened off to the left, tearing loose from the trailer tank, which, in turn, spun down the concrete road, tipping to its side, ripping open the side wall of the tank. The gasoline was vomitted onto the road, splashing toward the motor of the car, which was still running. The tractor of the semi came to rest on its top, its motor running as well. The flood of gasoline was vomited onto the road, splashing the car. When it struck the hot engine block and reached a sufficient temperature the fuel exploded, sending a gigantic ball of fire and smoke into the air.

The dogs in the gutter, terrified by the loud report, ran at right angles away from Highway Y-31. The mongrel, stiff from his fall, led the pack along the gutter bordering the state highway.

13

Pete pulled into a parking spot in the courthouse lot. From where he stopped he would be able to see the door through which Amy left the building. One minute after four-thirty the door opened, and county employees hurried outside, ready for the weekend. Pete and Amy hadn't discussed any plans for their time off, but he knew they'd come up with something. If anything, he hoped that he could introduce Amy to his daughter. It was time for the two of them to get to know each other.

When he saw Amy her eyes locked with his and she waved. He turned the ignition key and the motor roared to life. When she got in he slipped it into reverse, backing out of the parking place.

"You're free, slave," he said jokingly.

"It must be nice being your own boss." She lowered her window all the way, letting the fresh air flow in.

"Why not start your own business," he said, looking both ways before leaving the courthouse lot, "and find out how nice having all the worries can be?"

She reached over, playfully slapping him on the leg. "Anything would be better than working for Al. God, he's a stuffed shirt."

"Let's change the subject. Is there anything specific you'd like to do this weekend?"

Amy puckered her lips and stared through the windshield. "What's that?" She pointed to the black cloud of smoke rising into the air on the southern horizon.

Pete slowed the Bronco, staring at the tall, black column. "You've got me."

Before either could speak again the sound of a siren coming up from behind automatically made Pete duck for the curb. In a second or two the sheriff's car blasted by, siren wailing full volume, quickly diminishing as the emergency vehicle, its red lights flashing, roared down the street.

"Something's up. That's for sure," Pete said, looking in the rearview mirror before pulling away from the curb.

"I wonder what?" Amy turned to him.

"Ever chase fire engines?"

"That was the sheriff's car."

Just then another siren screamed from behind and the Volunteer County Fire Department roared by, not waiting for Pete to pull all the way over but dashing around him into the oncoming lane.

"That was a fire engine," he said, resuming the speed limit again.

"I know. What did you mean by chasing a fire engine?"

"You know. Chase the darn thing and watch a building burn. Come on. Let's do it. We've got no plans for right now. What do you say?"

Amy shrugged. "I'm game."

"I'm assuming that the sheriff and the fire engine are heading for that column of smoke. We'll head in that direction. S'funny. I can't think of anything other than farms that are down that way."

As they hurried along the street, heading toward the highway that would take them toward the smoke, Amy said, "Let's get back to the weekend. Did you have anything in mind?"

"How about meeting my daughter? I think it's time the two of you got to meet and know each other."

Amy smiled broadly. "Sounds great. What did you have in mind? Something like a picnic?"

Pete shook his head. "You and I were just on one. How about lunch Sunday and then going to the park? She can swing and ride the little merry-go-round and slide and teeter-totter."

"Okay. You've got a date with two women for

Sunday. What about tonight and tomorrow night?"

Pete grinned. "I'll let you decide on what we should do those times. Fair enough?"

"Just out of curiosity, why did you decide it was time the two of us met?"

Pete's grin turned into a frown. "Well, if Carol is bringing a guy, Uncle Mark, around, I figure it's time she met her Aunt Amy. Don't you think it is?"

Amy nodded. "I hope you're not using me to retaliate against Carol."

Pete's face softened. "Of course not. The two of you should meet sooner or later, and I guess now's as good a time as any."

When they picked up speed at the edge of town an ambulance zipped by, siren and claxon wide open.

"Boy, it sure must be serious," Amy said absently.

Pete didn't respond but kept to the speed limit. There was no sense in arriving too soon. That would mean running the risk of being told to drive on or at best to stay back. Then they wouldn't be able to see anything.

As Y-31 curved around, it became apparent that the black column was coming from very near the roadway. Pointing like an arrow, the smoke rose ahead of the Bronco. When they neared the intersection of the state highway Pete slowed and pulled off the road onto the shoulder.

They got out and walked toward the wreckage. Twenty or thirty people stood around, commenting on the cause of the accident and who might have been in the car. Both drivers, the word came to Pete and Amy, had been burned beyond recognition.

As they made their way up closer, Pete's eyes locked with Sheriff Little's, and they mutually nodded their greetings.

"You know Sheriff Little?" Amy asked.

"I just met him this morning. Remember? At Eppson's?"

"That's right. Gosh, I wouldn't want to be in law enforcement. Look at all the tragedy a person has to deal with. First the O'Malley boy, then Joe Eppson being found, half eaten by God-knows-what. And now a collision takes two lives. It must be depressing."

"Good way of looking at it," Pete agreed. "It sure isn't anything like the way Andy Taylor and Barney Fife worked, is it?"

Amy shook her head.

Pete crouched down to get a better view of the tractor cab that was some 50 feet or so away from them.

"Pete?" Amy said.

"What?"

"The sheriff is coming over here."

Pete looked up to see Duke Little approaching.

"Hey, Doc, you got a minute?"

"Hi, Sheriff. What's up?"

"I want you to see something. One of the paramedics pointed it out to me. Normally I wouldn't think anything of it. But considering the situation you and I were in this morning—the hell with it. Come on, I can show you better than tell you."

The sheriff eyed Amy, as if warning her to stay where she was.

"Can I come too?" she asked, knowing full well the sheriff didn't want her to follow.

Pete looked at the lawman.

"If she's got a strong stomach, why not? Come on." He motioned for her to follow him.

A highway patrol car that had been summoned by Little was blocking the state highway at one end and the sheriff's car was blocking it from the opposite direction.

"The paramedic asked me if I thought this was unusual. I think he meant it more as a joke. But, Goddammit, when I saw it my thoughts went back immediately to this morning. Look here, Pete." Duke threw back the corner of the plastic bag containing the remains of Chuck Adderly and pointed to the man's left upper arm. A piece, the size of a man's hand, was missing. The blackened flesh showed no evidence that it was a recent injury or that it might have been an odd deformity the driver might have had.

After a few moments passed, during which Amy turned and walked away, Pete looked at the sheriff. "Well?"

"Well? Well, what do you make of that?"

"What am I supposed to make of it?"

"What's it look like to you?"

The pieces of the puzzle fell into place for Pete, who had been steeling himself ever since the sheriff walked up to him and asked him to look at something. At first he didn't know what to expect. Then the sheriff had merely pointed and offered nothing in the way of explanation. But now—now the meaning of what the sheriff was implying with his dramatics became apparent.

"You think that a dog or some animal bit this man?"

"What other explanation you got?"

Pete shook his head and turned away. "I don't have any, but then, this sort of thing isn't in my bailiwick, is it?"

"You know animals. Right?"

"Right."

"Is that a dog bite or an animal bite of some sort?"

Pete shrugged. "I don't really know, Sheriff. I don't. For all we know the guy had a chunk of arm blown out in 'Nam or had some other sort of accident."

Duke looked perplexed. "Could it be? Could it be an animal bite?"

Pete thrust both hands into his pockets and hunched his shoulders. "Hell, I guess anything's possible. All right. Let's say it could be an animal bite. What about it? What has that got to do with anything?"

Duke looked frustrated now. "I—I don't really know. At first I thought if that really was an animal bite, then perhaps he had been attacked and that made him run the stop sign and cause the collision. But now that I've said it aloud, it sounds pretty dumb."

Pete shook his head. "Law enforcement isn't my cup of tea, Sheriff. Your theory makes some sense to me. But then, what the hell do I know?"

"Well, thanks for looking, anyway, Pete."

"Sorry I couldn't be of more help."

"If I need your expertise again, I'll get in touch with you. Is that all right?"

"Sure."

Pete turned back toward the crowd of people and found Amy standing with her back to the scene. Walking up, he put his arm around her shoulders and they hurried back to the Bronco.

Two miles west of the intersection, the dogs lay in an under-the-highway cow crossing, resting in the shade. In a while, once they were rested, they'd continue on their way, to the north of the state highway.

Trixie, head on her paws, lay on the edge of the pack, her eyes looking from one to the other of the members. This was her new family, but she still felt uneasy, unwelcome.

The black mongrel yawned and looked over his

charges. Noticing Trixie, he got to his feet and crossed the distance separating them. With a grunt, he lay down next to her and closed his yellow eyes.

Day Three

Saturday

14

Loco Louie carefully stirred the pot of "slumgullian" hanging over the small fire.

"Ain't never heard Mulligan Stew called that before," Boxcar Benny said, shaking his head.

"Slumgullian? Shit. That's what my mama called it back in '31. Fact of the matter is it was in a Hooverville pretty much like this one that I remember her callin' it that."

"Your mama was on the road?" Boxcar Benny asked, his eyebrows shooting up toward the dirty cap he wore.

"Had no choice, she didn't. My old man took off when the packin' plant shut down and—give me that salt you had—and we'uns was t'rowed into the street. Just like that." Loco Louie snapped his dirty fingers and took the packet of salt from his companion.

The heavy aroma of cooking filled the area around the box elder trees beneath which the men had set up camp. The tracks of the state-owned railroad lay fifty yards away. Here and there in the campsite evidence of old fires told mute stories of passing men—men who had opted for a life on the road as opposed to one of responsibility and social acceptance.

"When'll that there grub be ready?"

Loco Louie spooned some of the broth from the side of the pot and blew gently on it. When he placed it in his mouth he rolled his eyes. "It's good, but it needs somethin' yet. Don't know what, though."

"Let me try it. Maybe I can tell." Boxcar Benny took the spoon from the older man and sipped the broth he spooned out. "Shit! Tastes good to me. Let's eat."

"If'n you don't want a masterpiece, fine by me. I can tolerate most anythin' in my belly."

Filling two soup cans that had been scrubbed in the stream nearby, Louie handed one to Benny and sat back, leaning against the hole of one of the trees. They ate in silence and when Benny drained his can he stood and moved closer to the fire.

"When's the next train due?"

Louie shook his head. "Don't know for certain. This line runs one in both directions about three, maybe four times a week. I dropped off'n one day 'fore yesterday. It was goin' toward Laughton. That's a real bad one. The cops and sheriff'll run you outta town quicker'n anythin'." He pointed to the horizon, over which Laughton lay. " 'Course it came back the same afternoon. Just up there switchin.' "

"Think there'll be one today?"

"Could be. I sorta doubt it, though. Today's Saturday, if'n I recollect right. Seldom that trains run on Saturday in this part of the country."

"Well, I don't 'tend on walkin'. I'll wait right here for the next train."

"Could be one today, but I doubt it," Louie repeated, and moved to the fire for his second helping. "Better take it easy on the Slumgullian. It might have to last till Monday."

A gentle breeze ruffled the box elder leaves overhead, carrying a melodious note with it.

"Sh-h-h," Benny said, holding a finger to his lips.

"What's the matter?"

"I heard somethin'. Sounded like a whistle. Could be a train comin'."

"Shit!" Louie wheezed, sitting back down under the tree. "Wish to hell it was like the old days. Then a 'bo like you'n' me would know when the goddamn trains was arunnin'."

"Really somethin', huh?"

"You never seen nothin' like it. That line over there." Louie said, pointing toward the track, "used to be the Milwaukee. One of the best lines around. D'ya ever see their Hiawathas? *Geezus,* could those trains go. All orange and maroon and gray. Christ, they were pretty. And fast? Who-o-e-e! Now they run a few silver trains and the freights are goin' almost too fast for an ol' fucker like me to risk gettin' on. If it weren't for the state run lines I'd probably have to settle down in some old folks' home someplace. I—"

"Sh-h-h-h," Benny admonished again. The single throaty note of a diesel locomotive's horn was closer this time.

"Sounds like it might be three miles away or so. If it's goin' to Laughton, it'll be workin' up there for an hour or so 'fore it comes back. We can be ready to hop it then. Eat up, Benny."

Boxcar Benny grinned, showing the gap where his front incisors had been at one time, and emptied his tin can. Standing, he went to the pot for his third helping.

The black mongrel lifted his nose, sorting out the different scents riding on the morning air. A peculiar smell caught his attention, and the thought of the hot food the man used to feed him and the tan-and-black bitch before they ran away was dredged from his memory bank. The food had always sustained them, but it had never been enough. They had always been hungry then. They were usually hungry now. Perhaps the pack should check out this scent.

He licked his chops, recalling the sustenance they had achieved off the bodies of the humans they had killed. The taste was sweet to him and he felt it wouldn't be out of order to go after more. The smaller animals the pack tried catching were too crafty at getting away from him and the others most of the time.

Stepping through the tall grass surrounding him, the mongrel followed the spoor-ladened air. The pack fell in behind him, smelling the same thing. Tongues lolled from their mouths. Blood from the chickens still smeared one or two of the dogs. A German shepherd had a small feather caught between his teeth and although he had tried many times to remove it, it stuck tenaciously.

When they neared the source of the smells the mongrel stopped. Carefully searching the smell of hot food, he detected the strong smell of man. Turning, he found the others anxiously panting, waiting. They, too, had discerned the odors of man. They would eat well if they could kill.

The black mongrel growled softly and the pack quietly followed him through the tall grass. Off in the distance the diesel horn sounded again—two longs, a short, and a long—as it approached a grade crossing.

"D'hear that?" Louie asked.

"Yup."

"Let's finish this stuff off and get our things together. Then we can be ready to jump 'er when she comes back down, headin' fer Waterloo."

Boxcar Benny peered past Louie into the tall grass. "Hey, Louie, I think I saw somebody over there in the weeds. Turn around and—" He never finished the sentence as the grass parted and the black mongrel hurtled out into the clearing, straight at the seated men.

Benny leaped to his feet, knocking over the pot of food, and started running toward the trees on the fringe of the clearing. "Come on, Louie. Get up. That fuckin' dog don't look friendly, 'tall."

Before Louie could move the grass exploded with dogs as they charged into the campsite. Benny took a quick glimpse over his shoulder, quickly abandoning the idea of taking the time to climb a tree. Instead he dashed through the trees toward the track, running for his life.

Louie had barely made it to his feet when the black mongrel hit him full in the chest, sending him back to the ground, knocking the wind from the old man. The dog, without a moment's hesitation, went for the grizzled throat that lay open, exposed to him. His jaws locked on the windpipe, and any cries that Loco Louie might have made were squeezed off before they sounded. The mongrel ripped, tearing at the flesh, waggling his head back and forth until the skin, the flesh, and the vital components in the neck gave way. Blood spurted, not unlike a fountain, and the black mongrel greedily lapped it up.

Benny ran as hard as he could, coattail flying in the slipstream. A German shepherd, the one wearing a feather in his teeth, followed the fleeing man. Directly ahead, Benny could see the grade holding the tracks. Obliquely aware of the approaching train, he clambered up the steep embankment. The train bore down on him, and he screamed when the jaws of the dog locked on his ankle, keeping him from going ahead. The German shepherd pulled, growling the whole time, half dragging the body down the incline. Turning onto his back as he slid down, Benny kicked at the dog with his free foot and screamed even louder when a collie and several other dogs came running onto the scene.

Raising his free leg, he brought the heel of his shoe down on the snout of the dog attacking him. Instantly releasing his hold, the dog rolled down the hill, and Benny turned over on his belly to regain his feet.

The diesel engine roared as it passed the bloody activity below. The steel wheels on steel rails muffled the panting of the hobo and the barks and growls of the pursuing dogs.

Scrambling up the hill away from the animals, Benny pulled himself upright next to the track. He turned to look down the length of the train. Estimating the speed to be somewhere between 25 and 30 miles per hour, he turned to run with the boxcars as they moved past him.

The German shepherd, realizing his victim was about to get away, rolled to his feet and ran up the embankment, clawing the last few feet until he reached the top. Thirty yards away, he could see the man running, his hands outstretched, waiting for the right ladder and foot strap to come by. Gathering himself, the dog dashed after him, timing his leap perfectly as he left his feet to land full on the back of the man.

Benny lost his footing, sprawling foward and to his left, falling onto the rails. His scream was cut short when his body, splaying across the steel rail, belly down, split in two as the wheels of the boxcar above passed over him.

The dog, his ears standing erect, guarded his prize as best he could while the wheels continued clacking along. Tentatively reaching out, he closed his jaws on Benny's foot and pulled, the lower half moving easily toward him. When the cabooseless train passed, the other dogs that had stood patiently behind and alongside the German shepherd ran to the other half of the body, and the feast began.

In seconds the body of Boxcar Benny was torn asunder and the pieces strewn along the track right of way.

The black mongrel finished his feasting and, leaving the body of Loco Louie to those who were waiting, he stretched lazily and sniffed the campsite. When he came to the food that had spilled from the overturned pot from which the men had been eating he sniffed at it for a long time. It smelled very much like the food he and the tan-and-black bitch had eaten in the past. His tongue slipped from his mouth and he tasted it. Not quite sure, he tried it once more, then shook his head violently. It wasn't the same. Not as good to eat. Turning back to view the scene of the man's body being ravaged by some of the pack, he lay down.

He much preferred man over something so tasteless as the stuff on the ground.

15

The crowd of men sat quietly, staring at the sheriff, who had just finished speaking. A couple of uncomfortable coughs were followed by more silence. Finally one of the men put his hand up.

"Yeah, Al," Duke Little said. "Got a question?"

"Sure do, Sheriff. How come you told us in so much detail? That was pretty awful."

"Men, in the years that I've been sheriff I've never seen anything as horrible as the condition of Johnny O'Malley and Joe Eppson when they were found. You would have to have been there in order to appreciate the seriousness of this situation. Since you weren't, and, since I need as much help on this case as possible, I told you just about everything. I didn't leave anything out."

"So, why do you think it was dogs?" one man called out.

"That conclusion was drawn by Dr. Peter Reckels. Is he here?" Duke scanned the crowd, looking for the veterinarian, but he didn't see him. "Dr. Reckels is supposed to be here. When he arrives I'll let him tell you the reasons behind it."

"I find it almost impossible to believe," Carey Lewis said, standing up. "I've been hunting all my life and I've never seen a dog kill the way you described."

"Most of you men," Sheriff Little said, "were invited here because you are hunters or conservationists or outdoorsmen. As I understand it, dogs can be quite vicious if they get hungry enough."

"Couldn't a wolf have done it, just as easily as a dog?" someone shouted.

"As I understand it," Duke said, "there aren't that many wolves in the continental forty-eight, and those that are have just been reintroduced to the wilds."

"That's right, Sheriff. Besides," Carey Lewis said, "there isn't a single case of a wolf ever attacking a human being on record in this country and—"

"Make that in North America, Carey," Mike Kojinski called out from the opposite side of the room. "In Europe there've been cases, but almost always the wolf doing the attacking wasn't a full-blooded wolf but a cross-bred animal. Some dog, some wolf. Write wolves off the list, Sheriff."

"Anybody seen mountain lions around?" somebody called out.

A laugh went up from the gathering, and the sheriff called for quiet. "This isn't a laughing matter, men. Two people are dead. Two prize calves are dead. Those of you who are farmers should know the importance of protecting your livestock. Things are tough enough without your losing some animals to a pack of hungry dogs."

A sense of sobriety followed the sheriff's statement.

"What about coyote then?"

"Coyotes were mentioned, but I think—"

"I think," Pete said from the doorway, "the coroner only mentioned them because they belong to the same family as wolves and dogs."

"Come on up, Pete," the sheriff said, an expression of thankfulness crossing his face.

Pete hurried to the front of the room.

"Dr. Reckels here will tell you why he thinks the deaths may have been caused by dogs."

Pete didn't speak right away; instead he stared at the county map behind the podium. "What's that, sheriff?" he asked, pointing to the two red pins sticking in it.

"That's where Joe Eppson and the two calves were found," Duke said pointing to one, "and this is where Johnny O'Malley's body was found."

"I see," Pete said, turning back to face the men. "You see, when I was growing up on the farm, dogs usually gathered together at night, hunting, playing, mating, and what have you. You farmers know that. And they always returned home at night. Dogs are pack animals, just like wolves. When you have a house dog in town the family it belongs to becomes his or her pack. The same thing holds true on the farm, only there, in addition to the family, the animals become part of his pack and territory."

"Tell them about the pack you saw, Pete," the sheriff said quietly.

"I was just getting to that."

Before Pete could speak someone spoke up. "I know about dogs packing together. Hell, my Towser does it all the time. But he's always home in the morning—right where he belongs. When were the O'Malley boy and Joe killed?"

Pete turned to the sheriff.

"Johnny O'Malley was killed during the daylight hours. He was cultivating and when he didn't come home when his father thought he should have, Dan O'Malley went out into the field and found his boy's body. The time was somewhere between seven and eight o'clock in the evening. The night it rained. That was the night. He had to have been killed during the daytime."

"What about Joe?" the same man asked.

"The best the coroner could do was estimate within twelve hours or so. Dr. Reckels found the body and it was in the A.M. when he did. Now, hold your questions until Doc here is done." Duke Little gestured to Pete.

"For some reason when I heard about Johnny O'Malley, I automatically thought of him being found on the family farm. I guess the sheriff did say something about his cultivating, but I either didn't hear him or it didn't register. At any rate, the reason I asked about the second pin up there is, that is just about where I saw this pack of dogs crossing the road." Pete moved to the wall and pointed to Highway Y-31, which paralleled the oatfield next to the cornfield in which Johnny O'Malley had been killed.

"I still find it hard to believe that dogs could do what you're sayin', Sheriff," Tim McCatver said, standing up.

A murmur of agreement ran through the room, and Pete held up his hands. "Look, I'm a veterinarian. I find it just as hard to believe. I love animals. But the evidence, although it isn't completely overwhelming, is there for us to see. Right now, since I spotted a dog pack, and there have been two deaths that seem to have been caused by dogs, I think it only makes sense to keep our eyes open and be on the lookout for a pack of dogs."

"You'll have to show me before I believe dogs did it," McCatver said.

"In most ways I agree with you," Pete said. "Actually, most dogs wouldn't do this. But all it takes is a few that have been mistreated and are hungrier than all get out. Put those two things together and you got yourself a dog that's going to be pretty vicious if not outright dangerous. All

I'm saying is that the dog pack I saw has to be considered as a possible cause of the deaths."

"What do we do if they are the cause?" Greg Losberger asked.

"We'll have to hunt them down." Pete glanced at the sheriff. Perhaps he had overstepped his authority. All the sheriff had asked of him was to address the group and tell them about the possibility of the attacks having been made by dogs.

"Pete's absolutely right," the sheriff said, reaffirming Pete's contention.

Larry Jacobs stood up. "Can I say a few words, Sheriff?"

Duke nodded, and the man stepped away from his chair and into the aisle. "Fifteen years ago, when I was living in Minnesota, I was out bow-hunting deer. The guy I was supposed to go with got sick and I was out there alone. It was getting late and I hadn't even seen a deer, much less a track or sign, and was just about to track back to my truck. All of a sudden, from out of nowhere, a pack of fifteen or twenty feral dogs came charging at me out of the woods across a small ravine. They were about, I'd say, sixty or seventy yards away when I saw them. Believe me, I didn't wait around to see if they were friendly or not. I just took off. Thankfully, they had to track me once they got to the spot where I first saw them. In other words, I knew where I was going—to my truck—but they had lost sight of me when I ran into the woods on my side of the ravine. But I will tell you this much, I just made it back to my truck in the nick of time. I no sooner closed my door than the leader, a big, ugly German shepherd, leaped at the window. He came so hard, so fast, and wanted me so bad, he hit the window and cracked it. Luckily, it held. I've never been so scared in my life. I've hunted bear and elk with bow and arrow, but those dogs made believers of me and ever since I've always carried a sidearm with me whenever I go hunting."

The man sat down and a silence fell over the room.

"Say, what about bear?" somebody asked after several minutes went by.

"Not around here," Larry Jacobs said softly. "I believe the doc here. It was dogs."

"Don't say a bear couldn't kill like that," the questioner persisted.

"I've seen bear kills," Pete said. "The bodies of the two calves and that of Joe Eppson were mauled, but not in the way a bear would do it. There were, as I understand it, all sizes of bite marks on the arms and legs of Johnny O'Malley. Am I right, Sheriff?"

Duke Little nodded.

"That tells me right there that there had to have been more than one animal involved. Bears would bite, sure. But the marks would all be the same if it were a bear or a mountain lion or a lynx or any other animal you can think of. Wolves, coyotes some of the time, and dogs are about the only pack animals on the North American continent. Since there aren't any wolves or coyotes that we know of in this part of the country we've got one and one choice only. Dogs!"

"Doc, I've got three blue-ticked hounds. I sure as hell don't believe they would do what you're suggesting," Phil Sleeter said, standing up. "What about wolverines?"

Several of the men chuckled, but no one spoke until Pete coughed and said, "Wolverines are probably the most elusive animal in North America. They're mean and ornery and gluttonous when it comes to eating. Still, I know for a fact that Indians who trap for a living have had their traps stripped of bait and trapped animals by wolverines. Yet, they've never laid eyes on one in the wild. Besides, we're a way too far south for wolverines to be around here. I'm not remotely suggesting that your hounds or any of your dogs," Pete said, gesturing with a sweeping arm over the group, "are responsible. What we have are derelict dogs that are roaming free. They kill when they're hungry, which in itself is not bad. The bad thing is, they've killed two people. They've tasted human blood and flesh. That's the problem. It won't be unlike a man-eating tiger or man-eating lion in India or Africa. They'll soon learn, if they haven't already, that man is not that well protected when he's by himself in the out-of-doors."

"What sort of dogs were in the pack, Doc?" Jay Robertson asked.

"Actually they were too far away to really identify any of the breeds. There were different breeds, I'm sure. I think I saw a Doberman pinscher, but I'm not a hundred percent certain."

"What do you want us to do, Sheriff?" Jay Robertson asked.

"Now the fact that you're apprised of the situation is enough. If the dogs are spotted, I'll contact you. Personally, I think it would be a waste of time and the wrong time to go out looking for them."

"Why, Sheriff? There's more than enough of us to make up a couple of hunting parties," one of the men said.

"And where would I send you to hunt? That's the problem. If people saw fifteen or twenty men hunting for something, I feel a sense of panic might take over. No. I'm saying you forget about hunting dogs right now. Besides, we don't want any innocent animals killed. Leave your name and telephone number with the girl outside and where you can be reached at all hours. If the dogs are seen, you'll be notified. Be ready. Be prepared. That's the best we can do right now." Duke gazed at the men, confident he had made good points.

Pete glanced at the sheriff, who looked as if he were asking if the veterinarian had anything else to add. Pete shook his head.

"That'll be all, men. Thank you for coming and don't go in the out-of-doors unless you absolutely have to."

The men stood, filing out of the hall, talking in small groups as they went.

"Where will you be this weekend, Pete?"

"Here and there, why?"

"I'll feel a lot better if I can get a hold of you at any time. Can you leave your agenda for the weekend outside with Liz?"

Pete shook his head and smiled. "I suppose so, Sheriff." As he left the lawman behind he wondered what Amy would say to the latest wrinkle in his life. He had to be on call for the sheriff's department in case a pack of feral dogs was sighted. Well, if nothing else, it made his life a mite more exciting than it normally would have been.

16

Boxcar Benny's horrified eyes stared, unseeing, into the bright sunlight. The head rested at a jaunty angle to the track, totally unmindful of the train bearing down on it.

In the cab of the GP-38-2 diesel locomotive, Sonny Olson periodically checked the mainline ahead. This particular section of track called for a speed limit not to exceed 35 miles an hour. It was among the fastest tracks between Waterloo and Laughton. No matter. He calculated he could reach Waterloo by four o'clock, and that would give him plenty of time to get home, shower, and take his wife out to dinner for their fifteenth wedding anniversary.

Glancing over at Frank Bardman, his

brakeman, he said, "You got big plans for tonight, Frank?"

"The usual. Nothing out of the— What the hell is that?"

"What?"

"On the track. Up ahead. It looks like a head. A human head." Frank jumped to his feet, moving closer to the windshield. Stepping to the side, he opened the door and went outside.

"What? Where?" Sonny asked, straining his eyes. Then he saw it. "Oh, Jesus. It sure does look like a head."

The brakeman came back into the cab. "Looks like hell," Frank said as the engine passed over the gruesome sight. "It *was* a head. A man's head. I saw it plain as day. You'd better stop, Sonny."

Sonny pulled out his watch and calculated. He had just enough time, if he stuck to the speed limits, to reach Waterloo by four. He had to do something—but what?

"Hey, aren't you going to stop?" Frank stepped closer to him.

"Look, Frank, you've got to go along with me on this one. I've done you some favors over the years. Now you can do one for me."

"What the hell are you talking about?"

"Today's Marita's and my fifteenth anniversary. We've got a dinner date for tonight and she doesn't know it yet, but I've booked a suite at the Ramada Inn. If I stop now, I'll never make it."

Frank nodded. "Okay. What do you propose? We've got to do something about it, don't we?"

"Hell yes. I'll call the dispatcher and tell him what we *think* we saw. That way he can call the sheriff in Laughton and have *him* check it out. How far back was it?"

"Right after mile post nine out of Laughton. Okay, I'll go along with you. I can see your point about tonight. I can also see the questions and answers we'd have to go through, plus the forms we'd have to fill out for stopping the train to investigate ourselves. Besides, we'd probably be accused of hitting the poor sonofabitch."

Grinning broadly, Sonny picked up the radio phone. While he waited for the dispatcher to answer, he reached up and pulled the horn cord to whistle for a grade crossing.

Duke Little swatted an errant fly hovering around his coffee cup. He had decided earlier to leave the office before four o'clock. Nothing was happening to make it necessary for him to stay in the office. The dispatcher could call him if something did turn up. As long as there weren't any new bodies showing up or reports of dog attacks, he was happy to act as normally as he could under the circumstances.

Reports. That was the one thing that bothered him. Why hadn't there been any reports of a large dog pack made? Other than Dr. Reckels having seen a pack crossing the road not that far distant from where Johnny O'Malley had died, there hadn't been one single sighting. Was Dr. Reckels reliable? As far as he could determine, Pete Reckels was as down to earth as anyone he knew. Likable, a professional man, somewhat serious about most things, from what he could gather. For the most part he felt relatively confident that Pete Reckels had been a sober observer of a dog pack. That still didn't explain why no one else had seen it.

That wasn't exactly true. Johnny O'Malley had seen it, as had Joe Eppson. But they hadn't lived through the assault to report it. Were the dogs involved so crafty that they could travel around the countryside and keep out of view?

Duke puckered his lips and raised his coffee cup to drain it. The accident south of town seemed to be just that. An accident. But what about the piece of upper arm apparently missing from the driver of the Escort? Was that a normal feature of the victim? Or should Duke think of it as abnormal? He remembered seeing a documentary once about sharks. A diver had been attacked and a goodly piece of the man's calf had been bitten away. He recovered and went through life with a thin lower leg. Perhaps something like that had happened to the dead driver.

One of the first things he had done when he returned to the office was send out an inquiry to find out if such might be the case with the driver, Chuck Adderly. Until he got a report back, stating that the man had no physical deformities in the arms, he had to assume that the accident was an accident and nothing more. Nothing more? Two people had burned to death, if they hadn't been killed outright in the impact. He'd have to wait for the coroner's report on that.

But what if the driver had had two normal arms? What would the explanation be for the missing piece? It hadn't been that big, but it had been noticable enough for the paramedic to call his attention to it. He'd have to ask Pete Reckels if he had anymore time to think on it. To Duke, it looked like a dog could have bitten it, but the arm had been charred black and there was no way that he could be certain until he had more information from the coroner, Pete, and the inquiry he had sent out.

The telephone jangling brought his mind back to his office surroundings. Picking it up, he said, "Yeah?"

"A Porter Donovan from Waterloo is on the phone. He says he's the dispatcher for the Cross State Railroad. He wants to talk to you."

"Okay." He waited while he heard the connection being made. Then, "This is Sheriff Duke Little," he said when he thought he heard heavy, wheezing breathing.

"Ah, Sheriff, this is Porter Donovan over in Waterloo. I just got a call from one of my train crews. They reported that they think that they saw what might have been a human head on the track outside of Laughton."

Duke withered in his seat. There went his early

evening. "Where at, Mr. Donovan?"

"The engineer said it was between milepost nine and milepost ten."

Duke calculated in his head the approximate location. "Okay. I've got it. We'll take a look. Could I have the names of the crew in the event I need to talk with them?"

"Sure can. Sonny Olson's the engineer and Frank Bardman's the brakeman."

Duke waited a moment. "That's all?"

"Yup."

"What about the caboose?"

"Don't run cabooses anymore. Just two men to a train. Need anything else?"

"They didn't hit the poor sonofabitch, did they?"

"No. They reported as having seen it ahead of the locomotive. It was just lying there. I doubt like hell if it has anything to do with the road. Keep me posted, though, will you?"

"Sure enough. Thanks, Mr. Donovan."

Duke hung up the phone. It would be a lot easier for him to go out there than to send someone and have to sit around the office waiting for a report back. Standing, he grabbed his hat and strode to the door.

After telling the dispatcher where he'd be, he left the building and went to his car. Once he had turned onto the street he slowed down. Off to his right he saw Pete Reckels coming out of the supermarket. The same cute redhead that had been with the veterinarian at the accident site was with him again. He pulled over and honked his horn.

"Hey, Pete?"

Pete looked up at the sound of his name and waved to the lawman. "How's it going, Sheriff? Any report back on the accident yesterday?"

"Report?"

"About the arm. Where a piece was missing."

"Not yet. Say, are you busy?"

Pete glanced at Amy, who had come up behind him. They had shopped for groceries and were heading back to the apartment, where he had planned to cook dinner for the two of them. "I don't know why, but I'm almost afraid to ask what you've got in mind."

Duke smiled warmly. "If you have the time, I wish you'd ride out in the country with me."

"What's up?"

"Right now, nothing. I wanted to talk more to you about the dogs you saw and a couple of other things. If you have the time, I'd appreciate it."

Amy looked at Pete, a don't-you-dare expression crossing her face.

"How long would I be gone?"

Amy glowered at Pete.

Catching Amy's distress, Duke addressed her directly when he said, "I promise I'll have him back in an hour. Is that all right with you, Mrs. Reckels?"

"Oh, I'm sorry," Pete said quickly. "Sheriff, this is Amy Bondson, a friend—a very good friend of mine. Amy, Sheriff Little."

"How do you do, Sheriff?" Amy said icily. She didn't want her evening with Pete interrupted before it began.

"Miss Bondson. I hope you don't mind my taking Pete away from you for an hour. It *is* important."

Amy's face softened, and she forced a smile. "I'll hold you to an hour, Sheriff. If he's not back by then, I'll—I'll call the sheriff!" She smiled impishly.

"Let me get rid of this bag of groceries and I'll be right with you." Pete followed Amy to the Bronco, and after he had placed his bag inside he took the two Amy had been carrying. Closing the back door, he said, "I'll see you in an hour."

"Just a minute. You're not getting away without a preview of things to come tonight. Besides, if the Sheriff sees this, he won't be so cruel as to keep you away any longer than necessary." She threw both arms around his neck and kissed him. Her tongue jabbed into his mouth, wiggling about, exploring hidden recesses.

Embracing her, he returned the kiss.

Duke blew his horn. "Okay. Okay. I get the message. I'll hurry him right back to you, Miss Bondson."

Amy and Pete separated, both grinning, both blushing a bit. She went to the driver's side of the Bronco after Pete gave her the keys.

"Don't start anything until I get there," he said. "Remember, I'm coming tonight."

"For a minute there I didn't know what you

were referring to. 'Bye, Pete." She got in and turned the motor over.

When he was sure she was under way Pete turned back to hurry to the sheriff's car.

"We'll probably have to walk about a mile," Duke said. He pointed to a post emblazoned with the number ten, next to the right of way.

"What the hell did you have me come along for, Sheriff? All we talked about on the way out were dogs and the pack I saw. We'd talked about it all before."

Walking along the track, Duke said, "It doesn't hurt to go over something a second or even a third time. See, I find it funny that no one else has seen the pack."

Pete stopped walking and eyed the lawman suspiciously. "Meaning?"

"Meaning nothing. I don't doubt for a second that you saw a bunch of dogs. The thing I'm concerned about is the fact that they've been around long enough to kill two people and only one person has seen them. You. Are they that good? That sneaky? That careful that they can travel around and practically avoid being seen?"

"Well, for the most part they're going to hunt in the early morning and late afternoon and early evening. During the day, when farmers are in the field, they'll be sleeping someplace, assuming they've fed."

"So what you're saying is that they're moving when the chances of them being seen are at a minimum?"

"Not by design. Just works out that way."

They walked along for several more minutes without speaking.

"What's that down there?" Pete asked, pointing off to the right of the track.

The small clearing, perhaps 50 or 60 feet from the track looked as if it might have been inhabited at one time.

"Oh, that?" Duke said, grinning. "That's an old hobo jungle. According to my old man, it was called Hooverville back in the thirties."

"Hooverville?"

"Yeah. In honor of the president. President Hoover was blamed for the depression and lack of work. People lost their jobs, their homes, everything. They'd travel by rail and camp near the tracks. I—"

Pete stopped walking when the sheriff did and followed his outstretched arm. There on the track, perhaps 100 feet away, they saw the head of a man.

Half running toward it, the two men peered down when they stood over it. The eyes held their attention the longest. Terror, horror, shock. Absolute fright were etched forever into them. Cuts and abrasions marked the face where it had rubbed and rolled along the ballast of the track.

"Jesus Christ," Duke managed.

Pete turned away. "Can't blame that on a dog, Sheriff."

"Not yet at least. Christ, that's awful."

"Can't rule out anything until all the evidence is in. Who knows who or what did this?"

"What. What do you mean by *what*?"

"Maybe he was hit by the train."

"Didn't you say the report from the train crew said they saw the head in front of the engine?"

Duke nodded.

After looking over the immediate area, the sheriff stood up straight and stretched. "Let's go back in the jungle down there. Maybe the guy was a bum and tried jumping the train but fell off. We might find some evidence down there that'll tell us just that."

Pete followed the tall man off the track and down the embankment. Entering the clearing, the sheriff held up his hand, motioning for Pete to stop.

"Looks like something happened here as well."

"What?" Pete stepped around him and looked at the far edge of the clearing. The body of a man lay sprawled on the ground, his clothing ripped to shreds, his body torn open, his throat laid wide as if a second ragged mouth had been added.

Neither man spoke for several long minutes.

"You think it was the dog pack?" Pete turned to face Duke.

Shrugging, the sheriff said, "Who knows? Look here, the number of prints in the soft earth. Could have been dogs. Could have been almost any sort of wild animal that leaves prints like dogs."

"Meaning what? Wolves? Coyotes? Fox?" Pete turned away. "I thought you agreed that those were all ruled out?"

"I have. No, the thing I'm saying is that, at best, the prints are circumstantial."

"Circumstantial? We've found a body ripped open, killed the same way feral dogs kill, the entrails gone—nowhere to be found around here." Pete turned, checking to make certain that he was right on that point. "Dog paw prints all over the place. How can the evidence be circumstantial?"

"You sound as if you want it to be dogs."

"I'm just being reasonable. I've seen the pack. I've seen the bodies of their kills. Now I see their paw imprints. What else do I need, Sheriff?"

"You don't need anything, Pete. But I need more solid evidence. When were the prints made. Before, during, or after the death of this guy?" Duke waited.

Pete shook his head. "I hadn't thought of that."

"Right. And suppose the two of us had agreed on it. What would have happened then? Panic. People grabbing their shotguns and rifles and shooting every stray bitch and sonofabitch they saw. Can't have that. Somebody'll get hurt."

"What do we do now?"

"We don't do anything. I put this episode along with the other cases and continue waiting to have the pack sighted."

"Then you do believe that dogs did this?"

"More than likely, but until we run them down, we've got no case, have we?"

"I guess not."

"Well, let's get back to the car and call for help. I've got to get you back to your lady or she'll call the law down on me."

Pete managed a little laugh and followed Duke back to the track. Along the way they found what was left of the lower half of Boxcar Benny's body.

17

Pete got out of the sheriff's car and bent down to peer inside before closing the door.

The lawman frowned and said, "Tell Miss Bondson that I'm sorry about the time."

"It isn't that late. Besides, Amy's pretty reasonable. I'll tell her what happened and she'll understand."

"Thanks again, Pete."

"Any time, Sheriff." He closed the door and the car pulled away.

Pete turned to walk into the apartment complex. On the way he picked up the evening newspaper. In minutes he was knocking at his own front door.

"Who is it?" Amy asked without opening the

door.

"Me."

"Who's me?"

"Pete."

"I don't know anybody named Pete."

"You promised me something. I'm here to collect."

"Why didn't you say so?" Amy threw the door open and put her arms around his neck.

After kissing they separated and Pete said, "I'm sorry I'm late. The sheriff sends his apologies."

"What kept you?"

"Two more bodies."

"Oh, no. Who?"

"As far as could be determined, they were a couple of hobos or bums. Whatever you want to call them."

"What happened?"

"Well, after the sheriff called for some help, the coroner and he pieced together a story. He thinks the two men were probably in the hobo jungle near the tracks when the dogs attacked. One, the younger of the two, apparently got to his feet and ran for the tracks. From the condition of the body, or I should say the two pieces of the body, the train must have been going by and the poor devil fell under the wheels. At any rate, the pieces were found pretty far removed from the track. I agreed with the sheriff 'cause it sure looked like the body had been cut in half. The head was taken off too."

"Stop. Stop," Amy cried, holding her hands up. "You're forgiven. Just spare me the details. Are you sure that dogs did the attacking?"

Pete nodded. "The sheriff says the condition of the bodies and the prints in the soft earth are all circumstantial. But the evidence was good enough for me. I'm positive dogs did it."

"Why are you so sure?"

"Look, if it walks like a duck and quacks like a duck, and looks like a duck, the chances are it *is* a duck. The footprints, the condition of the bodies all tell me it was a dog pack.

"What's the sheriff going to do?"

Pete shook his head. "I don't know. He doesn't want to alarm the community and have people running around shooting every dog they see. But I wish to hell he would decide on a course of action sooner or later. The sooner the better."

While preparing their dinner, Pete and Amy talked about other things that didn't require a lot of concentration or carry heavy implications.

Just as they were about to sit down, Amy said, "What about Duchess?"

"What about her?" Pete asked, jamming a piece of steak into his mouth.

"Will she be all right?"

"Why wouldn't she be?"

"She's tied up outside."

"I don't think anyone will hurt her. Did you look at the paper when I brought it in?"

Amy shook her head. "Why?"

Pete reached across the table and picked up

the newspaper. Rifling through it in a hurry, he laid it back down. "Nothing about the pack. I was concerned for a moment that word might have leaked out."

"Isn't there anything?"

"About the deaths? Yeah. But just that they died. Somehow Little has managed to keep the gory details out of the paper, despite the meeting he held this morning."

"You mean that the press wasn't there?"

"Apparently, he didn't invite anyone from the media. Those who were there didn't talk to the right people, I guess. Otherwise it would be all over television and in the newspaper. You know how reporters go for something like this."

"But isn't that dangerous?"

"What?"

"Not informing the public."

Pete shrugged and cut another piece of meat from his T-bone. "I don't know. It's not my responsibility. However, I do more or less agree with the sheriff about not panicking the public."

"Back to Duchess."

"What about her?"

"Do you think she'll be safe?"

Pete nodded. "There won't be anybody out looking for dogs yet. Nobody knows, other than the coroner and the mortician, how Joe and the O'Malley boy actually died. Those men at the meeting won't say much. At least I hope they don't. And the two hobos have just been brought in. Not that many people know."

"What about the dogs?"

Pete stared at her. "I don't understand."

"Will the pack of dogs bother Duchess?"

"Oh, I see where you're going. I doubt it. First of all, I don't think the dogs will come into Laughton. It's too bright and crowded. It's too big. They'd be spotted for sure if they did—of course, they don't know that."

"Well, then, she might not be safe. Right?"

"I think she'll be all right. These dogs have gone wild. They're going to avoid man as much as possible."

Amy stared at him. "Pete? They didn't avoid Joe Eppson or Johnny O'Malley or these other two men. I think they'll come if they decide to."

"Well, the two men who were killed were ten miles or so from Laughton, and if the dogs' appetites were satisfied, they'll be lying up and sleeping tonight—not out roaming for food."

"You sure?"

"Positive as I can be."

They finished their meal in silence.

"Let the dishes go," Pete said, standing.

"Not very tidy."

"Well, I've got some things on my mind that won't keep."

"Such as?" Amy smiled demurely and looked away.

"Are you flirting with me? Or teasing me?"

"Neither. I thought we might compare notes. I've been thinking about some things, too."

"Such as?"

"Not here. Follow me," she said, taking his hand. Leading him through the small apartment, she walked directly to the bedroom. "Sit down."

Pete did as he was ordered and watched as Amy slowly, seductively unbuttoned her blouse. Her small breasts stood upright proudly, their nipples erect. Slipping from her blouse, she slid her jeans over her hips and dropped them to her ankles. She stepped from them and walked toward Pete.

He couldn't help being aroused. Whenever Amy did her little striptease he knew it was just for him. He bit his lip when he thought of Carol's attitude toward him and their lovemaking. She had thought of every excuse in the book. The last time he had had the opportunity to get even with his wife had been the start of their marriage's slide downward. She had come on to him, doing her best to seduce him, but he was in a peculiar mood, wanting instead to talk, to joke, to watch TV, to do anything but hold her in his arms.

"I—I can't, Carol," he had said huskily. "I—I might have herpes." It had been a joke, but one he was never able to undo. No matter what he said she didn't believe him. When he volunteered to go to any doctor she named she refused, saying he probably had bribed every doctor in Laughton. Two weeks later he had moved out of the hell he and Carol had created for themselves.

He looked up at Amy, who stood directly in front of him. She pressed his head to her breasts and he relaxed. They felt so good. So comforting.

Kissing them in a gentle way, he turned her body, lowering it to the bed on which he sat. In seconds he had stripped off his shirt, pants, and shorts.

Taking Amy in his arms, he kissed her softly, yet in a savage, almost frenzied way. She returned her own ardor to the man she loved, feeling that familiar tingle of passion arising within her lower body. Quickly spreading throughout her, the flames danced higher and higher, turning her coolness into a roaring inferno.

Pete's hands roamed over her body, kneading, pinching, massaging, arousing her even more than his kisses had. Lowering her back on the bed, he kissed her throat, running his lips first to one ear and then the other before spreading his lips to run his tongue over the fiery flesh. Spiraling outward from her breasts, he moved down toward her navel, where he jabbed her several times with his tongue before moving farther down. Kissing her pubic hair, he could feel her writhing as he kindled the coals of love they felt for each other.

Amy could sense Pete's arousal, his firm shaft pressing against her leg when he came back up her body, trailing his tongue in a wet, slippery path. Moaning, she gasped, "Now, Pete. Now. Do it now."

Positioning himself over her body, he lowered his hips until his penis touched her above the pubic hairline. She grabbed it, gently but in a ferocious way, guiding it to her vagina.

Thrusting forward, Pete drove it into her and she screamed in pleasure. Establishing their rhythm, they pumped their hips until both climaxed simultaneously.

Spent, they lay in each other's embrace, their breath slowly returning to normal. In minutes both dropped off to sleep.

The black mongrel, the pack immediately behind him on the hill, stared at the lights of Laughton below. He had come this way that one night when he had been by himself. That time he hadn't been very hungry, but he had smelled much food. Pungent odors had wafted to him from darkened areas, but he hadn't taken the time to investigate. Some of the pack was still hungry, and those who hadn't fed on the two men they had killed wanted something to satisfy themselves. The whole pack had moved out when the leader had left the area where they had been resting.

The dog started down the hill toward the blinking lights with the rest of the dogs right behind them. Sensing the newness of the situation, they padded along without making a sound, 37 dogs, some hungry, some not, but willing to try anything that might be found.

They came to a gravel roadway and followed it only because it was darker there than either of the two more smooth streets to the sides. The alley offered garbage pails and rubbish bags that had been put there to await the trash pickup on

Monday morning. Investigating each can, each bag as the treasure cove it represented, the dogs quietly, efficiently ate whatever they found. Because there were so many places to choose from, the animals were able to concentrate on eating and not fighting one another for bits and pieces of food.

An Airedale terrier, allowed to run before being called in for the night, confronted the pack, growling a warning. The black mongrel rushed to the fore, facing the dog. Advancing warily, the leader sniffed the air around the intruder. The growl, born deep within his chest, rumbled to the throat of the mongrel, and he bared his fangs. His yellow eyes reflected eerily in the distant light from the streetlamp at the end of the alley. The Airedale, not used to associating with other dogs, realized he was greatly outnumbered, and outweighed by the black beast confronting him. Drawing on a reservoir of knowledge that had lain dormant in his brain since birth, he dropped to his belly and slowly lowered his rump to the alley floor.

The mongrel growled again and the Airedale rolled over, exposing his soft underbelly to the leader. Accepting his submission, the mongrel haughtily turned away and moved back to the can from which he had been finding pieces of meat.

After awhile the pack moved on, farther into the confines of Laughton, but keeping to the alley. Suddenly, the black mongrel froze, reading the air coming toward him. He recognized the scent riding on the breeze. He had smelled it before. Growling to warn the others to remain quiet, he moved off in a direction, directly toward the source of the odor.

When the pack stood alongside the fence the mongrel voiced a whine and was answered immediately by a similar cry from within the enclosure. He could see the white figure outlined in the darkness of the yard. Effortlessly leaping the fence, the mongrel trotted up to the tethered bitch, sniffing the entire time, his body quivering with excitement. He picked up her excitation and they touched noses. No need for him to mate with her again. The time was gone and he could tell she carried a litter. He wanted her to come with them.

Whining, he turned and headed back to the fence. When he reached it he stopped, looking in her direction. She leaped at him, fighting the chain keeping her from going farther. She barked, a high-pitched pleading yip that, although heeded, went unanswered. The mongrel knew she couldn't follow. Vaulting the fence, he turned once more and eyed the prancing figure in the dark, looking more ghostlike, in her white coat, than real.

Without a sound, the mongrel turned and trotted down the alley, back in the direction from which the pack had come. The others fell in behind him.

Day Four

Sunday

18

Trixie closely watched the meadowlark on the fence post. The bird sang its territorial song, warning others of its kind to stay away. Trixie's tongue hung from one side of her mouth. Oblivious to the other dogs around her, she still felt ill at ease with the pack. The black mongrel had lain with her at night, when she slept, ever since she had deserted her home.

A low rumbling growl from the pack leader brought the collie's attention back to the hay field in which the dogs hid. The mongrel stood at the edge, watching some buildings that, when Trixie looked, reminded her of her own home. The smells were wrong, but from what she could make out from where she lay the buildings weren't all that different.

When the mongrel dropped to his belly the pack froze. A man, walking from the nearby barn toward the house, held the dog's attention. Without getting to his feet, the leader inched forward, toward the man, looking for a better point of attack.

Myron Sayman hurried toward the house. He had to get his coveralls off and hair combed or he and the family would be late for church. They had seven miles to go before reaching the city limits and then sixteen blocks to the church itself. They usually cut it thin every Sunday, but the pastor, Reverend James Wagonston, was patient with those people who were poorly organized on Sunday morning. The fact that the late-comers even bothered showing up once they knew they'd be late seemed to be the salve for the clergyman's ego.

"Georgia? Are you ready?" Myron called when he got closer to the house. "Georgia? Are you and the kids ready?"

From deep within the house his wife shrieked, "Yes. Yes. *Yes!* For heaven's sake, Myron, we'll be ready in a minute."

Myron didn't flinch under the high-pitched, nasal verbal assault of his wife. Georgia reverted to it whenever she was under stress. It was her normal Sunday-morning voice. He grinned when he mentally pictured his children. He was proud. Twenty-year-old Bob was a wonderful help around the farm. His only shortcoming was the social life he kept, which usually meant he didn't get up at the crack of dawn the way Myron did. But Myron could understand that. He had been 20 once. He knew what it was like. Patricia, 18, had just graduated from high school and she had, for a change, stayed home last night. She had gotten up shortly after Myron had hit the bathroom. Seventeen-year-old Jack was up, but not wide awake, and if he got dressed by the time everyone else was ready to go, Myron and Georgia would be thankful. The two youngsters, Bonnie Lee, 14 and Mike, 10, were no problem and got enough sleep to allow them to get up and be ready before anyone else in the family. They were great kids and Myron had every right to be proud.

Just as Myron stepped into the house yard, Georgia threw open the door and said, "You haven't got the car out of the garage yet, Myron. Why not? Good God Almighty, how can you expect the rest of us to hurry and be ready when the car isn't even out of the garage yet?"

Myron brushed past her and into the entryway. Dropping the buckets inside the door, he pulled open the coveralls and wiggled out of them after stepping out of his rubber boots. The white shirt and tie and pressed slacks he wore worked a complete, magical change of appearance for the slightly built man. His shoes, polished to a high sheen, had been well protected and his sudden transformation from farmer to immaculate church-goer had been immediate and swift. "I'll get the car out, you make certain the kids are ready."

Turning, he left the entryway and hurried toward the garage that was a short distance from the house, toward the hay field that butted up against the house yard. At least he didn't have to lock the building at night. He would if he lived in town, but that thought usually made him work much harder to stay on the farm. Swinging both doors open, he bent down to prop a stick against the one door that liked to swing halfway shut just about the time he'd be ready to back the Ford out.

Myron didn't have a chance to straighten up. The black mongrel hit him with his 80-pound body, springing from the full-speed charge he had started into when he bolted from the confines of the hay field. The pack, swift on the leader's heels, closed over Myron, biting, ripping at his clothing, tearing at his arms, which vainly protected his face and throat.

"Help!" The single word rang through the farm yard. "Get the fuck off'a me!" Myron struggled with the weight of the dogs pressing him to the ground. For some reason, when the first animal hit him, he had gone down, face first, but managed to roll onto his back. That had been his biggest mistake. His front side lay open, exposed to the gleaming fangs of the dog pack attacking him.

When the Doberman pinscher's jaws closed on

his penis Myron screamed loudly, the high-pitched yell resounding through the open windows of the farmhouse. The dog pulled, tearing at the pants material. When a ripping sound met her ears the hunting dog worked harder than ever, jerking a strip of material away, displaying the white splash of shorts, showing through. A mighty tug from the strong animal bared his manhood, and her jaws closed on it, grinding, biting, ripping at the soft skin.

Inside the house, Georgia dropped her comb when Myron screamed. "Kids! Something's wrong. Something's happened to Dad. Come on." She ran from the first-floor bedroom on the opposite side of the house to the kitchen and through the entryway. Bonnie Lee and Mike were quick to follow, with Patricia bringing up the rear. Rounding the corner of the house, Georgia screamed when she saw the horde of dogs swarming over her husband, who lay strangely quiet. His feet, the only things she could plainly see, rolled back and forth, as if the weight of the dogs was moving him.

The growls and barks from the animals drowned out her scream.

"Get away! Get away! Shoo!" She picked up a rusty bucket that had been long ago discarded and hurled it at the dogs. A German shepherd turned when it struck his rear end, charging at the petrified woman. Soaring, he bore her to the earth, snapping at the arms that covered her face.

Georgia screamed again when the pain of the bites became too much, and she futilely beat at the large animal. Seeing her exposed throat, the dog attacked it, closing his powerful jaws on her windpipe. Georgia gurgled her protest, but the shepherd continued chewing, pulling, and when he got a sufficient purchase, yanked back with all his strength. The ensuing red fountain that blasted him in the face became his reward and he lowered himself to feast, ignoring the other animals that had come around to his prey.

The three children came to the screen door of the entryway. Mike, who was leading, stopped. "What's that noise? Why is Mom screaming?"

"It sounds like a dog playing," Bonnie Lee offered.

Patricia thought for a moment. It sounded like a dog—or dogs—but they didn't own one. "I don't think so, Bonnie."

"Well, let's find out," Mike said, pushing open the door. Stepping outside, he stopped when he looked around the corner. "Mom! Mom!" He ran forward to protect his mother, who lay beneath the German shepherd and four mongrels who were chewing on her arms and legs. The German shepherd, lying on top of the body, lapped at the blood from the huge wound in the woman's throat.

"Get away from her!" Patricia shouted, running forward to catch up with Mike.

Bonnie Lee, frozen into immobility for a split second, took up the cries of her siblings as she ran to help.

The first to fall, Mike, had his nose bitten off and throat torn out by the black mongrel who had left Myron's body when the shouts of the children first went up. Patricia, unable to stop when she saw the gore and carnage on the ground in front of her, finally managed to turn without slowing and made a dash for the back of the house.

"Get back, Bonnie! Get back!" she screamed. The tan-and-black bitch sprang at her and the sudden impact and weight of the dog carried Patricia to the ground, face first. Snapping at her buttocks, tearing the dress, the bitch ground her teeth into the 18-year-old's soft flesh.

Patricia rolled onto her back, her eyes widening in horror when she saw Bonnie Lee coming up from behind to help.

"No. Get back. Get in the house!" The bitch attacking Patricia positioned herself over the young woman's body, snapping at her, catching the bodice of the girl's dress in her fangs. Pulling back, she ripped it open, and in seconds her jaws closed on Patricia's unprotected left breast. The girl screamed, bringing her arms down from her face to beat at the tan-and-black bitch.

Without recognizing the sight of a dog bounding through the air over her and the one attacking her, Patricia was unmindful of her younger sister's screams as she went down under the assault of a male collie.

When the bitch saw the exposed throat of the

girl her jaws closed on it and it was soon lapping up the blood spurting from the wound.

A short distance away, Bonnie Lee screamed once before dying.

Jack, one shoe on and one foot bare, ran through the kitchen. What the hell was happening outside? It sounded like a free-for-all at the dog pound. Blasting from the entryway door, he stopped when he saw the pack and his sisters, brother, and parents under attack. He stood without moving when a large white mongrel hit him full force in the chest, sending him back toward the door step. His head struck, telegraphing the shock of the blow through it, then his body, and the last thing he felt was the draining of his sinuses as he sank into unconsciousness.

The dogs feasted, shredding then bolting down the viscera of the bodies once the abdomens were opened. A peculiar, contented quiet fell over the pack as they ate, undisturbed.

Inside, Bob stared at the ceiling. What a dream. Growling, screaming. People being called. But he couldn't recall any action, any pictures or motions or images that usually went with dreams. Had he actually dreamt it? Forcing his eyes open, he focused them until he could read the digital alarm clock. He'd be late for church. He'd make the whole family late for church. He'd never hear the end of it if he were the reason the family would be embarrassed by walking into the services once they had begun.

Jumping from bed, he called out. "Jack? Come here. I need your help. Get my blue slacks and blue shirt out while I brush my teeth and hair."

No answer.

"Come on, Jack. I'd do the same for you." Bob made his way to the bathroom without putting on his robe. Dressed only in his shorts, he dashed across the hall into the lavatory. He pulled his penis out and, while urinating, lifted the window to an open position with his free hand. He heard the contented growls of the dogs without recognizing the sound.

"Jack? Come on. I'll never do you another favor as long as I live, buddy! Get my pants and shirt out. Puh-lease?"

Still no answer. Only that peculiar sound coming from outside. When he finished urinating he hitched his shorts up a bit higher and took a quick look outside.

"Christ! *Christ, Jesus!*" He erupted from the bathroom, running as fast as he could for the kitchen and entryway. Where had all the dogs come from? His parents and brothers and sisters were being attacked. He had to call for help. No. That would take too long. He had to do something and do it right now. But what? Turning, he went back to the hall closet. Inside, he found the double-barrel shotgun his parents had given him last Christmas. Reaching up on the shelf for shells, he jammed two into the breech and snapped the weapon shut.

Retracing his steps to the kitchen, he threw open the door and ran out, tripping over Jack's body and the four dogs gobbling down his intestines. The shotgun sailed through the air, striking the ground in such a way that the first shell exploded. The dogs all bounded to their feet and, the black mongrel, seeing Bob struggling to his feet, charged. The man went down and, in microseconds, died, his throat ripped open.

The dogs settled back to their feast after a few minutes and didn't immediately hear the whine of tires on the macadam road that fronted the farm property. Tugging and pulling on Jack's body, the dogs slowly moved it, while fighting for rights to it, around the corner of the house.

Suddenly the black mongrel stopped eating. He heard something. Cautiously making his way to the edge of the house, he peered around the corner.

He watched the milk truck turn into the yard. The driver made his way toward the barn and stopped. The mongrel watched him get out and look around.

Bert Livermore peered around the farm. His hackles crawled of their own volition. He felt something. But what? The only sound was the truck engine idling.

"Hey?" he called, cupping his hands around his mouth.

No answer. Only that peculiar silence that

seemed unnatural. Then he realized what was wrong. He wished the Saymans would get a dog. Ever since theirs had been run over by a semi when the stupid sonofabitch was out chasing cars on the road the farm had seemed too quiet.

"Hey, Myron? Come on, I ain't got all day." He waited. Usually the farmer would come out of the barn, ready to have him load the morning's milk.

Surely they wouldn't be gone to church already. He didn't like working without the farmer being around. If something happened, he'd be blamed sure as hell.

"Myron? Come on. I gotta get going." He waited and looked toward the house. It would be unlike him to have overslept. He didn't know of a single farmer who had ever overslept. That was too much of a luxury in today's farming. Things were tough enough without being lazy and staying in bed beyond dawn.

Bert started toward the house. They had to be inside. Nobody was at the barn. If they were, they were deaf. When he got a third of the way to the house he saw the head of the black dog sticking around the corner. They *had* gotten a dog. But apparently not too good a one. The stupid thing hadn't even barked when he pulled into the yard. Nobody would be safe with a dog like that on guard.

Bert took too more steps and stopped, his eyes widening, terror-filled, as the pack suddenly blasted around the corner of the house, coming straight at him.

Instinctively, the man turned, running as fast as he could for the cab of his truck. He had left it open when he got out and leaped in when he got within five feet of it. Slamming the door shut, he started to run up the window. The Doberman vaulted through the air toward him. Just as the head of the bitch entered the cab, the window closed on her and her upper body was caught. Leaning as far away as he could, Bert, threw the truck in gear and lurched away from the barn. He made a crazy route around the yard before shooting for the highway, the Doberman hanging half in, half out of the cab.

The dog snapped at Bert, who sat in the middle of the seat, driving. Swinging wildly with his left hand and arm at the dog's bloody jowels, he managed to turn onto the road and floored the accelerator. He'd get going fast enough and then lower the window and push the goddamned beast out.

When the speedometer needle touched fifty he reached for the handle of the window, but without taking his eyes from the road, put his hand within the range of the snapping jaws. Instantly, the bitch locked onto Bert's hand and he screamed, taking his right hand from the wheel to beat at the snout of the dog. The truck swayed wildly as it careened down the road, first to the right, then to the left. Each time it came close to the shoulder it veered away, cutting across the road to the other side. When the left front wheel caught over the edge of the macadam the truck's steering wheel spun to the opposite direction and the milk truck rolled into the gutter, the tank rupturing as it crashed.

The truck rolled to the left, the weight of the vehicle smashing the Doberman and the window that had held it so effectively, cut the bitch in half. Her upper body, free, fell inside the cab, right toward Bert. The nerves controlling her jaws continued working, and they locked onto Bert's throat, choking him.

Milk gurgled into the gutter, creating a white river among the dried weeds.

When the dog pack finished its feast of the Sayman family the leader started for the road and the gutters that ran along both sides. Raising his nose, he caught the whiff of milk on the breeze and followed it. When the dogs reached the truck, they satisfied their thirst and, after sniffing the dead Doberman bitch's lower body, continued on their way.

19

Duke Little kept to the speed limit even though he felt tempted to turn on the red lights and siren and drive as fast as he could. He didn't like what was happening in his county. After Charley Teahart called in about the overturned milk truck and Deputy Ralph Cassidy had investigrated, the sheriff had been notified at home. Ralph had been extremely upset when he radioed the courthouse. The dispatcher had patched the call through to Duke's home.

"It's awful, Sheriff," Ralph had whined into his ear.

Duke ground his teeth. He hated it when Ralph whined like that. It had to be the result of stress on the job that made him do it. "What's awful, Ralph?"

"The accident. Jesus. I got sick. I did."

"Tell me about it, Ralph?"

"There was a dog in the truck. The goddamned thing was sliced in half. And here's the worst part. The fuckin' thing has got a hold of the driver's throat."

"What?"

"You heard me."

"And the driver's dead?"

"Correct."

"I'll be there. Don't let anyone see inside the truck cab. Understand?"

"Gotcha, Sheriff."

Duke had already been dressed, but not in uniform, and he had strapped on his gun over his suit pants and dashed out of the house, telling his wife to go on to church. He'd get there when he could. Rather than draw attention to himself by speeding and making a lot of racket, he had opted to drive the speed limit and he hoped the only one on the scene would be Ralph when he got there.

Up ahead he could see the deputy's car parked off the road and the shiny tank of the milk truck peeking over the verge of the road itself. Slowing down, he pulled in behind the other car and got out after turning on his emergency lights.

"Tell me about it, Ralph," he said tersely.

"Charley says he came by here about eight o'clock this morning. There wasn't anything wrong. No sign of Livermore's truck. I guess Charley was going to church 'cause he says when he came back this way at nine-thirty the truck was there. He stopped but couldn't see into the cab very well. He did see that the milk was almost all drained from the tank, though." Ralph kept his eyes on Duke, not wanting to look at the wreck or the gruesome sight in the cab.

Duke dropped into the gutter and began poking around the weeds. "Hey, Ralph, did you see this?"

"What's that, Sheriff?"

"Other half of the dog." Duke bent down to examine it and straighened up after a few minutes passed. He walked over to the overturned truck and stooped to peer in through the windshield. "It was a Doberman. A Doberman pinscher. A bitch."

"Pretty bad, ain't it, Sheriff?"

Looking around for a moment, he saw something in the milky mud. Bending, he examined it before climbing back to the road level. "It's not very nice. Call the coroner. I want to know the cause of death. It looks like the driver might have been choked to death, but the look on his face says he either died of fright or the choking made his eyes bug out like that."

Ralph turned to go to his car.

"Just a minute, Ralph. Did this Teahart happen to say anything about where the milk truck would have been coming from or going?"

Ralph puckered up his baby face and pretended to think for a long minute. "No, he didn't, Sheriff. Why?"

Duke peered back in the direction from which he had just come. The truck was pointed in that direction. "I think it's only common sense to assume that the truck was heading that way," he said, pointing over his shoulder, "and coming from up that way." He pointed in the opposite direction. For a moment he studied the farm that stood out on the horizon. "I wonder if perhaps the truck might not have stopped at that farm up the road."

"You sure got me, Sheriff," Ralph said. "I think I'll go call the coroner."

"Have you been waving people on by?"

"Sure have. I didn't think anyone should see this. So, I just waved 'em on by."

"Keep on doing it. I'm going to go up the road and ask at that farm if the milk truck had stopped there."

"Sure looks like there ain't a dog pack involved, doesn't it, Sheriff? Leastwise not in this accident."

"What makes you say that, Ralph?"

"The fact that there's only one dog."

"There's only one dog because that's all that got killed. Who knows how many were around here? I didn't look all that close when I was in the gutter, but I did see what looked like all sorts of paw prints where the milk made mud. I think, now more than ever, that Dr. Reckels is right. There's a pack of dogs-gone-wild on the loose. We've got to find them and kill them before any other strange things happen like this accident.

The fact that there have been four people killed by them already makes it of the utmost urgency. Call the coroner. I'll be back in a few minutes."

Duke went to his car and drove off toward the farm. When he pulled into the yard he noted the name on the mailbox. Sayman.

Sheriff Little stared at the small knot of reporters waiting for the first question regarding the news release he had just handed out.

"Why have you kept quiet about this until now, Sheriff?" one of the reporters asked, quickly scanning the impersonal report of eight new deaths.

"Because no one was absolutely positive as to the cause of death in the O'Malley case or the other three. We have definite proof now that the perpetrators were dogs."

"Dogs?" one of the reporters asked. "I see that here in the release. What kind of dogs?"

"Ordinary house dogs. Farm dogs. Hunting dogs. Domestic animals. They've gone wild."

"Is that possible?" a radio reporter asked, thrusting his microphone into Duke's face.

"Would you like to see the bodies of the Sayman family? I tell you, gentlemen and ladies, that it was the most horrible thing I've ever seen. I served in Korea and I've seen death there and here on my job as sheriff of Cramden County. But I've never seen anything like this before and I hope I never do again. We've got to hunt these beasts down and kill them."

"Aren't you afraid of what the local chapter of the prevention of cruelty to animals will say?"

"Off the record, please, they can go fuck themselves if they try anything. I'll arrest the first person who tries to prevent one of these animals from being killed. This is for the record: There have been eleven people killed by the dogs and one died in a truck accident because he was being attacked. For that reason and that reason alone, I'm declaring open season on the dogs that belong to that pack."

"How will you differentiate between dogs that belong and dogs that don't?"

"Because they *are* a pack. They'll stick together. Find the pack and kill all the dogs in it and the problem will be solved."

"What was the condition of the bodies, Sheriff?" a woman asked, holding up her hand, twisting a pencil between her fingers.

"I don't think you really want to know. You wouldn't be able to print it in your paper and the television people wouldn't be able to give all the sordid details. Just say that they were killed by dogs. If anyone knows how dogs kill, they can supply their own details. As I understand it from Dr. Reckels, a veterinarian, dogs kill like this no matter what they're hunting."

"Anything else, Sheriff?"

"Yes. Please tell people to stay on the alert. It's madness to go out after dark without some sort of protection. It's madness even to think about going without protection. I'm organizing a posse to hunt down the pack. Until we can honestly say we've killed every last one, I feel no one will be safe. Emphasize that and don't downplay it in the least. Got that?"

When there were no more questions Duke dismissed the reporters and turned to the short, stocky man sitting behind him. Harry Manning, the chief of police, stood and came forward.

"It's really as bad as all that?"

"Worse. All you'd have to see is how these animals are leaving the bodies. Can you have your men drive up and down streets warning people about the pack?"

Manning shrugged. "I don't know. That could get expensive."

"What? Calling in off-duty policemen to do it?"

The chief nodded. "I'll have to get permission from the city tomorrow. It—"

"Tomorrow? Hell, we could have more people dead by that time. I'm sending all of my deputies out into the county to warn everybody. The least you can do is the same thing here in town."

Manning shrugged again. "I'll do it, but I'm afraid of what'll happen when the city manager and the city council and that sonofabitching mayor finds out. My ass could be in a sling."

"If it's their ass you save, you'll get a medal and not a sling, Harry."

Manning smiled grimly and left the sheriff to order all off-duty policemen in.

Duke hurried back to his office and picked up the telephone. When the dispatcher answered he said, "Have you been able to contact the deputies?"

"Yes, sir."

"Have you started calling the list of names I gave you?"

"Yes, sir. Most have been home and said they'd be here at three this afternoon."

"Good. Those men are hunters. You did tell them to bring their rifles and shotguns, didn't you?"

"Yes, sir."

"How many do you have left to call?"

"Four."

"Did you get in touch with Dr. Reckels?"

"I'm afraid he's one of the four, Sheriff."

"Keep after them—especially Pete Reckels. Understand?"

"Got it, Sheriff."

Duke hung up. Where could Pete Reckels be? He felt he needed the veterinarian around to give advice. After all, none of the hunters who were being summoned ever hunted dogs before. They had hunted with dogs but never had they specifically gone after dogs. Where should they look? He hoped Pete Reckels had ideas and suggestions.

Right now Sheriff Duke Little's biggest concern was getting the word out about the dogs. When he thought of the seven bodies he had found at the Sayman Farm he shuddered again and got to his feet. This time he was going to be sick. Why he hadn't thrown up when he made the grisly discovery was beyond him. But now—now that he had relaxed for an instant, his body demanded equal time with his brain.

He just made it in time to the public bathroom down the hall.

20

A cool breeze flowed from the Wipsipanicon River through the park, rustling leaves and bushes making its presence known. In the trees overhead birds sang out and children ran about the park, playing spontaneous games of tag and hide-and-seek.

Amy lay back on the blanket she and Pete had spread on the ground. Her eyes closed, she smiled.

"Now what is that little grin about?" Pete asked, turning to check on Jenny's whereabouts. The small girl, sitting in the middle of a sandbox, worked at filling a bucket with a miniature shovel.

"I'm just happy. It's so peaceful and quiet here

in the park. I'm glad we came early. At least we have a choice spot and the place isn't crowded yet."

"And you wanted to sleep in this morning." Pete playfully jabbed her in the ribs. "Tell me, what do you think of Jenny?"

"She's precious. I think we'll probably become close friends if we continue the way we started."

"By that I assume you mean that she didn't act shy when I introduced the two of you."

Amy nodded. "She's certainly mature when it comes to meeting someone. I didn't expect 'How do you do, Amy?' "

Pete smily slyly. "I wish I could take credit for her manners and behaviorial habits. I can't. At least Carol is doing a good job in parenting when it comes to Jenny."

"Oh, I'm sure you'd have done just as well." Amy's face clouded and she turned away.

"What's the matter?"

"I was just thinking about the dogs you think are running loose."

"Think? I *know.* It's just a matter of time before they're seen and the law takes care of them. What made you think of them in the first place? We were sitting here having a nice conversation when all of a sudden you bring up dogs."

"I guess my thoughts sort of went out of control. We were talking about Jenny and the good job Carol is doing in raising her. The mention of Carol brought to mind the hurt she caused you and I thought of her as a bitch. I'm sorry but that's the way she comes across to me even though I haven't ever met her. She hurt you and that makes her a nasty person to me. A bitch!"

Pete turned away to hide his smile. Amy was protective of him and he enjoyed that. But he didn't want to encourage her to the point where Amy would become almost militant and say something in front of Jenny. Then if word got back to Carol there would be hell to pay and he might wind up having difficulty in seeing his daughter as regularly as he had over the past few months.

"I—" he began, but stopped when he heard a voice over a loudspeaker coming toward them. Spinning about without standing, he looked across the park and saw a police car moving along slowly.

"Pete, what's the matter?" Amy asked.

"Sh-h-h, I want to hear what's being said." He motioned for her to be quiet.

" . . . and stay there until it is reported safe to go about your routine affairs." The car continued approaching them.

"What's that all about?" Amy asked.

Pete shrugged. "I hope they repeat it. I only caught the last few words."

"Attention. Your attention, please! You are requested to vacate the park and city streets as soon as possible. This is an emergency." The loudspeaker boomed.

Pete looked at Amy, expressions of puzzlement crossing both their faces.

"By order of the Chief of Police and the Sheriff of Cramden County, all civilians are to go to their homes and remain inside. There is a pack of feral dogs on the loose, roaming the countryside. It is believed that these dogs are responsible for the deaths of eleven or twelve people. It is urgent that you comply with this order. People found on the streets will be escorted to their homes or to a place of safety. It is imperative that you go to your homes and stay there until it is reported safe to go about your routine affairs."

Pete could barely speak. Twelve people? What had happened? This was a calamity. He turned to Amy, who was already on her feet, gathering together the blanket.

"I'll get Jenny," he said, jumping up to grab the cooler before hurrying across the intervening space separating him from his daughter.

"I wonder what happened," Amy said as she put the blanket into the back of the car. She stepped aside to allow Pete to put the cooler in.

"Why do we have to go, Daddy?" Jenny asked, tugging on her father's pants leg.

"We have to move our picnic to Daddy's apartment." He bent down, scooping her into her arms.

"We could go to my place. There's the back yard," Amy offered.

"No way. They said everyone should stay *in* their homes. Not around their homes. If the dogs are in town, there'll be more deaths unless people obey the order."

"We can stay *in* my house just as easily," Amy said, going around to the passenger's side of the Bronco.

Pete boosted Jenny into the car and she clambered over to Amy's side. Amy took her on her lap after buckling her own seat belt in place.

"If you don't mind," Pete said, winding his way through the park's gravel roadway, "I'll take you two to my apartment. It's a little safer than your house from the standpoint that it's on the second floor."

"My God, Pete, you don't think that those beasts are going to go around breaking into people's homes, do you?"

Pete shrugged. "I don't know what to think anymore. If seven or eight more people have been killed, something pretty awful happened. I'm not taking any chances of anything happening to you two. All right?"

Amy nodded. "All right."

After parking the Bronco and hurrying into the apartment building Pete closed the door after him and went directly to the telephone. He dialed the sheriff's number, hoping he could reach the lawman and find out what had happened.

"Law Enforcement Center," the voice of the operator answered after several rings.

"Sheriff Little, please."

"Who's calling? The sheriff's pretty busy."

"Pete Reckels. Dr. Pete Reckels."

"One moment."

The line went dead and Pete impatiently tapped his fingers on the kitchen counter as he waited.

After several minutes passed the line reopened. "Pete? Is that you?"

"Yeah, Sheriff. What the hell happened?"

"I've been trying all morning to reach you. Let me tell you what happened."

Pete listened as the sheriff told him of the discovery of the Sayman family and the Doberman's jaws choking the milk truck driver to death. The veterinarian could feel his head spinning. It was terrible. Eight more people dead.

"Can you get away, Pete? Could you come down here to the Law Enforcement Center and sort of be an adviser on this thing?"

Pete didn't answer immediately. He wanted to be here with Jenny and Amy. "Why me, Sheriff?"

"You know dogs. You know how they kill and how they act. If I've got you here to pick your brains, I think we can end this situation that much quicker."

"When? Right now?"

"Most of the men who were at the meeting yesterday morning have been contacted and they're coming in with their weapons. We've got to organize some sort of patrol that will be equipped to kill these animals the instant they're sighted. I've called for a three o'clock meeting. Can you be here?"

Pete glanced at the kitchen clock. It was

already two-thirty. Amy and Jenny would be safe here on the second floor. There were two exits, but both had solid doors without windows. The windows themselves opened onto nothing that would allow a dog or trespasser entry. They would be safe while he went to the meeting.

"Okay, Sheriff, you've got yourself an adviser. I'll be there." He hung up and turned to find Amy's quizzical face staring at him. Without giving her a chance to ask he offered everything the sheriff had told him, including the slaying of the family and truck driver.

"You be careful, Pete," she said, waggling an admonishing finger. "I don't want you added to the list." Her face went dark. "You don't have a gun, do you?"

He shook his head. "I don't have time to hunt. Why?"

"Shouldn't you have some sort of protection? What if the dogs catch you between your car and the sheriff's office or the apartment building? Then what?"

"I think I'll be all right now. But maybe the sheriff can lend me a gun." He kissed her goodbye and turned to leave after hugging his daughter. He knew he'd be back. He didn't have an overwhelming sensation of doom harboring within him. He'd definitely be back.

"With the cooperation of the police department and the sheriff's department you men will be assigned to ride with officers and deputies for the night," Duke Little said, looking over the group of 25 men. "Some of you will be walking patrols here in town with officers. Each of you will be issued a permit for discharging firearms within the city limits. I'm going to turn over the podium to Dr. Peter Reckels, one of Laughton's veterinarians. He'll tell you what you should know about this dog pack. Incidentally, he's the only one living who's seen the pack as far as we know. Doctor."

Pete shook his head. What the hell did Little want? What did Pete know specifically about this particular pack? Nothing. He grinned sheepishly and walked to the lectern.

"I hope I don't disappoint you, Sheriff," he began. "True, I did see the pack and at the time, although I thought it unusual for a pack of dogs to be running in daylight, I didn't worry too much about it. Perhaps I should have." He went on to tell them about dogs running together at night but usually breaking up at dawn.

"Now, if you'll excuse me, I'm going to get a bit on the gross side. If there were eight people killed today, the pack has eaten. That means they'll probably be lying up, sleeping most of the day and probably tonight as well. If that's the case, the only way we'll find them will be to find the place where they're sleeping. I doubt if they have a permanent lair of any sort. This pack has apparently just moved into the territory, considering the sudden rash of deaths in the county."

"Well, then," one man said, standing, "why bother going on a patrol tonight?"

Pete held both hands up to quiet the murmuring approval of the question. "Remember, I said probably. I have no idea how many dogs are in the pack. Maybe all of the members were satisfied and won't be hungry. If that's the case, they *will* be sleeping. But if a few weren't satisfied, the pack as a whole will move out and hunt again."

The man, his question satisfied, sat down again.

Another stood. "I'm not sure I could kill a collie or police dog if they came charging at me."

"You'd better make up your mind now, friend. Because you'll only have a second or two to decide if you wait until one attacks you. If one charges you and you hesitate and he hits you right, you'll go down and you won't stand a chance if there's more than one. Believe me."

When there were no more questions the sheriff began assigning men to different deputies. The chief of police did the same, assigning men to walk with officers or ride in patrol cars.

"I assume you'd like to ride with someone, Pete?" Duke said after he finished.

"I hadn't really thought about it one way or the other."

"I'll put you with one of the policemen if you want."

"I don't have a shotgun or anything."

"We can issue you one," the sheriff said,

turning to Harry Manning, who had just walked up. "You got a seat in a squad car empty, Harry?"

Manning nodded. "Yeah. He can ride with Ben Rathe."

"Can you get him a shotgun or something?"

"Yeah, come with me."

Pete hesitated. "I'll have to call home and let Amy know I won't be home right away."

Duke gestured toward his office door. "You can call from in there."

After calling Amy, Pete was issued a riot gun by Manning, who then took him to meet Ben Rathe. Carrying the unfamiliar weapon in one arm, Pete followed the chief.

Ben Rathe was a heavy-set man in his early thirties. His moustache seemed a bit too small for his round face, but he smiled warmly and shook Pete's hand in a firm grasp.

After six hours of riding Pete was tired. He was ready to go home and fall into bed. The evening had crawled by slowly, and although he knew he'd be finished in another hour when Ben Rathe finished his tour of duty, he wanted to go home now.

"Hey, what's that?" Rathe asked, slowing the patrol car to a crawl.

"What's what?" Pete asked, sitting up straight.

"I thought I saw a big dog run into that alley." Rathe eased the car down the street, turning into the alley he had pointed out to Pete. Ahead, an Irish setter trotted nonchalantly next to a cocker spaniel. "Do you think they belong to the pack, Pete?" Ben asked.

"I sort of doubt it, Ben. I don't think that one or two would splinter off from the group. They could, but I doubt it. Probably a couple of dogs that just got out of their pens or were allowed to run loose for a while by their owners. Nine chances out of ten, their owners never once thought of the danger to their own pets. Stop the car."

Ben did as he was asked, and Pete opened the door. Stepping out, he kept the riot gun ready, just in case.

"Here, boy! Here!" he called.

The two dogs stopped and turned, tongues hanging out. Neither moved in the splash of light in which they stood.

"Kill the lights," Pete said.

Ben turned off the headlights and stepped out of the car, his sidearm drawn and cocked.

The dogs stood perfectly still until Pete called again. "Here, boy. Come on, that's the good fella. Come on. Here." He made a smacking sound with his mouth and the dogs, tails wagging, slowly approached.

"What do you think, Pete?"

"They're all right. Wild dogs either would have been running away or, if they were hungry enough, trying to attack us right now."

The Irish setter reached Pete first and licked his hand. The cocker spaniel ran up, looking for his share of affection.

"What do we do now, Pete?"

"I don't think it's a good idea letting them run. If a homeowner saw them, the guy could panic and blow 'em away. For that matter, so could one of the policemen or volunteers. I think we should try to take them to the dog pound."

"I don't think it's open until morning." Ben took off his cap and ran one hand through his thinning hair.

"We could take them to my hospital and put them in cages there. In the morning we can check on their owners. Both are wearing tags."

"Fine with me."

Pete opened the back door and coaxed the dogs inside.

The sound of a stream flowing into the Wipsipanicon River soothed the dog pack as it slept. The bellies of the dogs were contentedly full and most slept soundly.

The black mongrel opened his yellow eyes on occasion, surveying his charges. Until one bigger, stronger, and meaner came along to challenge him, he would rule with his iron determination.

Off to one side, Trixie lay sleeping. For the first time she felt at ease with her new family. Her belly was no longer empty and she slept soundly. Visions of rabbits darting through a meadow with her in full pursuit unfolded in her brain and she jerked spasmodically as she ran in her sleep.

Day Five

Monday

21

Mayor Kiley P. Crawford glared at the chief of police, Harry Manning. "I have never," he said, his voice low, controlled but nevertheless seething with anger, "heard of anything so stupid before in my life."

"But—" Manning said.

"No 'buts' about it. *Stupid.* For crying out loud! Calling in every available police officer to patrol the streets all night looking for a band of dogs that will probably never set foot inside the city limits was stupid, Harry. What possessed you to do it?"

"Well, when the sheriff—"

"If the sheriff jumped in the river would you follow him?"

Manning stared at the floor before straightening up. "What would you have said, Mayor, if the dogs *had* come into town and the extra police were instrumental in saving lives and in killing the dogs?"

"But that didn't happen, Harry. And it probably never will. Just make certain that this doesn't happen again. Do you realize how much money that cost the city last night? Absolutely irresponsible. That's what your actions were—irresponsible. Don't let it happen again or you'll be back pounding a beat or looking for another line of work."

Manning turned and left the mayor's office.

"We understand, Duke, that there have been twelve people, maybe even fourteen, killed, if we take into consideration the auto accident you claim could have been caused by the dogs. What we can't understand is calling in the off-duty deputies and having them use their own cars at county expense to patrol the county roads. How can you justify that?"

"Apparently the idea of twelve, fourteen people being killed and most of them being eaten by a pack of dogs gone wild doesn't bother you. Well, by God, it bothers the living hell out of me." Duke glowered at the people opposite him.

"Of course it bothers us," County Supervisor Bradley Owens said, looking to his left then right for confirmation from the other elected officials. "It also bothers us that you've spent needless money on something that will more than likely solve itself."

"Let me ask you a question," Duke said, leaning forward to rest his hands on the desk of the supervisory board's chairman. "If you were the dogs, and you found a new supply of food at hand, would you move on?"

Owens stared at him. "I don't understand."

"What I'm saying is there haven't been any reports from any of the surrounding counties or states telling of people being killed and eaten. I'd know about it if there were. It's obvious that the dogs killed a person for the first time here in Cramden County. That means they've turned man-killer. No one will be safe until they're all gunned down and shot."

"The county can't afford to hire extra men and pay out money for gas and oil like we did last night. In fact, it's doubtful if we'll approve the expenditure from last night. What do you say to that?" Owens jutted his jaw out.

"What I've got to say," Duke said, bristling, "is this. I'm an elected official. You people are elected officials. I'm trying to perform my duty. You're ignoring a dangerous situation—one that should be taken care of immediately—and you're worried about spending a few bucks. At the next election, believe me, I'm going to be refreshing a lot of memories about the time the supervisors didn't give a good fuck about the people who elected them."

Owens glared at the sheriff. "Watch your

language. There's a lady present." He bowed to Madonna Smith. "What makes you think it's dogs doing all of this killing? As far as I know, dogs don't kill people."

Duke told them of Pete Reckels's conclusions and the sighting he had made of the pack.

"But he didn't actually see the dogs killing anyone, did he?"

Before Duke Little could say anything, Madonna Smith, the only woman on the board of supervisors, said, "I don't think I can visualize my Pomeranian, Giant, killing a person. In fact, I've been sitting here trying to visualize just such a thing, and it's rather comical."

Duke turned to face the tall woman. "You wouldn't think it was very funny if a dog was tearing out your throat and then working at ripping open your belly to gobble down your guts, lady."

"Oh, my good God!" Smith said, throwing a hand over her mouth and struggling to her feet. She stumbled from the room but not before the sound of her vomit hitting the tile floor of the supervisors room could be heard.

"I hope you're satisfied, Duke," Owens said, standing. "That wasn't very nice, you know."

"Sometimes, the truth *isn't* very nice. I'm going to see if I can get a court order to allow you people to view the cadavers of the Sayman family. If I can, you're going to look and look long and hard. Then we'll see if you're willing to pass this thing off so lightly."

Spinning on his heel, Duke stormed from the room, slamming the door behind him.

Owens leaped to his feet and followed him. Throwing open the door, he shouted down the hall, "As far as the board is concerned, dogs had nothing to do with the killings. Dogs are *not* responsible and there'll be no extra patrols and no volunteers in the county. Do you hear me, Sheriff?"

Ignoring the yelling man, Duke turned into his office and slammed the door behind him.

Owens stood in the hall for a moment before realizing that a door across and down the hall had opened. Kiley Crawford stepped into full view.

"I couldn't agree with you more, Brad. I'm not allowing any patrols over and above the normal number in town. And curtailing the use of volunteers is an excellent idea. Why, untrained people walking around town with guns could get someone hurt. Don't you agree?"

Owens nodded and turned to reenter the supervisors office. He looked at his fellow supervisors, noting that Madonna Smith hadn't yet returned. "Duke is going to have to understand," he said, "that the county just doesn't have the money to run this type of operation. Apparently, the city doesn't either. We'll have to stand firm on this one."

The three men facing him nodded solemnly.

The sun had long since disappeared and the

pack worked in its own peculiar brand of group nervousness. The black mongrel growled when a collie and German shepherd began fighting. When the rumbling sound pierced their own growls and snarls the two quit. In the last day or two they had picked up two more members in the pack besides Trixie. Numbering almost 40 now, the pack was almost too big. They'd have to kill more often to satisfy so many.

But they had made a great discovery. Man was easy prey. Man tasted good. They could outrun man. If they were capable of making a decision, they had made it to follow the line of least resistance. Most of the animals, with the exception of the last three to join, had been running with the pack since before they had killed the first man. Each was vicious, mean, wild, and when they tasted blood the frenzy that came over the pack seemed to come from one source, one common intelligence.

The mongrel walked down to the edge of the stream and satisfied his thirst. The others followed suit and when the last had drunk his fill, the leader trotted back to the top of the bank and peered out over the Wipsipanicon River. He languidly turned his head north, then to the south.

Behind him, the pack grew restless. They were hungry and wanted to eat.

Turning once more to the north, the dog wheeled about and trotted off in a southerly direction, along the river's bank, toward Laughton.

The pack followed him, eagerly anticipating food.

22

"Much as I'd like to, honey, I think I'd better get home. The little lady'll be up waiting for me with the shotgun when I get there as it is." Jake Lanters squinted at the woman sitting next to him at the bar of the Office Bar and Grill. He couldn't remember her name. All he knew was, she wanted him to go to a hotel, spend 50 bucks on her and have "a party" as she put it.

"If you think more of your wife than me, then go ahead, big spender," Lila Brooks said, sneering the words. Slipping off the stool, she made her way down the bar toward the back of the room.

Jake watched her go, eyeballing her ass wiggle in three-four time while she walked in four-four march tempo. He imagined her naked. She had a helluva set of knockers on her and if he had met her a couple of hours earlier, there was no telling what might have happened. But it was almost eleven o'clock now and he should have been home by five-thirty. There'd be hell to pay, but time had just sort of slipped away from him.

Throwing a five-dollar bill on the bar, he stood. At 50, he found he couldn't stand up under the influence of alcohol as he had when he was younger. Shuffling his feet to make certain he didn't stumble, he went to the door and sucked in the cool night air. It was fresher than that of the bar he had just left. Now all he had to do was find his car and he'd be able to go home.

Walking in the opposite direction of the place where he had left his automobile, Jake soon grew more confused than he was when he left the bar. The damned thing had to be around someplace. When he came to an alley he stopped. Maybe he should have gone with Lila. There wasn't that much between he and his wife anymore, and a good roll in the hay might have sobered him up enough to at least find his car. A crooked smile crossed his lips when he thought of Lila running her hand along his leg, *accidentally* brushing the growing bulge in his pants. She apparently knew how to turn a man on, which was more than he could say for Jeannie, his wife. Now that he thought of it, he couldn't recall having been so aroused since he had been first married. Maybe he should go back to the bar and get Lila. Turning, he looked behind him. The bar was gone. Nowhere to be seen. How far had he walked? The Office Bar and Grill was on Third Street. He was on Riverfront. How had that happened? At least he knew now where he was and could get back to Third Street by going through the alley yawning before him like a hungry mouth.

Jake started into the black maw, half walking, half stumbling. He didn't see the two-by-four piece of lumber wedged between the step of a back door and a heavy trash bin. When he came to it his foot struck it and he cursed as he fell. His head struck the edge of the trash bin and the last thing he remembered was the smarting pain in his ankle where he had tripped and the rush of dizziness engulfing him as he sank into unconsciousness.

Ben Rathe didn't let the squad car move much faster than 15 miles an hour. Why should he? He'd only get finished with the tour of the riverfront and the seedy factory neighborhood that much faster, which meant he'd have to move uptown where there might be more action. Still, he found tonight rather unnerving. The streets were practically deserted. He recalled, after the first hour when he came on duty, that the traffic was super light for a Monday. Not that that particular day was any busier than Tuesday or Wednesday, but for every ten cars that should have been on the streets he figured he saw maybe one, and that one seemed to be hurrying someplace. In the last hour he recalled having seen exactly two cars. The sidewalks were deserted as well. People, regardless of the mayor's order to withdraw the extra patrols, were still reacting to the threat of the dog pack possibly coming into Laughton.

"Car Eight?" The radio crackled to life, breaking the strange quiet in the automobile. "Over."

"Car Eight. Go ahead," Ben said after picking up the microphone. "Over."

"What gives tonight?" Mary Jane Adams asked. "Over."

"Repeat. Over."

"I said, what gives tonight? There hasn't been a report of anything for the last forty-five minutes. It's downright scary. Over."

"I know where you're coming from," Ben said, picturing the slightly built black girl in his mind's eyes. Cute as anything he'd ever seen, she couldn't have stood much over five feet tall, if that. She wasn't a regular police officer and worked only as dispatcher. "Over."

"What's it like where you're at? Over."

"Hardly anybody on the street. No traffic at all. It's like being in a movie where the monster that ate Buffalo is ready to pounce on another city and its been evacuated. Over."

"Stay tuned. I'm going to check the other cars. Car Six? Come in, Car Six. Over."

The black mongrel padded along the riverfront. The going had become difficult since coming into town. Until they had reached the industrial section the pack had meandered along the Wipsipanicon River bank, entering the city park and then following the shoreline around until they came to the first loading dock at a warehouse. Swinging to their right, the animals had entered a street and, although there weren't any people around at that hour, they surveyed the area before continuing on their way. Now they were well within the riverfront area.

The leader stopped, raising his snout in the air. He smelled something. He smelled food. He smelled man. The scent became stronger when the pack passed the alley way and stopped, reading the air coming from it. Definitely convinced that a man was in the blackness someplace, the pack entered, moving slowly. The shadows became lighter shades of gray as they entered, leaving the bright street light behind. The mongrel's yellow eyes scanned the area in front of him and then he knew the man lay within striking distance. Why hadn't he moved to run? Inching forward, the black dog sniffed at the still form lying in the alley. When the man suddenly moaned he jumped back half a step and cocked his head to one side. Assured after a moment that the man wouldn't move anymore, he moved forward again until he stood over him. Straddling his body, the dog studied the supine man for another long minute.

Jake opened his eyes, and the growling black mongrel held his ground.

"What the hell?" Jake mumbled when he

looked up into the snarling face of the dog. "Get the hell away from me." He struck out with a fist, catching the dog in the ribs.

The mongrel lashed out with his teeth, catching Jake's exposed throat in them. Waggling his head back and forth, as if killing a rat, the dog pulled, tugging at the windpipe. Jake gurgled as he choked, desperately beating at the beast attacking him. His eyes grew wider when he saw the reflection of the other dogs' eyes in the half light of the alley.

Jake heard a soft tearing sound and a popping noise as a piece of his windpipe was pulled out. He heard a slushing sucking without realizing what the sound was, as his blood spurted out into the face of the dog, who swallowed in one piece the section of his windpipe.

The other animals, sensing the man's death, closed in and in minutes Jake's body was being devoured by the pack.

Ben Rathe glanced in the rearview mirror. Nothing, just like the street spreading before him. Downtown was as dead as when a snowstorm would hit in the midst of winter, except it was summertime and a more than pleasant evening. Since it had rained a few days before the air had remained cooler. But the people of Laughton were undoubtedly frightened. There could be no other explanation. They had been scared of the out-of-doors ever since hearing the news of a dog pack gone wild possibly invading the city limits. At first he had smiled to himself, thinking that people would begin questioning the sanity of the police and reporters making the announcement. But the more he thought about it, and the more he had talked with Pete Reckels on his last tour of duty, he was convinced that the dogs, if they did come into the city, would be a major threat to the citizenry.

Ben eased the car around the corner of Main and Eighth. He had to make his round of the riverfront before taking one last spin around the downtown area. Then he could think about going to headquarters and checking out. Tonight would be a snap. He hadn't made an arrest or seen anyone to warn about driving too fast or telling kids to break up their impromptu meeting on some street corner.

The squad car rolled along the street, making the only sounds that could be heard if there had been someone around to hear them, other than the driver.

The riverfront might offer him a drunk to carry off to the tank for the night. If that could happen he wouldn't worry about going stark raving mad. Thankfully, this was a rare occasion and wouldn't happen again in a thousand years. He hadn't joined the police force to merely drive around a deserted town to make certain there weren't any wrong-doings by nonexistent people. Ben craved action. The sort of action being a policeman would give him.

He turned onto Riverfront Drive. Even most of the taverns had closed up early. Lights from three bars still burned, their signs blinking enticingly to passersby, except tonight there weren't any. Riverfront catered more to the factory workers and people who worked in warehouses along the waterfront. Not that it was a skid row area, although if Laughton needed a designated area called skid row, Riverfront Drive would be selected.

When his headlights reflected from the eyes of a dog, standing in an alleyway, Ben slowed even more. Dog? What was a dog doing on Riverfront? He pressed the accelerator more and the car picked up speed. When he got within 50 feet of the animal he could see it was a collie, wagging its tail.

Ben relaxed. It wasn't a wild, vicious dog after all. Still, he felt he should probably investigate since the alert, as far as the policemen on duty were concerned, was still on. Besides, he needed something to break the damnable monotony he had suffered all evening. Then the collie turned and reentered the dark alleyway.

Trixie, her belly full, turned and walked slowly back in the direction from which the pack had entered the alley. When she reached the street she stopped, looking in both directions, sniffing the air. She didn't like this place. There were too many heavy odors and peculiar, greasy smells that bothered her. She longed for her home.

Where was her master?

Then she saw the lights of a vehicle slowly coming toward her. Perhaps it was her master. She didn't know, but she still associated man with her life of pleasantry on the farm where she had lived for the last six years. A whine, born of loneliness, threaded its way through her chest up her throat and she opened her mouth, her tongue lolling out partway. Blood stained her fur just above the lips, but she didn't mind that right now.

She continued staring at the bright lights as the car neared, until the black mongrel barked once. Turning, she hurried back to the pack. The leader spun about, trotting toward the far end of the alley, the others right behind him, turning the corner several seconds before the car entered the alley.

Ben shook his head as he signaled a left turn. Big deal. Chasing a dog to make sure it isn't vicious. He'd rather be chasing some desperate criminal who wanted to shoot it out in some strange place.

The policeman hit the bright lights when he entered the narrow passageway, lighting it up more than it had been. Allowing the idle of the motor to pull the car along, he peered ahead. The dog was gone.

A split second later he saw the body of Jake Lanters, its white skin that wasn't blood stained gleaming in the reflection of the bright headlights. Ben slammed the brakes on. What was that? It couldn't possibly be what he first thought.

Picking up the microphone, he said, "This is Car Eight. I'm in the alley between Riverfront and Third Street. I'm leaving my car to investigate what looks like a body. I'll be right back. Over."

The radio crackled. "Okay, Car Eight. Holding. Over."

Ben drew his sidearm and cocked it. He wasn't about to take any chances, not after the way Pete Reckels had told him dogs killed and how the bodies of the victims had been. He slowly opened the door and listened to nothing, other than the surge of his own heartbeat pounding violently in his body. Peering back behind the car, he searched for any signs of movement. Nothing.

Slipping one leg out, he stood up and withdrew the other. He gripped his piece, holding it at the ready in both hands. Stepping around the opened door, he walked through the flood of lights in front of the squad car.

He took one quick look. The body lay on its back, arms and legs, what was left of them, thrown out in all directions. Bits of clothing clung here and there, but for the most part the man was naked, dead and his belly ripped open.

Ben spun on his heel. "Aw, shit!" he managed before vomiting his last meal onto the brick pavement. Coughing, gagging, retching, he emptied his stomach and staggered back to the car.

"This is Car Eight. I've just found a body in the alley. It's been partially eaten and from what I was told by the vet who rode with me last night, dogs probably did it. You'd better warn the other cars that the dog pack is somewhere around the riverfront. I saw one but no more. Over."

"I read you, Car Eight. Anything else? Over."

"Yeah. What do I do for my stomach? I just heaved my guts out."

23

The tan-and-black bitch nipped at Trixie's heels, urging her to move faster. Trixie broke into a trotting sort of gallop and soon caught up to the dog ahead of her, the other bitch right behind her.

The dogs continued down Third Street, suddenly stopping when the black mongrel halted several doors away from the lighted entrance of a bar. He heard voices and held his position without moving. The others did the same and, looking like statues, the dogs stared at the lighted area 60 feet away.

"G'night, Toby," a woman's voice cried out into the quiet night.

"S'long, Lila. See you tomorrow night?"

"Probably. Pickin' sure sucked tonight. Ah, you aren't interested in a little action tonight, are you, Toby?"

"Naw. I'm too tired. 'Sides, I couldn't afford you. Not based on what I had run through the till tonight."

"Yeah. Things are tough all over, aren't they?"

"Sure are. 'Night."

" 'Night." The woman stepped out of the entrance way and stood for a moment, spotlighted by the overhead illuminated sign that spelled THE OFFICE. Undecided she finally turned and walked away from the bar and the pack of dogs, which she hadn't seen.

The mongrel raised his snout. *Man.* The man smell, only this time it had something extra with it. He snorted quietly, trying to cleanse his olefactory organ, to reexamine the air. When he tried he still identified the source of the smell as man—food—but another, strange odor was there. To him it made no difference. The smell of food was there—it was right—it was for him and the others. He stepped forward to follow the prostitute, who entered small pools of light cast on the sidewalk from streetlamps as she walked, only to be swallowed up in the dark.

Eddie Jorgeson rolled the glass between his hands. The goddamned thing was empty again. His capacity for liquor never ceased to amaze him—more so when he was loaded then when he was sober. The latter condition seemed to be more rare as the days passed.

"Hey, Toby. I'm empty again."

"Why the hell don't you go home, Eddie?

Christ, there's no business and I'm tired as hell doing nothing."

"Hey? What's wrong wit' my bus—bus-money?"

"It's not that. But what I'm going to make on that double shot of rye you want, won't pay the light bill to keep the lights on. Understand?"

"Turn the fuckin' things off and pour me another, goddammit!" Half expecting the bartender to wait on him, Eddie's head bobbed to his right and he peered out through the glass door. Where had the woman gone? She had been standing there one minute before. He had gotten a charge out of watching her walk. When she asked him to go to bed with her for $50 he had refused, knowing full well that the amount of liquor he had consumed would prevent him from performing adequately. Besides, he didn't have 50 bucks on him. But the question as to where she had gone puzzled him. He had listened to the bartender and the woman talking then, just like that, she was gone. It was amazing.

Eddie's eyes bugged when he saw the parade of dogs passing the door. The first one, a huge black mongrel, didn't even bother to look in and then Eddie saw the others, following him. Each had their attention on something that Eddie couldn't see. What the hell was going on? He stared some more and when the last one was gone he turned back to the bartender.

"Thanks for the drink, Toby." He lifted the empty glass to his lips and downed the air inside.

"What?" the bartender asked without raising his head from the girlie magazine he was reading.

"Shay, turn the channel, will ya? The fuckin' dog show is over."

"What?" Toby looked up. The television set was off. The guy was drinking out of an empty glass that he was shaking over his open mouth. It was definitely time to close up. "Okay, Eddie, that's it. I'm closed. See you tomorrow night." Toby got to his feet, walking around the bar toward his last customer.

When Toby helped him off the stool Eddie straightened up and said. "Puh-lese, shir, I can make it on my own."

"You driving?" Toby asked, suspiciously eyeing the man.

"No, shir. I'm the deshig-nated walker. I don't own a car anymore. Say, thanks for the dog show. That was nice of you, but it went by kinda quick."

"Yeah. Yeah," Toby said, helping the drunk toward the door.

"Never saw so many fuckin' dogs in town in one place before. Did it cos' you much to have 'em brought here?" He looked up into Toby's face.

"Geezus, your breath is awful. Do you want me to call you a cab?"

"Why would you do that? I'm not a cab."

"I think I'd—" Toby stopped. What had he said about dogs? "What dogs?"

"The ones you had paraded by the front door for me. Or was it on telebision?"

Toby frowned. Dogs? Hadn't there been

something on TV last night about dogs, and that people should stay inside and not go out? Sure. Lila had mentioned it, too, but he hadn't paid that much attention. That would explain why he hadn't been the least bit busy tonight. Not that Monday night was ever that much to run around the block about. But usually he had more than three people in. "You really saw some dogs, Eddie?"

"O' course, I did. Why?"

Toby set him down at one of the tables and said, "Stay right there. Don't move. I've got a call to make." The more Toby thought about it, the more the story came back to him. There had been some people killed someplace and the authorities seemed to suggest that the dogs that were thought to be responsible might be on their way to Laughton. Toby felt it was his duty to call the police. If he did, he wouldn't have to worry about anything where his conscience was concerned. If he didn't and something did happen, he'd never be able to live with himself.

After he dialed the police he went back to the front of the bar and found Eddie, head down on the table, fast asleep.

Slowly the pack closed in on the woman. They didn't hurry. They had no need. They could run her to ground anytime they pleased. It seemed as if the pack was almost indifferent, but as the woman covered several feet with each step, the pack was covering three times as many in their easy, lopping gait.

When a distance of 15 feet separated them from their quarry the black mongrel charged, leaping on the woman's back. She went to the sidewalk hard, in the shadows of a car parked along the street, which blocked out most of the light from the intersection lamp overhead. She screamed once when she rolled over on her back, only to stare into the growling, ugly face of the black mongrel, which was framed by the hungry-looking dogs of the pack, glaring at her around their leader.

"Car Eight? There's a man calling into the station, telling of a group of dogs one of his patrons saw pass by his establishment. Would you like to check it out, considering you're only a block or so away? Over."

"What about the body here in the alley? Is the ambulance and another car on the way? Over."

"The other car should be backing you up in less than a minute. The ambulance is on its way. Don't worry, from what you said, the body ain't going to get up and leave. Over." The woman dispatcher chuckled under her breath.

Ben frowned. That hadn't been the least bit funny. Off in the distance he could hear the wail of the ambulance drawing nearer. Just then, a squad car turned into the alley to come up behind his. "Okay. The other unit just arrived and the ambulance is coming too. Give me the address. Over."

"It's the Office on Third Street. You know the place? Over."

"Of course. Ten-four." He turned on his emergency lights and told the other officer where he was going before taking off down the alley toward Third Street.

The dogs, tearing and biting at the body of the prostitute, licked at the blood spewing from the gaping wounds. When the mongrel growled loudly they stopped shaking the cadaver. The leader peered into the distance and watched the lights of a car turning the corner. They stopped less than a block away and a man got out to run into a building. Turning, the leader studied the bloodied body of the woman for a moment. They'd have to abandon it. He felt threatened by the man in the car for some reason he couldn't understand.

Pivoting, he took off down the street away from the Office, away from the car and its threatening man, and away from the food they had just killed. Heading into the first alley they came to, the pack slowed when the leader did and stopped when he did. On both sides, smells of people food filled the air in the alley. Meat predominated the smells emanating from the garbage heaped up by the restaurants whose kitchens emptied onto the narrow passageway.

The mongrel reared up, pawing at the stuffed can, and promptly tipped it, sending a spray of discarded foodstuffs onto the ground. The dogs attacked it at once, some eating at the garbage on the ground, others rooting among and finding other such treasure cans.

The leader stepped back. He felt satisfied. He had fed well on the first man they had killed and had tasted the blood of the woman. Walking away from the pack, he followed the different scents in the alley until one led him to a storm sewer drain. Lying down on his belly, he stuck his head in, separating the pungent, damp smells into different categories. He smelled food. Live food. He had eaten on it before when he and the others had killed the scurrying little animals around different farms they had visited at night. Snorting to clear his nose, he read the different odors over and over until each one was imbedded in his brain.

After a while the pack, satisfied with the garbage, came up behind him and waited. When he finished he got to his feet and trotted off toward Riverfront Drive.

Ben Rathe stood outside his squad car, microphone in hand, peering into the street. "That's correct. He didn't say how many, but I believe the guy. After all, I found the body of a victim not that far away. Only yards in fact. Over."

"We'll dispatch another unit to help you and Car Fourteen. The duty captain says if you spot them, you're to radio in. Then we'll send you all the help you need. Over."

"Ten-four," Ben said, hanging the microphone on the dash after he got behind the wheel. He pulled away from the curb, cruising in the direction the prostitute had taken, according to the bartender. Wondering if she were all right, he hurried along toward the apartment house he had been directed to as the home of the whore.

Ben had traveled less than a block when he saw the white skin of an arm sticking out behind a car.

Grabbing the microphone again, he barked his location and information into it, waiting until the dispatcher assured him an ambulance was on its way. He pulled over to the curb and got out, his gun at the ready again. He wasn't about to take a chance of getting out unprepared and run the risk that the beasts were still around.

Preparing himself for the sight, he turned away at first glimpse but then, steeling himself even more, he forced himself to look. She had been killed, her throat torn open. But it was the sight of her breasts that held him in a viselike grip. Both had been bitten and pulled on until the skin at the top and inside had given way, flopping them over her ribs. Stooping, he touched her forehead. It was still warm. It hadn't been long. Strangely, her face hadn't been touched. Ben knew her by sight. She was in her mid-thirties and an attractive woman. A real knockout in her earlier years, he was certain, although he hadn't known her then.

The wail of another ambulance siren wound its

way through the city toward the police officer. As soon as the vehicle ground to a stop, Ben hurried to his own car. After notifying the dispatcher that the ambulance had arrived, he told them that he was taking off, that the body was still warm and that the dogs couldn't have gotten that far away. Ordered to go ahead with the search, Ben hung the microphone on the dash hook and pulled away from the curb. He had no idea where he was going to look. Where would dogs go after killing a man and then a woman? Where did dogs hide? He remembered Pete Reckels telling him that that was the big question. Since the dogs were more or less nomads even the veterinarian had no idea where the best place to begin looking might be.

All Ben could do would be to roam up and down the street, hoping beyond hope that he would spot them and that they could be shot.

The dogs froze when an automobile drove by. The driver, either too busy driving or not very observant, continued on his way without seeing the 40 dogs standing along the walk, not moving. Once the car had passed the mongrel took off again, hugging the walls of the buildings they passed, keeping to the shadows, as if he knew it would be more difficult for them to be seen.

They froze again when a taxi shot by.

Slowly working their way back toward the river, the pack had a box car sitting on a siding between them and the street when the patrol car drove by. Even though they couldn't be seen, the pack came to a standstill and didn't move until the mongrel started once more toward the river.

The pack needed a place to sleep, and some of the places they had passed on their way into town would offer such a haven.

In the back of the mongrel's brain the memories of the sewer and the rats that lived there replayed.

Day Six

Tuesday

24

"Did you understand my question, Mr. Mayor?" the reporter from *The Laughton Lantern* asked.

"Yes, I understood it, and I don't appreciate you people from the media trying to purposely make your elected leaders look foolish," Mayor Crawford said, his face red.

"I'll repeat the question for you, Mr. Mayor. Do you still maintain that the idea of curtailing the use of volunteers was a good one?"

"Where did you get that?"

"Those are your own words, Mr. Mayor. You said them to County Supervisor Bradley Owens in the hall outside your office. Isn't that right?"

"I—well—that is—I might have said something at the time that might have sounded like that, but I don't remember exactly what was said. Why is that so important? You people have stormed into my office demanding answers to questions about a couple of people being killed on the streets of Laughton. That's an everyday occurrence in a city such as Chicago, you know."

"I don't think it's necessary to remind you that Laughton is a far cry from Chicago, Mr. Mayor," Nick Woodson, the reporter persisted. "Besides, those two people might still be alive if the patrols had been maintained the way they were Sunday. Do you agree with that?"

"No. If those people were to die, nothing anyone could have done would have prevented it from happening."

Woodson grinned broadly. "Then you *are* saying it was a good idea to pull the extra people off patrol?"

The other news people in the room held their breath, waiting for an answer to the volatile question.

"All I can say," Crawford said, his voice dropping several decibles, "is that the people who died shouldn't have been where they were in the first place. As I understand it, the man was inebriated and the woman was a prostitute—a lawbreaker. Are we to shed tears over such people—such low-lifes?" Crawford immediately blushed, knowing he had said the wrong thing again. The paper and television would have a banner day with that one.

"What about you, Mr. Owens?" Cathy Johnson

from KREJ-TV asked, addressing the supervisory board chairman. "How do you feel about the killings? Will there be any more volunteers used on the county roads?"

Owens held his hands up and every eye in the room rested on him. Crawford had called him over when the reporters first invaded the mayor's office. Thus far the mayor had totally blown his image, the city's image, and was pulling down with him just about every elected official in the city and county. He had to say something that would soothe the press. For an instant his eyes locked with those of Woodson. The reporter smirked but said nothing.

"I feel all of us, the members of the news media, the mayor's office, and that of the county supervisors should be working together on this, rather than doing our level best to argue, infight, and make each other look silly and foolish." He glared at Woodson, who looked away.

Owens continued. "The manner in which the situation was presented to the mayor and the county officials was not made out to be of such an urgent nature. Had we known the severity of the predicament, I'm sure our decision would have reflected it. As it was, we acted without having all of the information. Just as I was called over here a few minutes ago I was about to call the Highway Patrol and the National Guard, requesting help in running these feral dogs to ground. Since the most recent attacks were here in the city I feel that there should be a concentrated effort to find their trail here and follow it."

The door at the back of the room opened, and Duke Little stepped in. Owens blanched at the sight of the lawman. The best he could do would be to pray the lawman didn't tell the news people exactly what was said. Owens felt he was fighting for his political life, thanks to Crawford's ineptness. At least Little hadn't heard the last statement. He was sure to read it in the paper or hear it on the radio or television, but by that time the dogs might be caught and everything would be back to normal.

"Are you saying that the police and the sheriff's office failed in their duty to inform you?" Woodson asked.

Before Owens could answer and before Duke Little could react, Cathy Johnson said, "What do you expect the National Guard and Highway Patrol to do?"

"If we can't find the dogs here in the city, we'll request air support from both the Guard and the Patrol. That way we can blanket the entire county in a couple of hours and save countless dollars in the process."

Duke, at the back of the room, bit his lip. He didn't want to get into a public squabble with the likes of Crawford and Owens. Turning the knob, he stepped out of the room without the reporters being aware of the fact that he had been there. To Duke, it sounded as if the supervisors were going to cooperate with him and let him run a complete search of the county after the city was covered.

Hurrying down the hall, Duke made his way toward Harry Manning's office. They might as well jump the gun and have their plans underway by the time word came to them to search for and hunt down and kill the pack of dogs.

Pete inhaled. It was going to be hot. According to the reports on television last night and radio this morning, the temperature would be over 90 degrees by noon. The few days of cool air had been great but now Laughton was about to reenter the furnace of summer.

He hurried down the steps, leaving the cool confines of the apartment house, to the Bronco. Cranking down the windows before he got in, he let the stale, already warm air out. He climbed in, and after turning on the motor, switched the air conditioning to high. A warm blast washed over him before the air changed radically to cool. After putting the window up he backed out of his parking place and headed for Amy's. He had called her as soon as he heard about the killings of the two people down along the riverfront. He had shuddered when he pictured in his mind the man and woman lying on the streets. Although there had been no description of the bodies, Pete felt confident that the pack was responsible. The reporter had said the condition of the bodies had led the investigating officers to suspect that the man and woman had been killed by dogs. An additional report had said that a patron of the

Office Bar and Grill had seen a large number of dogs run past the glass door of the bar.

Pete shook his head. He loved animals. He never would have entertained the thought of becoming a veterinarian if his feelings had been any less. Still, here was a situation wherein dogs, according to the sages man's best friend, had reverted to being wild like their ancestors of hundreds of thousands of years before. It was strange to say the least.

Turning into Amy's driveway, he slowed, stopped, and honked the horn.

Amy poked her head out the back door. "I'll be with you in a minute, Pete."

Switching off the ignition key, Pete got out and strode to the back door. A movement in the back yard caught his attention and he turned to look at the cream-colored Samoyed bitch in the yard. He entered the kitchen and found Amy about ready to leave.

"Do you think it's wise to leave Duchess tied up outside?"

"I do every other day. Why not today?"

"You haven't thought about the dogs being in town? Remember? I told you that two people had been killed."

"I wasn't that wide awake when you called. I thought you said something like that, but I wasn't sure. The stations had already given the news when I turned the radio on and the morning TV news won't be on for another ten minutes. What happened?"

"A drunk and a prostitute were killed last night down on Riverfront Street and in that neighborhood."

"And the mayor thought it was a waste of money to have volunteers with guns out to patrol the streets with the police. I wonder what he's thinking now?"

Pete shrugged. "No idea. But I think you should let me take Duchess to my hospital until this is over. She should have been in heat by now and if she suddenly enters and the pack gets a whiff of her, they'll be all over the place."

"I think that's going to extremes, Pete. Tell you what. I won't let her outside today. I'll put her in the garage and tonight you can take her for a run. Fair enough?"

Pete hesitated for a minute. The garage should prove to be safe enough even if the pack did come around. But what then? Wouldn't that be endangering the whole neighborhood?

"I'll even throw in dinner with homemade pie and an evening's entertainment that money can't buy. What do you say?"

"All right. Nine chances out of ten the dogs are back in the county by now anyway. Besides, your house is on the farthest edge of town away from the river. The dogs would have to come all the way through town to get here."

After putting Duchess in the garage Pete and Amy left for the courthouse.

Minutes later, when they pulled up into the courthouse parking lot, Pete turned off the motor.

"Where are you going?" Amy asked, turning to face him without getting out.

"I'm walking you to the door. Portal to portal service, my dear. Besides, I want to see the sheriff."

Without saying anything more, Amy got out and walked to the front of the car, where Pete met her. Taking her arm, he escorted her to the door and followed her inside.

"What time is good for tonight?" she asked.

"You're the hostess. Name it."

"Can you pick me up when I'm finished working?"

Pete nodded.

When they reached the county attorney's office he opened the door and held it while she went in. Al Niedles spun around. When he recognized his secretary and Pete he said, "You know, I'm almost ashamed to be an elected official of this county."

"Why? Good morning, Al," Amy said, covering her smile.

"Good morning. I just heard about the so-called press conference down the hall. Apparently, the mayor and the chairman of the supervisory board made total fools of themselves with the media."

"Wow," Pete said, "the press sure doesn't waste any time does it? What happened?"

Al told them the secondhand story he had heard from Cathy Johnson, the TV news reporter.

Pete could hardly help laughing. If the mayor and the supervisors had seen the condition of any of the bodies, they'd have called out the U.S. Army as well as the Guard and the Highway Patrol.

"All I can say," Niedels continued, "is that it's a darn good thing no one important was killed."

Pete and Amy sobered immediately.

"What the hell do you mean by that?" Pete asked, glaring at the smaller man.

"We can be thankful that it was a drunk and a whore who were killed. That's all."

Pete could hardly believe what the man had said. What did he mean by that? "What about Johnny O'Malley? Seventeen years old. Wasn't he important, to use your words? What about Joe Eppson? He was important. The Sayman family—all seven members—were important members of the community. And as I understand it, the man who was killed last night. Ah, Jake—Jake Lanters—was a small businessman. Married. Family. Important member of the community, Al."

"Well, I—that is—I never—I—I think you know what I meant, Pete."

"I haven't got the foggiest idea where the hell you were coming from with that one. I've got to go. Just a word of advice, Al. Don't say that to anyone else. Otherwise you'll fit in perfectly with the mayor and the supervisors." He turned to Amy. "You make certain you're ready for me tonight. I'll be here at four-thirty."

Amy winked at him without Al seeing her do it.

"Okay. Don't forget your promise to walk Duchess tonight."

Pausing at the door, Pete turned back and said, "Not with the entertainment you've promised for tonight," Pete glanced at Al, whose mouth hung agape. "She's rented a couple of movies for tonight, Al."

Amy turned away when the door closed, biting her lip to keep from laughing.

Pete hurried down the hall toward the sheriff's office. He found the lawman with a map of the county on the desk in front of him.

After saying good morning Duke looked at the map, tapping a pencil on the edge of the large sheet. "Where do you think the dogs might be right at this moment, Pete?"

Pete stepped around the desk to stand behind the sheriff. "Where were they last seen?"

Duke pointed to the area of Laughton's riverfront. "Here on Riverfront Street, a short distance from the place where the woman was found."

"And no one else saw them?"

"There were a couple of patrol cars down there after the bodies were found, prowling around, searching, but they reported nothing."

"Any reports from any other place in town?"

"None."

"If they're still close to town, I'd venture a guess that they might be along the river someplace. I understand that you and the chief are going to get the cooperation of the mayor and the supervisors. Right?"

'Yeah. Finally. It only took a couple of more deaths and the news media to push those chicken-livered patsies into a corner."

25

The dogs walked slowly along the river bank, keeping beneath trees and low growing bushes, preferring to stay close to the water that seemed to give a degree or two cooler breath of air. Behind them, in the north, lay the city where they had had to abandon two kills the night before. The loose food that they had found, the dead food they had eaten had given them sustenance, but the desire for blood and fresh kills pulsated through the pack with one beat, one purpose, one thought. The dogs wanted more human flesh to satisfy their appetites.

Most of the dogs, their noses to the ground, searched for any tell-tale sign or scent that an animal suitable for killing and eating was close by. Those dogs, such as Trixie, who had recently joined the band, loped along behind the others, carelessly smelling the ground, the grass and weeds, the spoors, no matter how faint they might be. In time, given enough exposure, the collie bitch would contribute to her own keeping, but for now she would be among those who ate last.

Overhead, the sun's rays radiated the fore-casted warmth, drenching the countryside in heat, sweat, and humidity. The dogs, their tongues hanging out, occasionally stopped at the river's edge to lap enough water to satisfy their thirst.

The pack had ranged a short distance from the river, criss-crossing various trails after they had left the city. A few animals had been killed and devoured on the spot. Several fights had broken out when two or more dogs became involved in disputes over ownership of a particular dead mouse, rabbit or bird. Birds had always proven to be the hardest prey to capture and kill. Those four-legged beasts confined to the earth like the dogs, themselves, were much easier to catch.

The black mongrel, a few yards ahead of the pack, stopped beneath the shade of a large tree. He was hungry, as were the rest of the animals. They had not stopped hunting for an instant since having to desert the two big kills they had made. Most animals they could kill were lying up in the heat, safe and cool in their burrows, waiting for nightfall before venturing forth. The dogs, hungry, would have to find a cool spot to rest and resume their search for food once the sun was gone.

Reversing his direction, the mongrel passed through the pack who turned to follow him. Heading back upstream seemed the right thing to do. They had been successful in finding large prey and had managed to kill some of them. The pack would have to find a place that would be cool and afford protection from the heat of the sun.

After retracing almost the entire route they had taken since leaving the city the dogs came to a large rock opening, protruding from the earth and feeding into the river. It had been passed on the down trip. The opening resembled more of a cave than a pipe or tube. The smooth rock work that formed the mouth had been carefully laid by hand years before to carry off the overflow of water from heavy rains and to tranport to the river the waste and refuse of the city. The only current function of the sewer was to carry rainwater since the city had built a sewage disposal plant between the river and the city. The constant flow of water trickling from the mouth was from that plant that changed the refuse to almost pure water and redeposited it into the river.

The black mongrel walked up to the opening, sniffing the cool air pouring from it. He recognized the smells and odors as the same ones he had discovered last night after having to abandon the second kill. Inside, there were small animals the pack could kill and, from the air coming out, he recognized it as a good place to rest and sleep.

He turned, surveying the pack with his yellow eyes. Facing the opening again, he slowly entered, avoiding the stream of water in the lowest part of the sewer.

The pack watched him go in, some cocking their heads to one side, then the other. Were they to follow him? Where was he going? They moved closer, noses in the air, reading the smells themselves issuing from the dark. One by one they entered, following their leader. Their soft padding feet made barely a sound as they moved. On occasion one or another would whine and stop immediately when the answer echoed off the roof overhead. Opting to move without making noise, the pack trotted into the blackness.

Trixie hung back. She had entered the sewer, hesitantly inching her way inside. The dark under her porch at home had always been welcome. Cool, dry, safe, she could look outside and see the world—her world from where she rested. But this strange place was frightening. Turning, she looked back. The bright sunlight pouring onto the river bank and the river beyond seemed more welcome. But the pack was going inside. She had to go along. She had no pack other than this. She had no family other than this. Ever since her human had not come back to the farm, she had been alone except for this pack.

Hanging back, she reluctantly followed the others.

Up ahead, the black leader, his eyes accustomed to the dark now, looked left and right as he moved. Shadows of deeper recesses off to each side would be investigated later. Farther on, he would find the small animals he knew lived in this place.

When a splash of light brighly illuminated the area ahead the dog stopped. Advancing warily, he entered the spot of sunlight gushing through the sewer drain overhead. He peered up. Strange muffled sounds filtered down from above as cars and trucks drove along the street.

When he looked off to his right and to his left, he could see two more tunnels. One on either side. At this junction an elevated walkway perhaps two feet above the floor of the sewer itself ran along both sides and in all three directions. Jumping to the higher level, he walked a few paces and lay down. The rock ledge was dry. The air was cool. He was tired. Resting his head on his paws, he closed his yellow eyes, choosing to rest instead of hunting for the small animals. Their stench was all around and after they slept they'd find the rodents and eat.

Trixie entered the cross junction and saw the other animals lying down or about to lie down on the raised ledge. She walked slowly forward and after seeing a spot moved on even farther until she came to an area where there weren't any other dogs. Leaping up, she circled and lay down. Her eyes rolled back and forth, a plaintive whine crying from deep within her.

The noise echoed for a second and she rolled her eyes even more. She didn't like this place, but the air felt good and she was tired. Laying her head on her outstretched front paws, she closed her eyes and dropped off to sleep.

26

The sound of low-flying aircraft filled the air over Cramden County by noon. Private planes had been pressed into service when it became known that the services of the Highway Patrol and the National Guard had to be acquired through channels. The mayor, under pressure, managed to get through to the governor, who in turn cut a few corners in ordering the state-owned craft into the air. It seemed that almost everyone who heard the account of the deaths and the possibility, albeit a firm possibility bordering on 100 percent certainty, that the cause had been a pack of domestic dogs gone wild, put the situation into a nonemergency, emergency status.

Bob Eyer, cruising at 1200 feet, watched for any sign of movement in the underbrush below him. If there were as many dogs as had been reported, he should see them with no trouble. He assumed they existed although he initially felt the report from the tavern seemed a bit far-fetched. After checking with the authorities who hired him he learned that the number of dogs was probably 35 to 45. The report from the bar had been blown up from 100 to almost 200. There was no way that many dogs could go undetected for very long. Bob had a couple of hunting dogs and he knew a little about the animals.

Picking up the microphone, he called the airport, which was acting as the central intelligence on this air search. "Calling Laughton Field. This is Plane Two. Come in, Laughton Field. Over."

"This is Laughton Field. Go ahead, Plane Two. Over."

"I've covered grid twelve four times. I've seen nothing. Shall I move onto grid four? Over."

"Affirmative. Cover it the same number of times, once in each direction. We've received word that the National Guard helicopters will be joining the search around sixteen hundred hours. Over."

Bob grinned. "Big deal. By that time we'll have covered the county a half dozen times. Over."

"The Highway Patrol has been centered in the western part of the state following the rock concert Sunday at Riverport. They'll try to get here, but I doubt if they'll make it much before sundown. Over."

Shaking his head, Bob said, "I read you. Any reports of anything that looks like a convention of canines? Over."

"Nothing from no one. Keep looking. If we're going to spot them from the air, I don't think they'll be seen much before late afternoon or early evening. Over."

"Why do you say that? Over."

"Because if they're hunting, that's when they'll do it. It's too hot to be doing anything like that today. It's almost ninety-eight out here right now. Over."

"That makes sense." Bob glanced at his watch, then at the fuel gauge. "It's almost fourteen forty-five now. I'll be coming in for refueling in an hour, unless they're spotted before then. Over."

"I read you. Good hunting. Over and out."

Bob replaced the microphone on the radio and banked his plane toward grid four, which would be over the Wipsipanicon River.

Captain Alf Edel landed at the Laughton Air Field at 1600 hours and after picking up a map of the county, which had been marked off into grid areas for more efficient searching, took off with his co-pilot, Jack Seggit. Criss-crossing the first grid assigned to them at a slower speed than the planes gave the pilot and co-pilot more of an opportunity to search efficiently. Whenever they came to a woods or stand of trees they were able to hover and look more closely through binoculars. The other helicopter that had accompanied them did much the same thing over their assignment.

Carol Reckels picked up the telephone ringing on her desk at *The Laughton Lantern.* "Carol Reckels."

"Hi, honey. It's Mark."

"Hi yourself," she said, dropping her voice and the professional tone with which she had answered the phone.

"I've got a great idea."

"What's that?"

"How about a picnic tonight?"

Carol hesitated. "Do you think that'd be wise?"

"Why? You mean about the dogs and such?"

"Uh-huh."

Mark hesitated for an instant. "Well, I wasn't suggesting that we stay out all night. After all, you have to go to work in the morning and I've got to get to the car lot by eight. What I'm suggesting is a quick picnic supper in the park before it gets late."

"What do you call late?"

"I'll have you and Jenny home by eight o'clock. Eight-thirty tops. The sun will barely be down by that time."

Carol wrinkled her forehead. "What does the sun have to do with it?"

"I heard a couple of hunters being interviewed

on the radio and they both agree that the dogs probably wouldn't hunt until dark. Besides, if it's as many as they say, a person would hear them coming a mile away."

"Well, I don't kow. Couldn't we just eat at my place?"

"Uh-uh. I've got something to talk over with you and I need a special place."

"I don't understand. What are you talking about?"

"Trust me. What time should I pick you up?"

Carol looked at the watch hanging from around her neck. "It's going on four-thirty. I don't have anything ready. I've got to pick Jenny up at the day-care center. I've got to change clothes—probably shower if it's as hot as everyone is saying—"

"If it'll help, why don't I stop at a fast-food place and get some chicken or something? You bring a bottle of wine. Deal?"

"That would help like everything, darling. Make it about six-thirty and we'll be ready."

"I love you," Mark said softly.

"I love you, too, darling." Without saying good-bye, both hung up.

Carol stared wistfully over her computer screen. She loved Mark—a lot more than she had ever loved Pete. Pete always had his animals and practice interfering. Why she had ever thought being married to a veterinarian could possibly approach her idea of living with a medical doctor still evaded her. Theirs had not been a happy marriage and she was bound and determined to make her relationship with Mark work. He made great money selling Subarus and seemed to know how to handle his finances. That would help her tremendously since she had difficulty making her money go as far as she'd like it to go.

Jenny's heart-shaped face formed in her head. The little girl looked somewhat like her as well as Pete. She'd be a constant reminder of her failed marriage, but the six-year-old's personality, a smooth combination of both parents, seemed to make up for her looks. The child was beautiful, but to Carol Jenny was half Pete and half her. Since Mark had come into her life she seemed to notice Pete's half less and less as time went by.

Focusing her eyes on the screen, she reread her story about the upcoming garden party soiree for charity at Mrs. Ellen Brown's home.

"If we're going to find those mutts," Alf Edel said, "we'll probably flush them out of a bunch of underbrush like that down there."

"Why not hover right over it for a minute or two," Jack Seggit said, glancing at his pilot. "If they are in there, that'll scare the be-Jesus out of 'em and we'll see 'em when they run."

"Good idea," Edel said, lowering the craft until it hovered a mere 30 feet over the stunted trees and brush that covered one corner of a meadow, which was bordered on either side by woods. The branches waved frantically in the down draft of the huge rotor, but nothing, other than two rabbits, fled the wind-torn haven.

"Nothing. Goddamn. I wonder where a bunch of dogs like that would go to hide?" Seggit asked.

"You've got me. How many times have we been over grid ten?"

"I think that was, yeah, that was the fourth time. I'd better radio in and get a new sector."

After they received their new assignment the helicopter moved off, closer to the southern city limits of Laughton.

"Hey, look down there," Edel cried and brought the craft to a stand-still in the air.

"What?"

"Look here on the map. See this red-cross mark? That's where one of the bodies was found."

"Yeah. How do you know?"

"While you were checking out the chopper the guy in the air terminal told me some of the details."

"Like what?" Seggit asked.

"Like how the guy was gutted and all his guts were eaten up by the dogs."

"Oh, Christ," Seggit said, gagging.

"No shit." Edel laughed at his co-pilot's discomfort.

"Jesus, I don't feel good," Seggit said, his face white. "Why the hell did you have to go and say that? I think I'm going to puke."

"Oh, come on. What the hell would you do if you had to go into combat?"

"That's not quite the same. What the hell's the matter with you, anyway? You a ghoul or something?"

"Naw. I just sort of get off, knowing all the sordid details of something like this. Maybe we'll see something really gross."

"I think you're a fuckin' weirdo, Alf. This is something I didn't know about. Knock it off, will you?"

"Hey, different strokes for different folks."

Seggit looked out the window on his side, failing to see the silly smirk on Alf Edel's face.

The black mongrel stood up, stretching to free his stiff muscles. The light coming through the drain opening above was still bright but not direct sunlight anymore. The air felt a bit more cool than it had when the pack first entered the storm drain.

Most of the dogs were still sleeping and those that saw their leader get up watched him with an intensity that belied their supine positions.

The mongrel walked slowly through the intersection toward the opposite branch of the one through which they had come. He walked slowly into the half darkness, which was lighted in the distance by more drain openings. When he reached them he found ladders leading up to the squares of light. Overhead, cars and trucks passed, horns honking, and the general hubbub of Riverfront Street traffic assailed his ears. He continued walking, reading the air, smelling the presence of the small furry rodents that lived here but that somehow managed to stay away from him.

After passing a dozen of the openings he heard even more noise and stopped at an opening over him. Rearing up, he put his forepaws on the fourth rung of the ladder leading to the drain. He caught the smell of man coming into the sewer despite the overwhelming dampness and odors filling the air in the sewer. He was hungry. The pack was hungry. For some reason he had wanted to reach the people through the opening overhead but found he couldn't negotiate the ladders.

Stepping back, he leaped but gave up after one attempt. He'd lead the pack out the way they had come in and search for food on the outside. The drain was a good place in which to sleep and look for the furry rodents, but it wouldn't sustain the pack with a ready supply of food. That would have to be found on the outside.

On the way back to the intersection where he had left the pack he saw a rat feasting on something that had fallen through the drain overhead. Charging it, he caught the rodent off guard and broke its back in his powerful jaws. The three-pound rat was quickly torn apart and the warm entrails and viscera gobbled down. The meat was left and the black mongrel trotted down the drain toward the others. When he reached them some still slept and those that were awake looked at him, hunger in their whines as they grew restless.

The mongrel did not want to go out yet. He had heard too many noises from overhead. That meant there were too many people. He was as hungry as the others despite the rat, but they'd have to wait until almost dark if they were to hunt successfully.

"For all we know the dogs are gone. Maybe in another county, I hope," the dispatcher said on the radio. "At any rate, the mayor and the supervisors are calling the air search off. You guys can come in any time you want. Over."

Bob Eyer banked his Cessna and headed for the field. As he understood it, the county had been covered by nine planes and the two National Guard helicopters at least four times since the first planes had taken to the air. If the dogs hadn't been flushed out by the noise and they weren't seen chasing after some of the animals that had been scared by the sound of low-flying aircraft, the dogs probably were gone. After radioing to the field he began his approach once he had been given clearance to land.

"I heard enough scuttlebutt around the courthouse that tells me the dogs are probably gone from the county," Amy said after strapping herself into the seat of the Bronco.

Pete turned the engine over and backed out of the parking spot. "I hope they're right. If people hear that, they'll go back to doing everything normally and not give a thought to the possibility that the dogs might still be in the vicinity."

"Don't forget you have a date with Duchess."

Pete grinned. "I won't. At least I feel like walking today, which is more than I could say yesterday. Staying up all night is not what it's cracked up to be." After volunteering to ride with Ben Rathe, Pete had become involved in a long drawn-out conversation at the Law Enforcement Center and then wound up riding with another officer until dawn. He had called off his appointments and slept in most of the day. The one thing he should have done he hadn't, and that was call Carol to make certain that Jenny was all right. He usually checked almost every day. He felt it would never give Carol ammunition to fire at him in the event she ever got a wild hair up her nose and tried to prevent him from seeing her. She could never use the argument that he didn't really care about his daughter and never checked to see how she was between regular visits on weekends.

"Since you're walking Duchess I think I had better stop at the supermarket and get some groceries. I wouldn't want you to be shortchanged with just an ordinary meal." Amy reached over, stroking Pete's arm.

By the time they reached home it was almost six and Duchess, whining in the garage, won Pete's attention and he exercised the Samoyed as soon as they got the groceries in the house.

He walked the dog for 15 minutes toward the countryside south of Amy's house. Turning, he allowed the dog to run free on the return trip. Duchess investigated bushes and clumps of weeds along the way.

Back in the yard Pete snapped her leash on and hooked her up to the line that allowed her to run the full length of the enclosure.

"How's supper coming?" he asked when he entered the kitchen.

"Give me ten and you can satisfy your animal appetite as far as food is concerned."

"I'll give Jenny a call and see how she is. I'll only be a minute." Pete walked into the next room and picked up the telephone. Dialing the number from memory, he waited. The ring had buzzed in his ear eight times when he began to feel uneasy. He hung up after ten and redialed, thinking he might have made a mistake. Again, ten rings brought no answer.

Puzzled, he went back to the kitchen, where Amy was beginning to dish up their evening meal. "There was no answer," he said simply and sat down.

27

"So you and Daddy and this Amy person were here at the park Sunday?" Carol asked, doing nothing to camouflage her mixed feelings.

Jenny looked up at her mother, her eyes widening with fright. What had she said that was wrong? After Uncle Mark had helped her up the steep sliding board ladder and she had flown down into his arms, she felt good. She must have said the wrong thing since her mommy suddenly sounded upset.

"Tell me about Amy, Jenny."

"She's nice," Jenny said, her voice dropping to a whisper. She shouldn't have said something to anger her mother. Whenever Daddy came over it seemed as though her mommy became angry at everything—everything Jenny did, everything Jenny said—at everything.

"Hey, Carol, lighten up," Mark said, interrupting.

"Butt out, Mark. I want to find out all I can."

"Come on, darling. Don't let this ruin tonight."

Carol turned on him. "Ruin tonight? What do you mean? It's already ruined. That worthless piece of—"

"Ah-ah. Not in front of Jenny," Mark said, head motioning toward the six-year-old.

"I—I'm sorry. Really, I am. Jenny," Carol said, turning to her daughter, "why don't you go play in the sandbox?"

Jenny's eyes widened, this time in wonderment. Her mother wasn't angry any longer. At least Jenny didn't think she was angry. Hadn't she said to go play in the sandbox? Maybe this time her mother wouldn't get angry at Daddy or at her. "Okay, Mommy. You wanna come, too, Uncle Mark?"

"Mommy and Uncle Mark want to talk, darling. Run along," Carol said kindly.

When the child had run to the sandbox Carol turned to Mark. "I—I'm sorry I got angry. But when I think of him with another woman I—"

"You're with another man. Should he be upset?"

"It's not quite the same."

"I don't get your argument. I'm sure he saw me the other night when I pulled up. He didn't stop and come back to confront me or anything. Why get upset over something so trivial?"

"It's not trivial. What kind of woman is she? How dare Pete expose my daughter to some unwholesome situation?"

"Ease off, honey. She's probably a lot like you. If Pete is dating her, I'm sure his tastes wouldn't change that radically after having been married to you. Besides, aren't you in some ways 'exposing Jenny to an unwholesome situation' by having me at the house and going on picnics with me?"

"You're not being fair. It's not the same."

"Oh, but it is. From what you've told me Pete loves Jenny. He'd never run the risk of hurting her."

"I suppose you're right. I just get upset when I think about the whole thing."

"Want to start the evening over?"

"How much time do we have left?" Carol asked, winking.

"Well, we've eaten. My watch says it's almost eight o'clock. I thought we could maybe go for a walk along the river bank. It might be a little cooler over there."

"What about Jenny?"

Mark looked around the park. He had selected this spot for its seclusion. Standing, he could see most of the area. "From what I can see there isn't another soul around. I suppose most people are on the defensive considering the dog attacks and all."

"I think we should go home," Carol said,

standing, suddenly ill at ease.

"In a few minutes. Come on. We'll go for a quick walk and then get Jenny and head for home. All right?"

"Will she be all right in the sandbox?"

Mark calculated the distance between their picnic spot and the sandbox at 40 or 50 feet. Behind them the Wipsipanicon River flowed another 30 feet away. "We aren't going that far. Come on."

On the western horizon the sun had dipped well below the lowlying hills that edged Laughton.

Trixie was hungry. Her belly was empty and she wanted food. She could smell the rodents in the drain pipe. She had killed rats on the farm but had never devoured one. She had recognized the smell of them as being edible but, because she had been well taken care of by her human, she had never bothered to eat one. Now the smells tantalized her. She wanted to eat. Getting to her feet, she looked at the leader, who lay with his head resting on his paws.

Others in the pack stirred. Some were already standing. The black mongrel lazily got to his feet and stretched. His yellow eyes fixed on the sewer drain overhead. The square was barely visible. The sun had gone down. By the time they retraced their steps to the opening of the drain, it would be safe enough and dark enough to hunt.

Without looking at any other member of the pack, the leader turned and loped down the drain toward the mouth.

The others followed.

"Sit down here, Carol," Mark said, indicating a fallen tree trunk that lay partway in the water.

Opting to sit on the ground and rest against the fallen bole, she said, "What's up, Mark?"

Sitting down next to her, he said, "Don't be so impatient."

Sliding down a bit, Carol lay back on the cool grass. It was nice here along the river. A gentle breeze washed over them from upstream. When Mark lay down next to her she snuggled in closer. She allowed him to slip his arm beneath her neck and when he kissed her she kissed him back, sending her tongue into his mouth, promising more than she felt she could deliver here on the river bank.

When they parted Mark smiled down at her. "Will you marry me, Carol?"

The dogs erupted from the mouth of the drain onto the river bank. The sun had gone down almost an hour before and the gloom of early night hung over the water. The black mongrel ran up to the top of the sewer opening, holding his snout in the air. When he stood there, not unlike a king about to address his subjects, he sorted the breezes. He could see nothing, but with his sensitive nose he could tell there were people upriver from where he stood. There were at least two—maybe three. Turning, he loped back down to the river bank and started upstream toward the park without making a sound. The long grass muffled the sounds of the pack as they made their way.

When they stood at the edge of the clearing that bordered the park on the south side the leader stopped and turned to glare at the others. Some lay down, others stood, but none moved to advance. When he was sure they understood he turned and made his way quietly, moving like a black shadow through the encroaching darkness. The pack fell in behind him, moving as quietly as the black mongrel.

"Oh, darling," Carol murmured, covering Mark's lips with her own. "Yes. Yes, of course I'll marry you."

Mark embraced her and they kissed again.

"I hate to be a party poop, but we should get going," Carol said after a few more moments. The sky, still a light shade of blue, belied the shadowy night holding the park. In a few more moments it would be dark and Jenny would be petrified. The girl wouldn't be able to see them where they lay, and she'd panic if she suddenly discovered she was alone in the park, without her mother visible. The fact that it was almost nighttime wouldn't help either.

"I guess you're right. Maybe we can finish at your place what we started here," Mark suggested.

"We'll see, once we get Jenny to bed."

Mark kissed her again.

The mongrel slunk close to the ground. He could hear them now as well as smell them. The others mimicked him, advancing at a snail's pace, each nerve aquiver. Each could smell food. Each was hungry. Each wanted to eat.

Then the black mongrel stepped into the small clearing next to the river. The man and woman were already on the ground, clinging to each other. He waited until the others had entered the clearing and had surrounded the couple.

A deep-throated growl rumbled through the dark and the reaction was instantaneous from the man and woman.

"Ah, no," Mark moaned when he looked up. "Jesus Christ. It's the fucking dog pack, Carol. What'll we do?"

When Carol opened her eyes she barely saw the black mongrel, upside down, standing behind her head. The lighter-colored dogs she could make out, and a sense of unbridled fear and panic surged through her body. She opened her mouth and screamed one word. "Je-e-en-n-ny!"

Jenny patted the sand into the box that the chicken had come in and leveled it off. It would make a grand cake for their dessert.

Then she froze when she heard the cry come to her from the river bank where her mommy and

Uncle Mark had gone. What was wrong? Did her mother want her to come there? That must be it. She'd better hurry. The last thing she wanted was to upset her mommy.

Clambering to her feet, she brushed off the sand from her bare legs and started running to the river.

The black mongrel and the tan-and-black bitch reacted instantly when Carol screamed her daughter's name. Leaping forward, the mongrel caught Mark in the throat with his powerful jaws. Carol had time to cover her front with her arms just as the bitch jumped on her. But the onslaught of the others biting, tearing, gnashing at her exposed legs and arms, brought her, struggling, to her knees. She beat at the dogs, but their weight forced her back. The Airedale pulled at her blouse, ripping it to shreds. Her bare breasts fell free and the Airedale closed its jaws on one, biting with all his might. A shower of blood spewed out, covering him and another bitch, gnawing at Carol's upper arm, which half covered her other breast. When the pain of the tearing flesh registered in her brain she screamed.

Jenny, running full tilt toward the spot where she thought her mother had gone, heard the second high-pitched, terror-filled cry and stopped. When she stood still she could hear the growls and half barks and yelps of the dog pack as they devoured the woman who was still alive, and the man who lay half in, half out of the water, his eyes bulged out, staring unseeing into the night.

Puzzled by the strange sounds, Jenny stood transfixed for a moment. Something was wrong. She knew her mommy had gone in this direction, but what were a lot of dogs—at least they sounded like dogs to the child—doing in the park? She half turned, facing the sandbox to her left and Uncle Mark's car in front of her. To her right the sliding board stood skeleton-like in the gloom.

What should she do? Go to the river and find her mommy? Go to Uncle Mark's car, where the dogs couldn't get her? But if she did go to the car, could she reach the handle to get in? Maybe she should just go back to the sandbox and play in the dark and wait for her mommy.

Maybe she should call for her mommy. "Mommy?" she ventured in a frightened voice.

Nothing. No response. But had her mother heard her? Perhaps she should call louder.

"Mommy?" Louder this time, but still no answering call other than the sound of the dogs coming from the direction of the river 60 to 70 feet away.

"Mommy!" she cried out in her loudest voice.

A cocker spaniel, waiting to push into the feast, heard the cry and turned to investigate, along with several other, smaller dogs who were waiting. Stepping through the bushes, the cocker saw the girl. At the same instant, the dog growled, bearing its fangs.

Jenny, looking at the bushes, from which the animals were coming, barely saw the form of the dog step through. Then she saw another and another coming into dim view in the dark. They didn't look very friendly.

Jenny glanced at Uncle Mark's car once more before turning to run to the sliding board. She clambered up the ladder, getting as close to the top as she dared. She remembered how careful she had been, with Uncle Mark right behind her to make certain she didn't fall. Now Uncle Mark was nowhere to be seen and she had to climb up there all by herself.

When her foot touched the first rung the cocker, followed by the others, sprung from the bushes, running as fast as they could at the child. By the time they reached the bottom of the ladder, Jenny hung precariously from the sixth rung, over their heads.

The dogs barked, froth slipping from their lips as they growled.

Frightened, Jenny climbed another step up, then another and another until she sat at the very top. She'd have to be careful or she might go sliding down and then those mean dogs would get her.

Below, the dogs leaped up toward her, failing miserably to achieve enough height. One, a nondescript white dog with black spots, put his front paws on the third rung and peered upward, barking, growling, snapping at the distance separating him from what he knew was food.

On the river bank Carol's stomach had been torn open, as had Mark's, and the dogs feasted on the entrails and viscera. Their contented sounds crossed the distance to the five dogs barking at the base of the sliding board. Concerned that they might miss out on a more sure thing, first one, then another, and finally the balance of the attackers turned, running toward the bank.

When they had finished devouring as much of the couple as they could the dogs followed their leader into the park, their noses to the ground, hunting for more food and prey.

Twelve feet overhead, Jenny Reckels clung to the safety rail around the top of the sliding board, her scent being wafted away on a breeze too high for the pack to smell.

Day Seven

Wednesday

28

"The police department and the sheriff's department urge everyone to stay indoors. The whereabouts of the dog pack is unknown at this time. It is extremely important that people who do not have to go outside their homes today stay inside. Only people who have essential employment indoors should consider going to work today.

"Again, the bodies of two people, Mark Phalen and Carol Reckels, were found last night in the city park by a city patrolman making a routine tour through the park. Although Officer Ben Rathe did not see the dogs, the county coroner has determined that 'the cause of death was multiple animal attack—most probably feral dogs.' The condition of the bodies is reported to match that of the other victims.

"Six-year-old Jenny Reckels, daughter of one of the victims, was found clinging to the top of a sliding board, having apparently taken refuge there when the dog pack attacked her mother.

"In other local stores, Wiley Used Cars has declared bankruptcy after a series of court cases involving—"

Pete turned off the radio. He looked up at Amy. Both their eyes were red from lack of sleep and from weeping.

Raising his cup of coffee, Pete said, "If I live to be a hundred, I'll never get over the shock of seeing Rathe at the back door with Jenny in his arms last night."

Amy reached across the table, gently patting his arm. "Try to forget, darling. It'll only hurt more if you concentrate on it."

"I know. But God, that's an awful way to die." He shuddered. "When it was people I didn't know it almost got to be routine. Christ, I was the big expert on dogs and how they act. I feel so goddamned rotten, it's unbelievable."

Standing, Amy moved to the stove and picked up the coffee pot. "More?"

Pete nodded and held his cup out. "Make another pot. I'm not going anyplace just yet. I don't think I could if I had to."

"Don't reprimand yourself too much for being the expert. If you hadn't gotten involved, the sheriff would never have gotten Jenny to you as quickly as he did."

"I suppose that's true. I wonder just how all this will affect her."

Amy spooned coffee into the basket. "I'm no child psychologist, but if what the officer said is the case, it shouldn't be any more traumatic than losing her mother in an auto accident."

Pete stared at her. "That would be traumatic, wouldn't it?"

"What? Losing her mother in an accident?"

Pete nodded.

"Of course it would. But considering the fact that it was pretty dark, and that Jenny was twelve feet off the ground and quite some little distance from where Carol died, I don't think it's going to bother her. At least, not as if she had actually seen the killing."

Pete shuddered. After turning on the stove Amy went to him. She wrapped her arms around his head, pressing it to her breasts. She felt him relax a bit.

"I guess," he said after several moments, "Duke Little should be thanked for deducing Jenny was my daughter."

"There aren't that many Reckels in town. It didn't take Sherlock Holmes to figure it out."

"That's true, but if you hadn't met him in the supermarket parking lot, he would have had no idea where to find me."

"Okay, we'll make Duke Little a hero. Satisfied?"

He looked up to find her smiling. When she winked he returned a forced grin of his own.

"I never once thought I'd get Jenny under circumstances like this. There were times when I thought about taking Carol to court to fight for my right to have her. But I always considered what a fight over her would do to Jenny. I guess that's why I always backed off. Now she's my responsibility. It's sorta scary."

"Scary? How?"

"A man raising a daughter. That can't be the easiest assignment in the world."

"It's been done before. What are you afraid of? Woman talk?" She playfully poked him in the ribs.

"Well, it would be easier if she were a boy."

"You chicken. Unless I've been misinterpreting our relationship, I think I can take over for you if the going gets tough."

Without speaking, Pete embraced her, then kissed her.

"Where's Mommy?" Jenny asked from the doorway of the dining room that opened onto the kitchen.

Pete and Amy broke their embrace. Jenny stood, arms hanging at her sides, hair mussed, wearing the same sunsuit she had had on at the park.

Pete hurried to her, scooping her up in her arms. "How's my precious little girl this morning?"

"I'm fine, Daddy. Where's Mommy?"

Pete swallowed. "Mommy had to go on a trip, darling. How do you feel?"

"I'm hungry. Can I please eat?"

"Of course you can, Jenny," Amy said, going to the cupboard to find a box of cereal. She brought out Frosted Flakes and poured some into a small dish.

"I'm beginning to see a new side of you, Amy," Pete said, sitting Jenny down at the table. "Frosted Flakes? What's an adult doing with Frosted Flakes?"

"Hey, I like them. Wantta make somethin' outta it?" she said, grimacing like a tough and rolling her hands into fists.

Pete chuckled despite his depression and sat down next to his daughter. "Where were you last night, Jenny?"

"Do you think you should?" Amy asked, pouring milk on the cereal.

"I've got to. Otherwise I'll never know what I can say around her or what I can't. I don't know if she saw any dogs or if she'll panic every time she sees one in the future." Turning back to Jenny, he said, "Do you remember?"

Nodding, she spooned some flakes into her mouth.

"Where?" Pete asked, pushing for an answer.

"Mommy and me and Uncle Mark went on a picnic."

"Did you have fun?" Pete asked when he saw no fear on her face.

Nodding, she took more cereal. "Uh-huh! We—"

"Don't talk with your mouth full. I'll wait." Pete

reached out, stroking her mussed up hair.

When she finished she said, "I played in the sandbox and we ate chicken. Then Mommy and Uncle Mark went for a walk."

"Where to?"

Jenny shrugged.

"Did you go along?"

"Uh-uh. I played some more in the sandbox. Then the puppies came."

"Puppies?" Pete glanced up to find Amy hanging on every word the child said.

"Uh-huh. And they weren't very nice. I heard them barking and stuff in the bushes. I didn't know what to do."

"Were you afraid?"

"Uh-huh. I didn't know where Mommy was and I was real scared. I thought about going to Uncle Mark's car. But I decided to go up on the sliding board instead. I was scared up there, too, when I saw some of the puppies come out of the bushes after awhile. There were all kinds of them. But they didn't see me."

Pete waited a moment. "Then what happened?"

"I was up there a awful long time. I thought about sliding down, but it was so high. Uncle Mark slided down with me before and I was afraid then. So, I just waited."

"And then the policeman came and got you down?"

Jenny nodded. "Uh-huh."

"Wow," Pete managed, getting to his feet.

"She's pretty darn brave, you know?"

Amy nodded and bent down to hug Jenny.

Rubbing his tired eyes, Pete went to the window and looked out at the back yard. He had put Duchess in the garage when he came back last night and would have to get her out before he left. Now he was exhausted, having been up since Rathe brought Jenny at 11 o'clock.

One day, sometime in the future, he'd have to tell Jenny about the manner in which her mother died, but for now she was all right. She should grow up and be normal, without any phobias resulting from last night where animals were concerned. He wouldn't relish the day he'd have to tell her. He hoped time would dim the memories and he'd be able to gloss over the more gruesome and graphic details.

The jangling of the phone from the dining room brought him back to the kitchen.

Amy left to answer it and when she called Pete he reacted slowly.

"Who is it?" he asked, taking the receiver from her, clamping his hand over the mouthpiece.

"It's the sheriff."

"Sheriff? I owe you," Pete said without saying hello.

"It's my job, Pete. Can you come down here for a meeting? We've got all sorts of problems, the least of which is trying to keep the people of Laughton from panicking."

Pete turned to Amy. "Can you take care of Jenny? Call in sick or something?"

"I'll tell Al what really happened. He'll understand."

Pete went back to the phone. "Sure. What time and where?"

"Here at the courthouse, in half an hour."

"I'll see you then." Pete hung up the receiver and turned to go back to the kitchen. He still needed one more cup of fresh coffee to make certain he got to the law enforcement center wide awake.

"Gentlemen," Chief of Police Harry Manning said, holding up his arms for quiet. "I don't want to minimize the problem we have on our hands here. Sixteen people, maybe eighteen have been killed by this pack of wild dogs. People in the city and county are terrified. The mysterious thing about all of this is, only two people have seen them and lived to tell the tale about it. Pete Reckels and a patron of a bar Monday night."

Pete stood up. "There are three of us now, Chief. My daughter saw them in the park last night."

"Okay. I stand corrected. The reason I say it's mysterious is because the planes and helicopters flying over the county and city yesterday didn't turn up a thing. They saw nothing. Absolutely nothing. Our problem is to figure out where that many dogs could hole up and never be seen."

A man held up his hand, standing at the same time. "How many dogs are there, Chief?"

Shrugging, Harry said, "We have no exact count, of course. The man in the bar said there were quite a few, which of course doesn't tell us much. Plus, his condition at the time is suspect."

A murmur of laughter swept across the room.

"Our big question is," the chief said, quieting the room full of men, "how do so many dogs disappear so quickly? Where do they go? Where are they when they aren't killing?"

The chief of police continued for several more minutes and Pete studied the group of men. There were off-duty police and sheriff's deputies as well as several who were on duty and in uniform. The men who had been contacted to serve in volunteer positions during the weekend had, for the most part, shown up. There were those who had to go to work, but most of them had made arrangements to be at the meeting.

When Pete looked at the dais again Sheriff Little was addressing the men.

"As far as we know, the first victim was either Johnny O'Malley or Joe Eppson." Little pointed to the map of the county on the wall behind him. "We have reason to believe that the dogs may have been responsible for the car/tanker accident in which both drivers died. Then, two hobos died close to the old Hooverville jungle out along the tracks, west of Laughton. On Sunday, the Sayman family was wiped out, as was the milk truck driver." He indicated each location where a killing had taken place and which was marked with a large red tack. He moved to a map of the city.

"Again, as far as we know, the pack then got into town on Monday night. A man and a prostitute were killed several blocks apart. Neither of their bodies were—were—were eaten very much. We think the dogs were probably disturbed by the police unit that found both bodies. Then, last night, the last two victims were killed in the city park."

As the sheriff droned on, Pete studied the map. It seemed to be the way the lawman had said. Staring at the two tacks that represented Carol and her boyfriend, Pete noticed the river and followed it upstream, and downstream. There were probably caves and things where the pack could lay up during the day. If that were the case—. He held his hand up.

"Could the dogs be hiding in any of the small caves that are on the river bank?"

"Yesterday one of the helicopters went up and down the river, looking for such caves. Those they found, they hovered near, hoping that the sound of the helicopters would frighten the pack and bring 'em into daylight. Nothing happened. In addition, those caves aren't deep enough to allow the dogs to go in far enough to be out of earshot."

Pete nodded and listened intently when the sheriff continued. Then he saw something on the map that apparently everyone had overlooked. He wasn't that familiar with the opening, but he knew where it was in relation to the park. If it were accessible, the pack could very easily be *under* the city.

Standing, Pete said, "Can I talk with you and the chief for a moment—in private, Sheriff?" It would do no good to have a lot of armed people suddenly heading for the storm drain opening along the river bank.

Duke Little glanced at Harry Manning and, when the chief nodded, Duke stepped off the dais and followed the chief and Pete into the hall.

When they were alone Pete said, "I think I know where the dogs are and I want you two to come to the city park with me right now."

Duke studied Pete for a moment and, when he saw the chief nodding, said, "All right, Pete."

29

"I wish to hell you'd tell where you're taking us, Pete," Duke said from the back seat.

"Yeah. I don't like it either," Harry said from behind the steering wheel of the squad car he had taken.

"Look, I'm just almost certain about this thing. I think I know where the dogs are hiding. If I'm right and we can locate them, we'll have them right where we want them. If I'm wrong, we can start looking someplace else."

"Why not just tell us?" Harry said.

"If I had told you back in the courthouse, you probably would have dispatched a squad car with a police officer in it to investigate. Then we'd have had to wait until he reported back.

Right? In the meantime, I get antsy, you two get nervous about it, and all three of us telegraph to the men who were at the meeting that something is up. If the dogs turned out not to be there, then all of our anxiety would have been for nothing. This way, we don't get the volunteers and other officers upset. I hope it makes sense."

Harry glanced in the rearview mirror, nodding his head when he saw Duke doing the same. Harry had dismissed the meeting, telling those who had attended to be on the alert. If they were needed, they'd be called at home.

"I still don't see why you're so mysterious about it. Can't you tell us now?" Duke asked, a pleading tone in his voice.

"Look, Sheriff, I'm not particularly fond of the idea of being away from my little girl right now. She's in good hands, but I'd just as soon be there than here. Humor me. All right?" Pete was exhausted and mentally flinched when he realized how he was addressing the two heads of the law enforcement agencies.

"Okay, Pete. Have it your way."

The squad car moved into the park and around the cinder path toward the river. When they were a mere 20 feet or so from the site of the two deaths, Harry stopped the car and got out when Pete did. Duke followed.

"Okay, show us," Harry said.

Duke led the way since he had been called in last night and knew exactly where the bodies had been found. Stepping through the bushes, he waited for Harry and Pete to follow.

"Right here," he said, pointing to a small grassy clearing.

Pete forced himself to concentrate on looking for paw prints and to forget about the fact that the woman he had loved, had married, and had had a child with, had died here within the last 24 hours.

"It looks as though," Pete said, kneeling and closely examining the ground near the bushes where grass didn't grow, "the pack might have gone into the park after—after they finished," He stood. "I think it'll be smarter for us to backtrack them if we can."

Without waiting for a comment from either man, the veterinarian started to move north along the river bank. In several smooth areas of ugly, brown-colored sand and ground, he found nothing that would indicate that the dogs had come this way. Turning, he retraced his steps to the grassy clearing and continued south. At first he thought he might run into the same lack of spoor, but he found an area parelleling the path he had followed that showed dozens of tracks.

"Here," he said, pointing to the spot.

Harry and Duke stepped around and looked.

"All right. So they were here at one time. Where are they now?" the chief asked.

"Most of the prints show them going north. So they came from the south.'"

"I understand that, Pete. But I'm with Harry. Where are the dogs now?" Duke stared at the younger man and waited.

"We'll know in a few minutes if I'm right. Come on." Pete started walking along the path in a southerly direction until it ran out at the edge of the park. Then striking out through some tall grass and weeds, he followed what looked like a trail of some sort. "I think the dogs came through here and look," he cried, pointing to his right, "there's another one coming from the direction of the park and the city. They join right here."

"But when were these trails made?" Harry asked.

Pete shrugged. "It had to have been sometime within the last twelve to fifteen hours or so. The grass hasn't had a chance to completely straighten up. Come on." Again he struck out, but stopped when the chief called out.

"Do we know for certain which way they went? Couldn't they have come in the opposite direction?"

Pete turned and came back. "Possibly, but I'm betting that they'd found a place they feel safe in during the daylight hours. If I'm right, they've gone south—not toward the city. There weren't any tracks along the river bank to the north and if they were in town someone would have reported them by now."

"Go ahead," Harry said, resignation hanging on each word.

Climbing a small hill, Pete found the grass and weeds had thinned out and the trail had disappeared. But he knew he was heading in the right direction. Coming down the opposite side of the small hill, he stopped and pointed. "What's that?"

Harry, coming up behind him, stopped, and Duke did the same.

"Why, that's the storm drain. Why?" Harry turned to Pete.

"You think they're in there?" Duke asked.

"Why not? It's long and deep. They could be under the courthouse and city hall right now, and no one would ever know it. Any noise or commotion at the mouth of the drain wouldn't even be heard by them if they were in far enough. If the helicopters hovered out here, yesterday, the dogs, assuming they were somewhere in the drain system, probably wouldn't have heard it or felt threatened if they had. Not like they would have if they were holed up in a shallow cave like those north of the city."

Without waiting for the two men to comment, Pete started out once more, hurrying to the mouth of the sewer drain. When he was almost to it, he stopped, waiting for the other two to catch up.

He pointed to the muddy ground around the mouth when they came up alongside him. "There's your proof, gentlemen."

Hundreds of paw prints of various sizes were visible in the muddy earth around the opening where the constant trickle of water poured out.

Once more Pete started walking. He skirted the

muddy area as best he could and continued south of the drain. After several minutes, he came back. "There are some tracks down there but only coming this way. The tracks in the mud here show that the dogs went in and then came out before going back in once more."

Duke crouched down, looking more closely. "Damnit. You're right, Pete. We've got the sons-ofbitches now—right where we want them."

"I'll radio back to the station and get the men down here right now," Harry said, striding off.

"Hold it, Chief," Pete yelled.

"Why, for crying out loud? We've got them cornered, don't we?"

Pete shrugged. "I don't know. How many drains lead into the river?"

Harry glanced furtively at Duke and shook his head. "I'm not certain about the drains. That we can find out with no problem. But, assuming we can effectively block the drains, can't we just go in and blow 'em away?"

"You have to remember that dogs can see a lot better in the dark than we can. Sure, we can take lights in with us, but what about missed shots? Wouldn't bullets ricochet off the walls? Somebody could get killed."

"Yeah. I see what you mean. It is a problem. But we'll think of something," Harry said.

"What about gas?" Duke suggested.

"We'd have to check with the water department and the health department," Harry said. "What would be wrong with fencing off the openings and starving them to death?"

"Aren't there sewer rats in there?" Duke asked.

"I guess so, Duke. Will dogs eat rats, Pete?" Harry turned from one to the other.

"Of course. They'll eat just about anything if they're hungry enough—even human beings."

The three men fell silent for a moment.

"What about poison, Pete?" Duke asked, his eyes lighting up.

"That might work. But how are we going to get it to them?"

"Good question. Right now," Harry said quietly, "it seems as though the dogs are holding the upper hand."

"Well, until we think of something, what can we do about containing them?" Duke asked.

"Why not close off the park? It's the easiest way to get here. That'll keep people away from the drain," Pete said.

"That makes sense," Harry said. "What about posting a car at the main gate and closing the others?"

"Good idea," Duke agreed.

"Then," Harry said as an afterthought, "I'd better get another couple of men down here at the mouth to make certain no one comes around here."

"To be on the safe side, Chief," Pete offered, "why not arm them with shot guns or rifles? If the dogs decide to come out, they can drive them back in, until we have a plan worked out."

"All right, I can see that."

"You go back to the squad car and radio for the back up units, Harry. Pete and I will stay here until they arrive."

Harry started back toward the park and the squad car.

"I feel like I just found Judge Crater," Duke said, his eyes lighting up.

"Who?" Pete turned to him. "Who the hell's Judge Crater?"

"Oh, he's a judge who disappeared a long time ago. Nobody ever found a trace of him. They don't know if he just decided to disappear or if he was murdered or what. I guess every lawman in the country was looking for him back in the thirties or whenever it was that he dropped out of sight."

Pete nodded. "I see."

"At any rate," Duke continued, "what seemed hopeless yesterday appears to be coming up solved today."

"I hope you're right."

"About what?"

Pete pointed to the drain.

"You said they were in there. Are they or aren't they?"

"More than likely they are." Pete frowned.

"Then what's the big deal trying to 'queer' the case now?"

"I'm not trying to queer anything. I'm just being realistic."

"How? How are you being realistic?"

"Well, the dogs have eluded all efforts to find

them up to this point, haven't they?"

Duke nodded.

"Maybe they've got another way out of the sewers, one we don't know about."

"That could be. But even if they're not in the sewer now, the guards will get them when they come back."

"Of course, you're assuming they're going to come back."

"Where else would they go?"

"Where else did they go before they found the sewer? I'd guess they've only been in there—if they are in there—since Monday night, since the man and woman were killed on Riverfront."

"You're saying they may or may not be in the sewer? You're saying that a bunch of dogs are smarter than we are? You're saying—"

"Don't get upset, Sheriff. These aren't human beings we're dealing with. They're animals. They have an instinct for life and survival that can be awesome at times. Right now, they're in a better position than we are."

"I don't follow."

"If they're in the sewer, and I'm almost positive they are, they have more going for them than we do. They've got a much better defensive position than we do offensive. If they decide to come out, they're going to know about us a lot quicker than we know about them—unless they come out barking and I doubt they'll do that."

"So," Duke said, turning when Harry came up to them, "what do you suggest we do?"

"I'm thinking of a plan right now. If we're lucky—real lucky—it might work. If it does, the menace is over."

When he didn't offer anything more, the sheriff and the chief fell silent, and the three of them waited for the police to arrive.

30

Pete fidgeted as the chief of police glared at the telephone in his hand. Duke paced back and forth in front of Harry's desk.

"I—" Harry managed but was obviously interrupted.

Pete turned away. It was apparent that Harry was not getting through to George Throckmorton, the water commissioner.

"But, I—" Again the chief was cut off. Fuming, he looked up, glaring first at Duke then at Pete. "Listen to me for a moment, George, Goddamnit! For Christ's sake, this is urgent. Important! I wouldn't ask these things unless it was absolutely necessary. I—" He ran his free hand over his forehead when he was interrupted again.

Turning away, Pete frowned. If they didn't get cooperation soon, it would be too late to think about containing the dogs tonight.

"All right, George, we're going to come to your office and plead our case in person. Maybe that'll convince you. I don't think you're taking this as seriously as you should." Without waiting for confirmation, Harry slammed the receiver into its cradle and stood. "Come on. We're going to Throckmorton's office. Pete, be ready to explain the severity of the situation. As a veterinarian, you know dogs better than we do."

Harry stepped from behind his desk, cramming his police cap on in the same instant, and headed for the door. Duke fell in behind him and Pete brought up the rear. Matching the two officers stride for stride, Pete wondered what the small entourage must look like to the uninformed. Harry took the steps two at a time and when he reached the top, leaned against the wall catching his breath.

"God, I should know better than to do that."

"You all right?" Duke asked.

"Yeah. Give me a minute."

Pete stepped back as if he were helpless to assist the chief in catching his breath and waited for him to do so. Duke cast a furtive glance at Pete as if to say, be patient. We'll solve this thing one way or another.

"What did George have to say?" Duke asked as Harry slowed his breathing.

"The sonofabitch doesn't want to do anything.

He kept quoting the law to me. We can't do this because of that ordinance and we couldn't possibly think of trying that because it violates the state law and so on and on. We've got to convince him to bend the law for a few hours or by God I'll hold him responsible. I'll have the bastard's job, if not his head." Harry stepped away from the wall when a pretty young girl, a secretary in the county recorder's office walked by. When she had passed, he said, "Come on. I'm fine."

He led the way down the hall and stomped into the outer office of the water commissioner. The startled secretary looked up.

"May I help you?"

"George is expecting us," Harry snarled and hurried past her desk, throwing open the door to George P. Throckmorton's private office.

"What the—? How dare—? Oh, it's you, Harry. I told you on the phone that what you're proposing is in direct violation of city ordinances and state laws, not to mention federal regulations." Throckmorton stood up behind his desk.

"Sit down, George," Harry barked. "This is Pete Reckels, a veterinarian. He's going to tell you in graphic detail why you're going to cooperate." Harry turned to Pete and winked at the veterinarian as if to say, lay it on thick.

"The best I can do is tell you about Joe Eppson and the two hobos who were killed." Pete launched into a bloody account, winding up with the fact that one of last night's victims had been his ex-wife and that his child could very well have been a victim as well. When he finished, he stopped, leaning forward over the commissioner's desk, staring into his round, mustached face.

"Now see here," Throckmorton said, spluttering as he stood, "if you think you're going to blame me for what's been happening, you're completely off base. How can you even think such a thing?"

"Nobody's accused you of anything, George—yet," Harry said, tacking the last word on in an ominous way.

"What do you mean?" Throckmorton asked.

"If you don't cooperate with us, and more deaths result because we can't flush the animals out, news of your decision not to help is going to be spread all over the pages of the *Lantern.*" Harry glowered at him.

The heavyset man stared back at the chief for a brief second before dropping his eyes. "You realize, of course, that you're blackmailing me."

"I prefer coercion to blackmail, George," Harry said quietly. "It seems to fit better, considering everything."

Throckmorton sat down heavily, an expression of defeat crossing his features. "What do you want me to do? How can I help?"

"That's better," Harry said, pulling a chair up opposite the desk. He motioned for Duke and Pete to do the same. When they were seated, he continued. "We'll give you the ideas we've come up with and you tell us if they'll work. All right?"

The water commissioner nodded.

"One of the things we talked about was gas."

Throckmorton looked up, his eyes wide. "No. That's impossible. Gas would seep through the entire system, possibly coming up through sewer drain openings and into the street. I shouldn't have to tell you that if the gas is going to be strong to reach and kill the dogs wherever they may be in the system, it's going to kill people or make them awfully sick."

"Couldn't the drain openings be sealed?" Duke asked.

"Out of the question. First of all, it would cost a ton of money. Let me pose a question to you, gentlemen. What if it rained while the drains were sealed? The streets would flood and there'd be hell to pay. I'm afraid gas is completely out of the question."

Harry looked first at Duke, then at Pete.

"Besides," Throckmorton continued, "the poison could pollute the river eventually. I'm sure you people are aware that Laughton is already under fire from the E.P.A. for pollution from our old sewage disposal plant."

"But under the circumstances, wouldn't the E.P.A. look the other way?" Duke asked.

Shaking his head, Throckmorton said, "Let me ask you something. What's wrong with just going into the sewers and killing the animals? I'd happily give you permission to do that."

"That would be like going into a cage filled with wild lions and taking a slingshot along for protection," Pete said.

"Aren't you exaggerating a bit, young fellow?" the commissioner asked.

"All right, I'm stretching it a bit. But I know dogs, and I'd be the last one to think of just going in there with a rifle or shotgun for protection."

"Why?" Throckmorton leaned forward.

"Only four or five men could go in at a time. They'd have to walk abreast so that they could fire their weapons at once. The dogs can see much better in the dark of the sewers than any man can. There are about forty dogs in the pack. That means that even if all five men fired at once and each one hit a dog, there'd be thirty five or so coming right at them while they were reloading."

A deep silence fell over the room.

"I see what you mean," the commissioner said finally.

"How many drains like the one near the park are there, George?" Pete asked.

"Four. Why?"

Pete looked around the room. He had to tell them of his plan. It seemed that it was their only option.

"The dogs *will* come out at night. We know that," Pete said.

"Yes," Duke agreed, "but out of which opening? There are four."

"More than likely they'll come out the one they went in. They'll follow their own scent to find their way out. Dogs rely almost completely on their sense of smell to track, to identify, to feed. The only reason they might use one of the other drain openings is that they discovered one or all and have already used them as well as the one near the park."

"So, what are you suggesting?" Harry asked, a glimmer of hope in his eyes.

"I've been thinking about the terrain around the opening ever since we left there earlier. I propose we station men around the opening, out of sight, so that their movements won't alarm the pack."

"I thought you said the dogs would rely on their sense of smell. Would they be alarmed if they did see the men?"

"I wouldn't want to take that chance if it's the only shot we've got at them."

"I see," Duke said, nodding.

"But the tough thing is going to be holding them there long enough to shoot them. I think we should bait them with some meat and have it laced with poison. When they stop to eat some of the meat, the men could open fire."

Harry smiled. "Yeah. It would be like a shooting gallery, wouldn't it?"

"Sort of," Pete said. "The good thing about this plan is that it should work at the other three openings as well, in the event the one by the park isn't used. We'll have them when they come out to hunt tonight."

"How many men should we try to have at each opening, Pete?" Harry asked, standing, as if to leave.

Duke got to his feet, as did Pete.

Before Pete could answer, Harry turned to Throckmorton. "Thanks, George."

"I'm sorry I couldn't be of more help. If there's anything I can do, let me know."

"I'll do that," Harry said, striding for the door.

"About the number of men," Pete said when they were in the hall, walking back toward the stairway, "it would be ideal if we could have one man per dog. That way we'd be assured of getting them all. But I would think if the men are close enough, say within hand weapon range, or shotgun range, that perhaps seven or eight men at the most could handle the situation."

"I think, with the number of volunteers we had at the meeting and the fact that those who couldn't be there because of work would be available after supper, we could manage that pretty easily," Harry said, turning to Duke. "I assume we can count on your department, Duke?"

"Of course. Even though the drains are within the city limits, this calls for cooperation right across the board."

"Say, Pete," Harry said, holding the door open to his office. "Won't the dogs smell the men waiting for them?"

"Yeah, you said that they really depend on their sense of smell more than any other," Duke said, dropping into a straight-backed chair in Harry's office.

"We can camouflage the smell. Deer hunters and elk hunters do it all the time." Pete grinned.

"How?"

"Just have them stand in some wood smoke from a fire for a minute or two. That smell will cling to their clothes and skin. The dogs won't notice the smell of man until it's too late."

"Do you want in on this, Pete?" Harry asked.

"One thing I'm glad of is that veterinarians don't have to take an oath like the Hippocratic Oath doctors take. I'm not that swift on the idea of killing any animals, let alone mass killing, but this case is entirely different. These dogs have killed a lot of people. They won't change even with a lot of care and affection. They've become killers and they've undoubtedly cultivated a taste for human flesh. They've got to be killed."

"So, do you want in?"

"Yeah," Pete said quietly.

Harry picked up the telephone and dialed a number. "This is Chief Manning. Bring a loaded riot gun to my office right now." He hung up and looked at Pete and Duke. The hunt was under way.

31

The sun had all but disappeared, leaving behind on the horizon one super bright pinpoint of light as it hung just below the hills west of Laughton. The men, crowded together behind bushes and several barrels, waited patiently. The last order given them had been not to utter a sound. Each man had allowed the smoke from a wood fire to wrap around him, permeating his clothing and covering his skin and hair. Although the wind was blowing gently from the east, Pete had still insisted on the smoke bath for fear the wind might shift capriciously at the most critical of moments—when the dogs were about to leave the drain.

Fifteen yards in front of the yawning mouth, 75

pounds of guts, half-cooked beef tallow, and chicken parts lay on the ground. Each piece, each pile of bait had been laced with strychnine.

Now the men had nothing to do but wait. Those officers who had been on guard had departed when the crew of eight showed up. Four men were stationed above and behind each side of the drain, to avoid firing into each other. At the focal point of their firing angle lay the poisoned bait.

When the last sparkle of sunlight had abandoned the western horizon, Pete looked at his watch: 8:51. In not too short a time it would be dark, and they'd be at a definite advantage when the dogs came out. He was positive the pack had not left the sewers by some other drain, since a squad of eight men was posted at each opening, poisoned bait in front, duplicating the scene in which he found himself. If the dogs tried to leave, he, along with the others, would have heard gunfire, and they would have been told that the pack was no more.

Ray Kingsbury, perched behind a barrel opposite Pete, wiggled his nose. That damned smoke had triggered his allergy and he had been fighting for the last hour the terrible urge to sneeze. The tickling in the back of his throat had grown to monstrous proportions and had invaded his sinus cavities, where the feeling grew by the minute at first, and now by the second.

His eyes, watering, blinked spasmodically. If

he could sneeze just once, he'd be able to cope with the allergy from then on. Without warning, without a chance to prepare to breathe through his mouth and quell any sneeze that might be forthcoming, the allergic reaction won and a loud sneeze broke the silence.

Pete and the men on his side froze. Looking across, Pete could see the man wiping his nose and eyes. Poor fool probably couldn't control it. He only hoped that the dogs hadn't heard it, in the event they were moving toward the opening.

The black mongrel raised his head. He had heard something. Something from the general direction of the place where they had come into this cool spot. The noise had wound its way back through the tunnel, growing and receding in volume as it echoed and reechoed from the walls. His yellow eyes, ever on the alert since awakening a few minutes before, scanned the intersection where the pack lay sleeping and resting.

He got to his feet and stretched lazily. He was hungry. The others would be hungry when they woke up. It was time to go. He gave a short, deep bark and the pack scrambled to its feet, quickly alert.

Without hesitating, the dogs followed the black mongrel into the black maw, away from the grayness of the place they had slept, toward the river and open air where they could hunt and feed.

Pete edged his way over the top of the opening, breaking his own rule that no one move once they were in position. But there he was, going to check on the guy who had sneezed. If there would be more sneezes, the man had to get away from the vicinity as soon as possible. Surely an ill-timed sneeze would alert the dogs, if the one hadn't already.

When he got close to Ray he whispered, after exhaling most of his breath, "Are you all right?"

Ray nodded. "I had to sneeze just one time. I should be all right."

Pete frowned. "Unless you feel you aren't going to sneeze anymore in the next ten minutes or so, you'd better get the hell outta here. If you haven't already alerted the dogs, the next sneeze might."

"I'll be all right. I promise."

"Okay." Pete made his way back to the other side, taking up his position when he got there.

The mongrel, ever on the alert, stopped in the mouth of the drain. Holding his nose high, he read the breeze that suddenly picked up, coming to him from across the Wipsipanicon River. It was fresh. It was clean. It was devoid of nearby animal life, which meant the pack would have to range outward and hunt. When he lowered his head he caught the smell of meat. Food. Dead food. The others coming up behind him smelled it, too, and anxious whines wound their way out of the drain opening. The mongrel growled at the pack and they fell silent. He tentatively stepped forward until he stood half in, half out of the sewer. The trickle of cool water flowing along the bottom of the drain washed over his paws, but he didn't seem to mind. He had located the meat, perhaps 40 feet in front of the drain. Cocking his head, he studied it, his yellow eyes taking in every aspect of the food. Hesitantly stepping out, he approached the pile of guts.

Pete froze when he saw the large black head move out of the shadows and stop. The sonofabitch was leery. That was a mark of a dog gone wild. Completely lacking in trust for anyone and anything—even what appeared to be an easy meal. The dog stepped out farther into the night. Where were the rest of them? Surely there had to be more than just one dog.

Watching him approach the meat, Pete raised the riot gun to his shoulder, releasing the safety without making a sound. The other men did the same, all waiting for the appearance of the other animals. Pete tensed when the dog lowered its head to peruse the pile of intestines. The dog ran its nose over every exposed inch of the guts before moving to the half-cooked beef tallow. That should make his mouth water. The dog examined it and turned away, giving an equal amount of attention to the chicken parts and entrails lying around.

Then the men tensed even more as the rest of the pack slowly came into view. There had to be at least 40 animals when the last one, Trixie, left the shadows of the drain.

From where he was situated Pete could see the hackles on the back of the black mongrel stand. Then he heard the dog growl and the others backed away. Pete shook his head in an admiring way. The black leader had picked up the smell of poison and was warning the others away.

Pete slowly squeezed the trigger, knowing that his shot would be the signal for the others to start the slaughter. The instant before he completed the squeeze of the trigger, the black dog turned and looked up to see Pete outlined against the darkening sky.

Just as Pete realized that the dog had seen him, he fired, but the dog vaulted away, running full tilt toward the pack. The pack, immobile for a microsecond's time, started after the leader at the sound of Pete's shot.

The other men fired and the ensuing staccato reports of hand-held weapons, shotguns, and rifles filled the air. By the time each man had exhausted his weapon's magazine, those dogs not hit or killed were gone from sight. Scattered about, near the meat and toward the trail the black mongrel had initially taken, the bodies of dead and wounded dogs lay. Those who were still alive, yelped, crying in pain, writhing on the ground.

"Hold your fire, men," Pete called out and started down the small hill that would take him to the bloody carnage below. The others, standing to stretch first and get rid of the kinks that had settled into their joints during the hour they had waited, followed.

"Jesus Christ!" one man said softly. "They're ordinary house dogs, ain't they, Doc?"

Pete nodded. "Ordinary, but gone wild."

"This is awful," Ray Kingsbury said. "I didn't think they'd be like this. Christ. Some of 'em are cute."

"Hey, Doc," one man called to Pete, "looky here. A good-looking collie."

Pete turned and stepped closer to the man. Bending down, he examined the lifeless head. He knew the dog. It was Joe Eppson's collie, Trixie. "God, that's a shame. I know the dog." He went on to explain how and from where he knew the animal. "She must have gotten pretty hungry out there on the farm and so she went with the pack when it passed nearby again."

One of the officers stepped closer to Pete. "I've counted thirty-one dead or wounded dogs. What do we do about the injured ones?"

Pete swallowed the lump in his throat and said, "Kill them. It's the only safe and humane thing to do. Shoot them right in the middle of their heads, here," Pete dropped to his knees and pointed to a spot on Trixie.

Once more gunfire filled the air and the acrid smell of spent gunpowder tore at the senses of the men.

When the noise died away Pete motioned one of the officers over to him. "That meat had better be picked up before some innocent animal comes by and eats it."

"What do we do now that some of the dogs got away?" The policeman asked.

Pete shrugged. "I don't know what the sheriff or the chief will want to do next. We got most of them. I was hoping we'd get all of them. I only hope that no one else gets in their way tonight."

The officer to whom Pete had been speaking turned away and ordered two of the other policemen to take care of the poisoned meat. Another was dispatched to radio for the humane society to come pick up the carcasses of the dead dogs.

Ten minutes after the shooting stopped the chief of police and sheriff pulled up in their respective cars.

"Did you get them?" Duke asked Pete when he came up to the veterinarian.

"I wish. We got thirty-one, but I'd venture to guess that seven or eight got away. Our problem still isn't solved. Any ideas?"

Duke shook his head, as did Chief Manning, who had arrived just in time to hear Pete's answer.

"Shit!" Duke said softly.

"Now what do we do?" Harry asked.

"I think we will have to continue telling the public the truth. We didn't get all the dogs and the problem still isn't solved. Everyone must stay alert. The consequences for not staying alert are too horrible," Pete said, stifling a yawn. His body ached. Even his mind seemed to be tired. He had been up since the previous night when Ben Rathe had brought Jenny to him. He had been unable to sleep after that, not that he had tried. Instead, he and Amy had sat up talking. Talking about the awful deaths that Carol and Mark had suffered and about the future Pete had to look forward to now that Jenny was his complete responsibility.

"Say, Pete?" Harry said, stepping closer. "These dogs, except that collie over there, seem to be pretty small. Do you mean to tell me that this is all the size they were?"

Pete shook his head. "The ones that got away are pretty good-sized. There was a black mongrel that seemed to be the leader. I'd say he'd go maybe sixty-five, maybe seventy pounds. There were another half dozen or so that were almost as big as the leader. They're the ones that got away."

"Well," Harry said, "what's our next move then, Pete?"

This time Pete couldn't control the yawn, and his mouth opened widely, gapping in the chief's face. "I'm sorry, Chief, really. I'm just so damned beat, it isn't funny anymore. I don't know what I've been operating on all day, ever since you called me this morning, Sheriff. I had promised myself then to take a nap."

"Hey, Pete, you've done more than your fair share in this. You go on home. Harry and I'll do the worrying and thinking. Maybe we should have been doing it from the very beginning."

"What the hell do we know about dogs, Duke?" Harry asked. "I'm putting Pete's name in for a citation or something that will give him the recognition his efforts deserve."

"Great idea, Harry," Duke said, slapping Pete on the back. "In the meantime, Pete, go home and go to sleep. You look like you could fall asleep standing up."

"Gotcha, Sheriff," Pete said. "Hey, can I take the riot gun along?"

"Better ask Harry. He's the one who issued it to you."

Before Pete could turn to the chief Harry asked, "Why, Pete?"

"Well, there are still some pretty big dogs running loose and as an ordinary citizen I'm not in the safety of my home. I just want some protection with me when I get out of the car and go inside."

"You got any shells left?"

"I think I emptied it. That thing really fires fast."

Harry called over one of the policemen who carried a riot gun and had his vest filled with extra ammunition, still on. "Randall, load Dr. Reckel's gun for him, will you?"

When the piece was fully loaded Pete checked to make certain the safety was on and said, "Good night, gentlemen. It's not been a pleasure. If you need me, don't call until about ten tomorrow morning."

"You got it, Pete," Duke said. "Incidentally, where will you be? At your place or at Miss Bondson's?"

Pete hesitated for an instant. Jenny was with Amy. He wanted to be with the two of them. "I'll be at Amy's. Her number's in the book. G'night."

Pete plodded toward the city park where he had left the Bronco and quickly got in. The last thing he wanted was a confrontation with the remainder of the dog pack without some sort of protection.

He turned over the motor and pulled away. The riot gun sat on the floor, pointing toward the ceiling of the vehicle and the right window, which was closed. Within ten minutes he'd pull into Amy's driveway, go inside, and collapse. He needed that.

32

The black mongrel bolted the instant he saw the flash vomiting from the pipelike thing the man held to his shoulder, bounding ahead to full speed within two or three strides when the explosion erupted in his ears. He felt the pain of tiny pinpoint bites in his left rear haunch and, yelping his agony, ran as fast as he could command his legs. In less than three seconds he had knifed his way into the tall weeds and grasses that lined the river bank and headed north toward the park.

The German shepherd, the tan-and-black bitch, the Airedale, a mongrel, and a good-sized Spitz took flight as close to and right behind their leader as they could possibly get. The sound of the guns being fired and the yelps and cries of those members of the pack who did not get away quickly enough receded in the distance. The dogs dashed after their leader, bellies hugging the earth, fore legs stretching out in front of them for as much ground as they could pull in with one stride, rear legs pushing forward, propelling their bodies even faster.

The black mongrel ignored the pain in his rear, concentrating on running and making certain that they weren't about to meet anymore men with noisy pipes. He made a large half circle through the park as he slowly altered his course from north to northwest to west to southwest and, finally, in a direct southerly course.

Following him, the pack made their headlong flight through a dumping area and managed to avoid detection when they passed two of the other stakeouts positioned near the two drains that emptied below the one they had just left. The mongrel heard the men talking and laughing and he ran even faster through the night. Unaware that the dogs were even close, the men continued making noise, covering the escape of the remaining pack. From the corner of his right eye he could see the lights of Laughton bouncing about in the distance as he ran.

After the lights became fewer and farther between, he slowed and then stopped, his sides heaving, his saliva-dripping tongue hanging from his mouth. Dropping to the ground, he twisted about to lick at the pain in his rump. Now that he had stopped he realized the pain was not as bad as it had felt at first. The other animals dropped to the ground to catch their breaths, panting, waiting.

Ten minutes after stopping the mongrel stood and stretched. He felt fine. His hunger pangs returned. Looking behind him toward the direction from which they had come, he could barely see the fuzzy spots of light that represented Laughton. To his right, toward the west, he could see the occasional lights of the neighborhoods that edged the town. Raising his snout, he read the air streams coming toward him. The wind had shifted from the gentle breeze that had come from the east to a steady zephry riding out of the opposite direction.

Then he caught the smell, an odor that he knew. It was familiar, and he whined. The others caught his tentative attitude and stood, facing in the same direction. Catching the scent of another animal on the wind, the pack collectively whined and turned to face their leader. They were all hungry. They all wanted food.

Stepping away from the spot in which they had rested, he continued whining as he walked. The closer he got to the author of the spoor, the quicker he walked, until he broke into a trotting pace.

Pete pulled away from the traffic light. Now he could move toward Amy's house without having to stop anymore. The effort to brake the Bronco to a stop had seemed almost painful to his tired body and legs. He slowed for an intersection and, when he glanced to the right, caught sight of the riot gun. A mighty yawn rippled through him. Although he knew he was breaking the law by carrying a loaded gun like that in his car, he couldn't care one way or the other. If they wanted to arrest him and take him to jail, it'd be fine with him since he could probably go right to sleep—even in jail on a hard bunk.

He grinned and bit his lip. He had done more for the community in the role of a volunteer than anyone, including the sheriff and the chief of police. It was ironic that he had no weapon, and it would have been even more so had he had to leave the park unarmed and then confront the dog pack.

The streets were deserted. Not only here in the residential neighborhood, but downtown had been just as dead. He felt strange. Maybe the feeling could be described as eerie—like something out of a grade B horror movie. If the pack wasn't found and killed, the remaining dogs might just keep on running and leave the Laughton area completely. That would suit Pete fine. He didn't like his town having to go to bed with the sun, the people frightened to come out of their own homes.

The houses were fewer and farther between and, in the distance, he could see Amy's little house, the last one on the street. He liked it out here. It was quiet and peaceful and still close enough to downtown that the distance could be covered comfortably in less than five or six minutes.

When he was almost on top of the driveway he slammed on the brakes and grinned foolishly. He'd almost driven right by. Turning in, he pulled the Bronco up alongside the house and turned off the motor. A shower would feel great. All he had to do was get out of the car, walk in the house, and tell Amy he wanted to take a shower. The amount of effort that it would take almost overwhelmed him, but he opened the car door and got out.

Slowly walking along the side of the house, he went toward the back door and stopped when he heard a dog bark. *God! The pack!* No, he was getting paranoid. It was Duchess. Since the pack was not completely destroyed he thought it better if the Samoyed was in the house or the garage. Opting for the garage, since he wouldn't have to undo the task of taking her out of the house in the event Amy didn't want her inside, he released the tether chain and walked the bitch to the small building. He opened the door and coaxed her inside. Ignoring her pleas for an ear rub or affectionate petting, Pete closed the door and locked it.

Half stumbling up the steps, he entered the kitchen and locked the door behind him.

When Amy saw him she ran to him, throwing her arms around his neck.

"Are you all right?"

Pete nodded and quickly told her what had happened. He finished with, "I'm pretty beat, hon. Bushed, tired, half dead—you name it, it fits me. I want a shower and a hundred forty-eight hours of undisturbed sleep. Possible?"

"Of course. I'll sit guard and blow anyone away who tries to wake you up. Deal?"

"You don't have to go to that extreme. How's Jenny?"

"Fine. You didn't try calling here to check on her, did you?"

"As a matter of fact, no. Why? Were you gone for a while."

"No. The blasted phone has apparently been out of order ever since I called Al this morning. At least that's the last time I tried using it. I went to the neighbor's house and called the telephone company. They said it would be sometime tonight or tomorrow before they could look into it. So, you won't have to worry about the phone ringing tonight and being disturbed."

"That's fantastic. No interruptions of any kind. I love it. What did you and Jenny do all day?" He yawned.

"Pete, she's so beautiful. A lovely child. And intelligent? I can hardly believe it. We really hit it off. She asked about her mother again and I went along with your idea that she had to go on a trip. I hope that was all right."

"It should be." Pete yawned again.

"I'm sure in time she'll be able to handle the information."

"I'm glad the two of you hit it off. I think it's going to be very important that the two of you like each other."

Amy smiled. "That'll be easy—at least for me, it'll be easy. She's your daughter and a lot like you."

When Amy's face clouded Pete caught the subtle change and said, "Okay, what's wrong?"

"Wrong? Nothing, really. It' just that today, when I wanted to take her outside, she caught a glimpse of Duchess and didn't want to go."

"What did you do?"

"I thought about people who have an auto accident and are urged to get into a car and drive as soon as possible after the fact, just so they don't lose their nerve. Do you know what I mean?"

Pete nodded and waited for Amy to continue.

"It took a little doing and convincing, but I got her to go out into the yard and pet Duchess. Of course, Duchess is such a sweetheart herself that it didn't take much and the two of them were friends in no time."

"I'm glad of that. It would be a helluva note if a veterinarian's daughter wound up hating animals."

"Are you hungry, Pete?"

He laughed tiredly. "I hadn't thought about it. Now that you've mentioned food, I suddenly realized I haven't eaten any lunch or dinner. Just a quick cup of coffee."

"You relax in the living room and after I make

something to eat I'll call you."

The black mongrel stopped in the center of the empty field. Not too far distant, he could see the lights of several widely spaced houses. The smell he had tracked this far was coming from the house on the end. Cocking his head to one side, he studied the fuzzy lights and then walked forward, slowly, one step at a time, stopping between, to examine the air. The smell of a man, faint, indistinct, rode with the smell of the bitch that predominated the breeze. She was there. Maybe he could get her to come with him this time. The man smell renewed his hunger and he instinctively stepped forward.

The pack settled in behind the mongrel, walking when he did, stopping when he did, reading the air. They didn't whine, but their muscles knotted together in a tense way as they anticipated the animal on the other end of the scent spoor.

When the mongrel came to the street he didn't hesitate but continued walking toward the driveway and the car parked in it. He passed the Bronco and advanced to the fence surrounding the back yard. A quiet whine seeped from his throat and he effortlessly leaped the 42-inch frame. One by one the others followed him, entering the back yard. The pack was deathly still as the mongrel searched for the white bitch. He checked out her kennel and her favorite resting spot. The smells were strong, but the bitch was nowhere in sight. Then he heard her plaintive whine from the garage. Turning, he trotted to the door, following the scent line. He could hear her inside and whimpered his answer.

Duchess, her tongue hanging out, whined again in the garage, begging the mongrel and the others to come to her.

The black dog reared up, putting his paws against the door. He sniffed the upper reaches of it and fussed loudly before dropping back to the ground.

The other dogs milled about, sniffing the yard. The German shepherds stepped up onto the back porch, sniffing at a plastic garbage bag, pawing at it. Enthused over the prospect of finding food, he wailed loudly, giving half a bark.

Amy turned down the burner under the pan of soup, to let it simmer while she made a couple of sandwiches for Pete. When she heard the whine and little bark she didn't react immediately. Then, stepping toward the door, she called out to Pete, "I'm going to bring Duchess in. She's crying something awful. Besides, I don't think it's a good idea to let her out all night with the pack running loose." She reached out for the knob but found it locked.

Pete nodded. "Okay, hon. Just hurry with the grub. I'm almost ready to drop off to never-never land."

Then Amy's words registered. He had put Duchess in the garage. What had Amy heard?

Springing to his feet, he yelled. *"No-o-o!"* and made a dash for the kitchen.

Amy was just unlocking the door and turning the knob to open it when Pete burst into the room. Turning to look at him, she continued opening the door and the German shepherd hurtled through.

Amy screamed, falling back under the attack of the dog. Pete continued across the kitchen. The dog slithered across the room toward him, losing his footing as he hit the slick linoleum. The animal spun around in half a circle and Pete quickly scooped the dog up from behind, heaving him through the open door into the faces of the pack that had gathered and was charging up onto the porch toward the kitchen entrance.

Flying about like bowling pins, the dogs scattered in all directions as the German shepherd struck them. Pete slammed the door and locked it.

"Check the windows to make certain that they can't jump through any that are close enough to the ground."

Amy ran from the room to do as Pete ordered.

"Where's Jenny?"

"Upstairs," Amy cried as she slammed one after the other of the windows down.

"Get her," Pete yelled from the kitchen, peering through the curtains into the blackness of the back yard.

The mongrel leaped at Pete's outlined figure in

the window and his snarling face came within inches of Pete's. The yellow eyes burned into Pete's and he shuddered. Drawing the shade, he did the same to the other three windows in the kitchen.

"Call the police," he said when he heard Amy coming.

Amy entered the kitchen, carrying a sleepy-eyed Jenny. "I can't. The phone's not working. Remember?"

The awful truth smashed into Pete's consciousness and he turned to face Amy. "I'm going to draw the shades. If they can't see us or smell us, they might forget about it and leave."

He ran into the dining room, pulling the shades of the four windows there. The dogs, having sensed movement in the house paralleled Pete's route through the rooms, barking, growling, jumping at him whenever he appeared in a window to pull down the covering. In the living room he drew the drapes shut and breathed easy for a moment.

When he reentered the kitchen he found Jenny crying softly.

"It's all right, darling," Amy cooed into her ear.

"Let me," Pete said, taking his daughter.

"Don't let the puppies get me, Daddy," she sobbed. "I'm afraid."

"Don't worry, sweetheart, Daddy won't let the doggies get you. They're outside and we're safe and sound inside." Looking up at Amy, he said, "But I've got to do something."

Just then the sound of a body hitting the window in the kitchen door broke the quiet of Pete's statement.

"What?" Amy asked, taking Jenny back.

"I haven't got the foggiest. But if they're that hungry that they'll try to hurtle through a closed door, there's no telling what they'll try if they find out the windows will break."

"Here," Amy said, handing him a butcher knife.

Pete grinned bitterly. "That won't do much good, I'm afraid. What I need is—*the gun!* The riot gun. I left it in the Bronco. How stupid can one person be. *Jesus Christ!*"

"What gun? What's a riot gun?" Amy asked, her eyes widening.

"Remember? I told you the police issued one to me for the hunt tonight. We got most of them, but the larger dogs got away. That's what's left of the pack in your back yard."

Jenny and Amy both screamed when another dog leaped at the square of light that the kitchen door window represented.

"We've got to do something. If they can break in here, I'm not sure we could protect ourselves unless we locked them out of a bedroom or something."

"That damned telephone," Amy managed. "And there isn't that much traffic along here—especially after dark."

"What about the neighbors?" Pete asked.

"You know how close the next-door neighbor

is? Six lots away. Besides, they seldom come over here. What are we going to do, Pete?"

The dogs continued yammering outside the kitchen door, bounding against it.

"First I want Jenny to do something for Daddy and Amy. Can you, honey?" he asked, turning to take his daughter from Amy.

Sobbing softly, Jenny nodded. "What?"

"Daddy's going to put you in a bedroom and into bed. I want you to promise Daddy that you'll stay there. Will you?"

"For how long?" She wiped tears from one eye.

"Not very long. Amy's going to make a bunch of noise and Daddy's going to get a gun and shoot all the nasty puppies. All right?"

Jenny thought for a moment before nodding. "Don't be long, Daddy."

Hugging her tightly to him, Pete said, "I won't be, darling." He handed her back to Amy and they hurried to Amy's bedroom, tucking the child in bed. Pete turned out the light but left one on for comfort for his daughter when he saw how dark it was.

"I'm going to close the door so we don't disturb you too much, Jenny," Pete said, pulling the door tightly shut.

"What are you talking about? How can you get the gun? You said you left it in the Bronco."

"I want you to create a diversion in the kitchen. Yell, scream, bang pots and pans together. Anything to draw their attention. When you've got it I'll go out the front door and around to the

Bronco. The gun's in the front seat. I can get it and then—good-bye, dogs."

"I'm scared, Pete. Will it work?"

"You got any other ideas?"

She shook her head and said shakily, "No. But damnit, you be careful or else."

Pete grinned at the threat and stepped to one of the windows that looked out over the driveway. The Bronco was so near and yet so far. Could he make it to the passenger's side and grab the gun in quick enough time to be ready to fire when the dogs came at him. He was positive they would attack once they heard the car door open.

"Get ready, Amy," Pete said stopping in the kitchen doorway. "Just make a bunch of noise. I won't leave the kitchen until I'm positive they're all back here."

"You'd better not even think of leaving until we know where all of them are," she said, picking up two pans. Stepping closer to the back door, she slapped them together. The ensuing bang brought a brief second's worth of silence from the back porch.

Pete pulled back the curtain just as the black mongrel sprang at the window again. There was an awful lot of dogs on the back porch. They had to be all there.

Amy continued shouting and banging the pans together and watched anxiously as Pete stepped into the dining room. From where she stood she could see him checking the windows along the driveway as he went toward the front of the house.

Pete could see no animals anywhere along the side of the house where the car was parked. When he reached the front door he wrestled with the decision of closing it or leaving it open for a quick retreat in the event a dog came at him before he got to the Bronco. Thinking of Amy's and Jenny's safety, he closed the door quietly behind him, making certain it was latched.

Taking a deep breath, he stepped away from the front of the house and quietly yet hurriedly made his way to the side where the car was parked. Stopping at the corner, he marveled at how loud Amy sounded, banging the pans together and shouting at the top of her lungs. Somewhere lost in the cacaphony but coming through whenever Amy stopped to take a breath or the dogs all coincidentally stopped barking, Pete heard Jenny crying. He had to hurry. It must be hell for his little girl.

When he stood next to the passenger door he tried the button then bit his tongue to keep from cursing. The door was locked. He had to go around to the driver's side.

Stepping carefully, he made his way, quietly opening the door when he reached it. The courtesy light went on, flooding the interior and the immediate area around the vehicle with light.

When the dogs stopped barking Pete scrambled in, grabbing the riot gun in one motion. Jumping out, he barely managed to release the safety when he saw the dogs hurdling the fence, charging straight at him.

He pulled the trigger and the Spitz and Airedale went down, caught in the same blast. The smaller mongrel came full tilt toward him with the German shepherd right behind, and next came the tan-and-black bitch.

Pete pumped furiously, ejecting the spent shells, inserting fresh ones with each motion of his left arm. The riot gun roared each time and each time it spoke dogs fell, cut in half, others with heads blown off. Barking, shotgun reports, the yelping and screaming of wounded and dying animals filled the night air.

When the last shell ejected and no more were in the magazine to be released into the chamber Pete stopped pumping. The dogs lay at his feet and back along a bloody trail toward the fence. It was over. The dogs were dead.

Then he saw the black shape jump the fence, coming straight at him, his yellow eyes blazing in the light from the shade-drawn windows.

Acting instinctively, Pete threw the gun into the air, catching it by the barrel. It was hot. His hands burned, but he hung onto it, swinging it with all his might at the black mongrel as he sprang at Pete. The stock caught the dog along the side of his head and diverted his path through the air, making him land to the side of Pete, toward the house.

Instantly back on his feet, the dog leaped

again, before Pete could swing full, and knocked the man off his feet. The gun went flying and Pete stared into those horrible yellow eyes that were no farther away than half a foot. The gleaming fangs came at him as if in slow motion, and Pete threw one arm up that was caught in the dog's mouth.

Snarling, growling, his foamy saliva flecking Pete's face, the dog ripped at the veterinarian's arm, pulling, tearing, trying to get rid of it to enable him to get at the man's throat. Instead, Pete forced his arm back, knowing that as long as the jaws were around his arm and the head was forced back, the dog wouldn't be able to bite him anyplace else. Rolling over, Pete straddled the mongrel's body.

Pain flooded through Pete. Nausea sent his mind reeling, but he still pushed back, arousing the dog's fighting instincts even more.

Pete's blood mixed with the saliva and the frothy combination poured down the dog's throat and splattered the man's face. Pete's arm felt numb, and he could hear the dog's molars rubbing against the bones in his forearm. He wanted to vomit, but knew he'd be dead in a minute or two if he did. He gagged, retching, but continued the pressure against the dog's mouth, reaching out with his free hand to push the back of the animal's head toward his arm.

"You want to bite me? Then, goddammit, bite me, you sonofabitch!" Pete yelled.

Pete could hear the dog choking more than he

had before. Would it be safe to release the pressure and go for the animal's throat? He waited, pushing all the harder. What if his bitten arm proved to be useless in choking the dog? His arm had to be mangled badly, but he would be dead if he thought of his wounds for any longer than a second.

The dog's eyes bulged as he choked, gagging on his own saliva and Pete's blood.

Pete could see the dog's tongue hanging out to one side, caught between his own teeth and Pete's forearm. That was why the dog couldn't swallow efficiently. Feeling him grow perceptibly weaker, Pete sensed the moment of truth was at hand and released his grip on the back of the dog's head. Instantly, he gripped the dog by the throat, and when the jaws released his mangled arm his other hand closed with his good one. His wounded arm and muscles worked perfectly.

The dog coughed, reacting immediately. Writhing about, he tried to break loose from Pete's grip. Pete continued, exerting pressure on the throat. He could feel the dog's windpipe working frantically, trying to bring in air, but each time the dog exuded some stale air, Pete closed even tighter.

Pete heard someone screaming and suddenly realized it was he who was screaming with pain and rage and a beastial sense of justice. With one last surge of strength he closed as tight as he could and held. The dog wiggled, doing its best to tear free of the deadly grip holding it to the ground. But the animal's wind finally gave and the body went limp in Pete's grasp.

Continuing to hold the neck of the dog in his aching hands, Pete didn't realize at first that the dog was dead. A gravelike quiet filled the night and he eased his cramped fingers back. The instant he released the animal, blood began pouring from his torn left arm. It looked awful.

Looking up at the dining room windows, he saw Amy holding Jenny in her arms. He struggled to stand, barely making it. When he looked again the window was empty and he heard the door in front open and Amy calling. He stumbled toward her as she rounded the corner and nearly collapsed.

Amy slipped her free arm around Pete's waist and helped him up the steps.

Inside, the phone rang merrily.

Epilogue

Karl Jurgens sat back in his chair, feet on the desk in front of him. He looked up to see the figure of a man standing in the doorway.

" 'Bout time you got here," he said.

Ted Riffleman stepped into the office. "You ready to go and get your brains fucked out?"

"Sure. Why not? What else is there to do on a Saturday night? All I gotta do is close up and turn the dogs loose."

"You still got the same ones?"

"You bet your sweet ass, I do. After that black mongrel and tan-and-black bitch got away the last time I made sure no dog would ever break out of or into my yard again."

"I remember you tellin' me how you were goin'

to pour concrete along the bottom of the fence. That was a slick idea, all right. Sure musta worked if you ain't lost no dogs since."

"I've had the same two males ever since the other two got away. Come on, let's go." Karl stood and turned off the lights. After locking the door he closed and locked the gate, the only way into or out of the junkyard. Walking along the fence, he pulled on a piece of rope and the gate to the dog pen squealed loudly as he lifted it. The two males, one black, one white, tore out of the pen, racing around, loosening their muscles.

Karl turned and hurried to Ted's car and got in. They roared off in a cloud of yellow dust.

The two dogs ran immediately to a spot nearest the hill that rose behind one side of the yard. There, where large boulders had not been moved to allow wet concrete to be poured, they stopped. First one, then the second, wiggled between two large, rounded rocks. On the other side, they began digging at the hard earth where they had been spending the last few nights after discovering this place while chasing a rat.

They worked patiently, and whether they broke through tonight or the next made no difference. In time they'd be free.